Cult
A Delaney & Murphy mystery
Jack Adams

Atlas Productions

Cult

First published 2023.

Copyright © Jack Adams and Helen Goltz

Proofread by: Emma Bramley.

Cover design by: Atlas Productions. Image by Malivan_Iuliia, Shutterstock.

PLEASE NOTE: This book is written in British- Australian English.

Chapter 1

Then...

    Nathaniel Delaney stood his ground, arms folded, a serious look on his young face. Sure, he was only 11 years old and didn't go to the rich school or have the latest shoes or wristwatch, but he knew when he was being tricked.

'Everyone's coming along, and we're all going to do it. It'll blow you away,' Griffin Maxwell was saying to Nathan's best friend, Adam Murphy. Griffin turned his attention to Nate. 'You don't have to come. Adam doesn't need you there.'

Adam stepped in. 'Thanks, Griffin, yeah, maybe,' he said with a shrug and nudged his best friend, Nate, to walk away. 'See you at school tomorrow.'

It took a second nudge and a shove to get Nate to turn around; Adam was usually the follower. They grabbed their bikes and headed away from the park oval where Adam's school friends had been playing football to their favourite place – the river near the lunatic asylum, with its huge trees for climbing and cool river for swimming. Nate's ill humour faded as he raced ahead on his bike, setting the pace for Adam to catch him, and catch him he did. The boys whooped as they turned into the bush track, down the path and skidded to a stop at the river's edge. It was shallower; it had been for a few months with the dry, but the water was inviting even if there was less of it. The spotted gums towering above them provided some relief from the day's heat, and neither boy feared the looming River Park Lunatic Asylum in the background.

Nate whipped off his shirt and ran into the water. Adam followed him in, rising at a depth where they could stand with their shoulders immersed below the waterline. Last year, it had been over their heads.

'I don't like him,' Nate told his best friend. He ran a hand through his wet hair, wiping the water from his eyes.

Adam shrugged, not that Nate could see the movement below the water line. 'He's alright. He's popular.'

'You only think he's alright because he wants to hang out with you, go to your place, and meet your mum. He's probably got a house like yours.'

'Don't know. I don't really want to do a séance anyway,' Adam said.

'Me either. I heard they were dangerous. Why would you call back the dead when they're gone? What if they don't want to come back, and they get angry that you're pestering them?'

'Yeah, exactly. What if they stick around, and you can't get rid of them?' Adam's blue eyes widened at the horror of it. 'That'd be worse.'

'That would be super freaky,' Nate agreed and began to wade into the shallow water. Adam followed. Nate grinned. 'We should sneak up and scare the crap out of them.'

Adam laughed, then shaking the water from his dark hair, asked, 'Why don't you like him?'

Nate said nothing for a while. Adam was his best friend outside of school, but Griffin Maxwell went to the same private school as Adam and was trying to make Adam his best friend; Nate was sure of it.

'I just don't,' Nate said and shrugged. 'Are you going to go?'

'Nuh, not if you don't,' Adam said.

Nate smiled. All was well in the world again.

Chapter 2

Now... twenty years later...

Dr Adam Murphy's eyes narrowed as he drove toward the office building he shared with his best friend, Nate Delaney, in the Stones Corner village. The business was about to celebrate its first anniversary and had been a success. He wasn't sure a private investigator and a psychologist sharing office space was a good idea at the time, but he was up for the challenge. Lord knows most of Nate's ideas were crazy, but they'd gotten away with them up to now. Scoring Jessica Johnson as the office manager was a great move on Nate's behalf, even if Nate was in love with her and couldn't admit it. Adam figured it would soon come to a head one way or the other; he just hoped they didn't lose her. The team surprisingly fitted with his mentor and now supervisor, Robert Ware, on board to work on class actions and Danielle in and out to do Nate's surveillance work.

Adam's eyes cased the street as he approached the building's car park. It was three weeks until *the* wedding – his famous and beautiful model mother, Winsome Keeley, who never fell out of the spotlight as the nation's *It Girl*, was marrying his godfather, Jack Bernham, the *Voice of the Nation*. Jack was arriving next week to do two concerts before the wedding. Jessica couldn't wait, apparently.

Adam groaned. A photographer and a cameraman sat near the entrance to the underground car park. Next to them was a young girl with a writing pad and iPad who looked straight out of university. She was dressed like she was going to the opening of an event, so she'd be angling to get on camera. He couldn't understand the fascination with fame. Nate explained Adam knew no different, having grown up with it in his face, but it appeared to be in everyone's face these days.

He hit Jessica's number on his phone.

'Delaney and Murphy,' she answered, 'Oh, it's you, the Murphy half.'

Adam chuckled. 'It's the better half. Anything newsworthy in the street that you know about, or are the three media folk outside the building waiting for me?'

She sighed. 'Sorry, Adam, you're the target. They buzzed to see you earlier, and I said you wouldn't be back today.'

'Nice try, thanks, Jess. You'd think they could find something better to do... like find a real story,' he said. As he drove closer, and they saw him through the front windscreen – the only window in his car that wasn't heavily tinted – they stood and grabbed their gear. Adam tried to avoid making eye contact with them, but they had targeted his black Mercedes – a 30th birthday gift from his mother – and there was no escape.

'You are news, babe, whether you like it or not,' Jessica said. 'As Rob would say, stay cool and don't lose it,' she quoted his supervisor, 'or you can take Nate's advice – 'Stay calm and don't become the headline.''

'Yes, thanks for that, coach. See you in a minute.' He disconnected and stewed.

What's left to say for the love of God?

Yeah, I'm really happy for Mum and Jack.

Did I see it coming? Sure did; they've been going out for a while.

No, I'm not the former prime minister's love child. My father is James Murphy.

Move along; nothing to see here.

He touched his auto remote to put the garage door up and expected them to run down into the car park and harass him as he exited his car. And that's just what they did. A few flashes went off, and he swung his car around them and pulled into his designated car park next to Nate's vacant spot and Jessica and Rob's car park. There was no avoiding them.

The young woman introduced herself as he exited the car, flicking her dark hair back behind her shoulder.

'Hi Adam, Felicia Cooper, *Entertainment News Today*, can we have a quick interview?'

'I've got a client meeting, but fire away,' Adam said, knowing Nate would be proud of him for agreeing. He tried not to grimace as he did in all his media shots, according to his ex-wife, Stephanie – who continued to use his surname and be employed as his mother's publicist. He kept walking to the annoyance of the cameraman.

'Are you playing a role in your mother's wedding?' she asked, giving him a smile that said she was interested in more than an interview.

'Yes, I'm the son,' he said, and she laughed.

'Cute! Will the former prime minister's family be invited?' she asked, and Adam reined in his anger. The rumours about him being the product of an affair between his mother and the prime minister before his parents' hurried marriage meant a lifetime of speculation about his heritage. The fact that he looked like his father and the prime minister did not help.

'I haven't seen the guest list,' he retorted.

'Really?' she asked, surprised. 'Have you thought about modelling or performing like your famous mum and soon-to-be stepdad?'

'Nope, I've no talent for entertaining.'

'Who are you taking as your plus one?'

Adam stopped the interview right there. His girlfriend, Kelsey, was not for public consumption. She had had a tough childhood; Adam was witness to it when they met for a moment in time through the bars of the asylum. She was wary of people, and he would not give her a starring role because his mother couldn't live without being in the spotlight.

'I'll let you out here,' he said, opening the door so they could exit the front while he took the stairs up to his office. They ignored the offer and followed him up the stairwell.

'I'm free if you need a date,' Felicia said and laughed. The cameraman and photographer joined in, not averse to winning Felicia's affection.

Adam found Jessica waiting with the door ajar.

'Sorry, Felicia. I've got to run,' Adam said and hurried in. Jessica waved and added, 'Have a great day,' as she closed the door.

'Thanks. For fuck's sake,' he muttered.

'The prime minister question?' Jessica asked, knowing him well enough to know what would rile him.

'That was the second question. The sooner this wedding is over, the better.' He sighed, moving into his office as the photographer took a photo through their open office windows. He heard Jessica snapping the Venetian blinds closed.

'It's safe to come out,' she called, and he returned to the reception area again.

'Thanks for that.' Adam glanced at the clock on the wall. 'I've got to get to the prison for the group therapy session in thirty minutes, and I hope they don't follow me there.'

The buzzer went, and Jessica returned to her desk, frowning, expecting to see the three media crew again. Then, she brightened. 'It's Dan, and I've got a brilliant plan!' She buzzed in Nate's researcher, Danielle, who ran up the stairs impressively fast for someone in high-heeled boots.

'Doesn't Dan have an access key and the keypad number?' Adam frowned.

'She does. But she always presses the buzzer and then heads up,' Jessica said and shrugged. 'I think she likes to give me a heads-up she's on the way. I appreciate it.'

'Okay,' Adam said, making a note to think about that later. He went to the door, glanced out, and confident that no reporters were waiting for him outside the door, he opened it for Danielle, who came in as she always did – hurried and full of energy as if the party was waiting for her so it could start.

'What's happening? Why are all the blinds closed?' she asked and glanced into Nate's office, then rolled her eyes. 'I knew he'd forget about our meeting.'

'Doesn't matter, we need you, perfect timing,' Jessica said.

'Oh, well, it's nice to be wanted, thanks.' She looked from Jessica to Adam. 'Why do you need me?'

'Beats me,' Adam said, looking at Jessica.

Danielle moved to Adam and gave him a quick hug which he winced through. She always hugged him hello, amused by his reaction.

'You know you see me pretty regularly these days. We could drop the hugging; we're not long-lost friends.'

'You'd miss it, I know,' she smirked at him, and he saw Jessica suppressing a laugh.

'World's gone mad,' Adam said with resignation. 'What's your brilliant plan?'

'Dan can be a decoy,' Jessica explained. 'The media were out the front, probably still are.'

'Yeah, I saw them and gave them a wave. I told them I could tell them all they needed to know about you, Adam, if they wanted an exclusive.' She gave him a wink.

'Sure, you did. When's the book coming out? That'd be a good doorstop,' he said with a smile, knowing they didn't come more loyal than Danielle.

'You know I wouldn't.' She nudged him.

'I know. You wouldn't break under interrogation,' he agreed.

'True.' She beamed, happy for the praise and turned to Jessica. 'I'm not sure if I look enough like Adam to be a decoy, though.'

'Get out of here. Only our mothers can tell us apart,' Adam played along.

'If you two are quite finished?' Jessica rolled her eyes. 'Haven't you got a meeting to make?' She didn't wait for Adam's response. 'Here's the plan. Adam takes your car, Dan, and heads off to the prison for his meeting. They won't be looking for him in it.'

'But I need a car,' Danielle wailed. 'I'm not waiting around for Nate.'

'Well, that's even better because you can drive out in the black Mercedes, and the media will rush to talk with you; by that time, Adam is away.'

'My car?' He frowned.

'I know you love that car,' Jessica said, rolling her eyes. 'You can meet Dan in the next street and swap over.'

'Or I could just bring it back later when I meet Nate again. I don't mind you driving my Mazda. If you wanted to fill it up as well, that'd be fine,' she joked.

'It's a good plan,' Adam conceded. 'And yeah, just bring my Merc back later, but make sure you do. Don't whip it, and make sure you stop at the red lights. They've got cameras now, you know.'

Danielle gave a cheer. 'I have to visit a couple of ex-boyfriends then, show them my new car and what they're missing out on,' she joked. 'But

I'll be back before the end of the day. I'm parked on the back street, so that'll be perfect. You can slip out the side while I drive out of the garage.'

Adam rolled his eyes. 'Let me get my stuff, and we can go. Mazda...' he muttered as he headed to his office.

Chapter 3

In years to come, Skye Lyons would regret not reading the fine print, but then, in her enthusiasm to sign a modelling contract, the fine print seemed so unimportant. To think that someone wanted to give her a three-year contract was a dream come true. Her parents had said models were a dime a dozen, whatever that meant – they didn't even think or talk like they lived in the 21st century. How would they understand new reality markets for fame? But the owner and founder of the *Fidelium Wellness Studio,* Griffin Maxwell, understood.

Three years of studio work, content making, modelling, and an enormous share of her own profits from subscribers at the end of the three years, not to mention a profile and fanbase that could see her go on to bigger gigs like reality shows and brand appearances. It was validation that she had something unique. That's what Griffin told her. He was gorgeous and charismatic, and he said she was a shining light, fresh and beautiful; she would be a star. *Give me the pen and let me sign.* And sign she did. The first week had been so great. Had she been lulled into a false sense of security? She had surrendered her phone as expected – it distracted from the wellness aspect of the camp –and was shown to her new quarters. She met Leaf, her roommate, who looked so similar they could be sisters. Leaf was lovely, and they exchanged looks of excitement as they were given the tour, met other girls, saw the studios where they would do their acting classes and record content, and visited the hair and make-up studios.

'I can't believe it,' Skye had whispered to Leaf as they followed the tour guide, an experienced model in the third year of her contract.

'I keep pinching myself to make sure I'm awake,' Leaf giggled.

In the first week, they worked with an actor, were groomed, made some exciting content, and enjoyed nights in the spa. At night, Leaf would be assigned work in other areas. Skye never questioned it because she was summoned to visit Griffin. She was the chosen girl, which didn't make her many friends. Jealousy was rife amongst the ladies, all waiting to fall under his gaze, and with Skye the flavour of the day, another model had fallen by the wayside.

To celebrate their first week completed, Skye was told to expect a reward tonight after dinner – a visit to the VIP House and to take part in some serious acting with Leaf – to say she was excited was an understatement.

'Is this what you have been doing at night for the past week? Going to the VIP House?' Skye asked as they dressed earlier.

'No, I've been doing content for subscribers who want live stuff at night. You've been too in demand to attend,' Leaf teased Skye, who blushed with pleasure.

'What's the night content about then?' Skye had pushed.

'Just posing, photo sessions, that sort of thing,' Leaf had said non-committedly, which Skye thought was weird, but she wasn't complaining. Who would? Everyone wanted to be with Griffin Maxwell, and he chose her to romance.

But tonight was different. The only other man in management on the site, Zach Crowder – Griffin's solicitor who dealt with her contract – had collected them in his car after dinner. Skye had seen some of the girls flirt with him, but he wasn't attractive with his wiry build and thinning hair. He was, however, powerful and always wore expensive suits. And power was an aphrodisiac. He was known as the Producer in the Wellness Camp and could be charming when he turned it on.

They drove out of the front gates of the grounds, around a looped road for a short distance, and then back in behind the studios before entering an underground car park. Before they went below, Skye saw the exterior of the building – a huge, imposing structure with darkened windows and no sign of life. Zach parked, and the three alighted from his expensive black car, a Lexus.

'This way, ladies,' Zach said, using his security card to access the lift and building. 'You both look gorgeous, by the way.'

They thanked him, conscious of the need to please. In his dark grey suit, he looked like a man comfortable in his own skin, but he was not Griffin. Skye suspected he wanted to be. They all wanted Griffin in some form or other.

Zach opened the door for them and led them down several hallways with closed doors on either side. There were no windows in the hallways, but the venue spoke of money. Beautiful soft lamps lit the way, and the carpet was plush. Gold-framed paintings of old-world scenes filled the hallways. It was like being inside a private, exclusive hotel. So quiet, so lush.

Zach's phone rang, breaking the silence – he was allowed a phone – and he paused. 'One moment, please, ladies,' he said and frowned at the name on the screen before answering with a lowered voice. Skye and Leaf admired the paintings but could not help but overhear.

'—he's been banned from here.

'—don't approach him unarmed. He's dangerous, unbalanced...

'—how the fuck did he even get in here?'

Both ladies were now looking at Zach, and he closed his eyes, his face flushed with anger.

'I'm on my way. Put Griffin on alert. We may need to lock down. You know what he did to one of the girls that—' He stopped on seeing the girls and added he was on his way, hanging up. 'I'm sorry, Skye, Leaf, there's an emergency.' Zach glanced down the hallway and then back at them. 'If you could both head to the door at the end, enter and lock it, you'll find a producer in there expecting you. I won't be long.'

He hurriedly turned and, running a short way back from where they had just come, exited through one of the doors behind him.

'Holy crap, what's that all about?' Leaf asked and bit her lip concerned.

'An unhappy customer? But I thought all the customers were online subscribers.'

'Maybe not. Maybe here in the VIP House there are real clients. Come on, let's move,' Leaf said and started towards the door, which seemed a million miles down the hallway. Skye hurried after her.

The world went black. Pitch black. The two women stood, stunned, motionless. In the dark.

'Oh, my God.' Skye said, the hairs on her arms standing up. 'What's going on?'

'I don't know but if the lights are out, is the security system down too? Could anyone just enter?' Leaf asked in a whisper. 'Do you think that guy is loose in here?'

It was so dark; Skye couldn't see her hand in front of her. 'I don't know, yes, maybe. Have you been here before? In this building?'

'No, I don't know it or where anything leads to. We've got to get to the room down the hallway.' Leaf gripped Skye's arm like a lifeline.

Skye could hear Leaf hyperventilating. That wasn't her real name any more than Sarah's name was Skye, but they were given names upon arrival at the *Fidelium Wellness Studio*. Nothing here spoke of wellness.

Skye's heartbeat thudded in her chest, and her breaths were short and sharp, fearful.

'Oh my God, oh my God,' Leaf panted. 'What's happening? Are we going to be murdered?' She huddled beside Skye, and they pushed themselves along the wall in the dark hallway, listening. Skye felt the texture of the wall beneath her fingers. Carpeted. Soundproof.

'What is this place?' Skye whispered, the words coming out sounding strangled.

In the dark, she could only just make out Leaf's silhouette but could feel the tremors and shaking of the other girl's body.

'I was promised three years of modelling and content making,' Leaf said. 'We're going to die.'

'We're okay, we'll be okay,' Skye said, stepping up. She didn't believe it or feel that brave. Suppressing a cry, she whispered, 'I want to go home.'

'Me too.'

Her thoughts raced from survival to running to confusion. *I didn't sign up for this.*

'Hurry, we can feel our way down to the end,' Skye said, dragging her hand along the carpeted wall as she headed towards the far end of the hallway.

They heard a thump behind them, and both reeled around. A door opened, a sliver of light, a dark, tall shape that wasn't Zach.

Leaf screamed. They were in darkness again.

'Shh,' Skye whispered with urgency where she imagined Leaf's ear to be. She tugged Leaf along.

'I'm here,' a voice said in a whisper somewhere near them. A male voice, and both women cried out in fear. Skye flattened herself against the wall and waved her hand blindly around her in an arc, her fingers touching something straight ahead.

'Who is there? Who are you?'

There was the sound of running, a thump further up the hallway and then the only noise was Leaf crying. Skye tugged her to keep moving forward, staying flat against the wall. Whatever or whoever it was, was no longer there or they were watching. Maybe they had those green night vision glasses and could see everything, every emotion and movement, and were standing closer than she knew. The thought filled Skye with horror, and she reached out again but felt nothing in front of her.

'We have to go back,' Leaf said with hysteria in her voice.

'Shh, we can't go back,' Skye whispered. 'Zach said to go forward.'

'Zach!' Leaf screamed, and Skye flinched at the roar of Leaf's voice in the hallway. 'Help, Zach!'

'Shh, for God's sake, shut up, shut up!' Skye hissed.

They waited and stood... nothing. Far away, on another level, they heard a woman's faint but undeniably frightened scream.

'He's up there, on another floor,' Leaf said with relief. 'I can't die. No one knows I am here. No one would look for me.'

Skye realised she was in the same situation. She had told her parents not to contact her, that she would be out of range while studying, and that she'd contact them. It was what she wanted; she had insisted.

Behind them, somewhere, there was the faint sound of male laughter. Deep, guttural.

'Who's there?' Leaf called out. No answer.

'Keep going, move,' Skye said, edging along. Then she screamed as something touched her. She wheeled around, thrashing out with her arms but only hitting Leaf. 'Something touched me. Someone.'

'Keep going to the door at the end of the hallway, or we can find a fire exit,' Leaf said, shuffling along in the dark and stepping up at last.

Skye stopped dead. Someone was breathing near them. They were definitely no longer alone.

Leaf screamed, primal, terrifying, loud. She released her grip on Skye.

And then Skye realised she was alone.

'Leaf?' she whispered. It was more of a pleading. She could hear whimpering and realised she was making the odd keening sound.

There was a sound. She strained to hear it – the sound of something heavy being dragged along the floor.

Out of nowhere, a beam of light appeared under a door at the far end of the hallway, making Skye shield her eyes from it. It was the room Zach told them to go to, and the producer must be there. She took off running towards it but glanced over her shoulder to where Leaf had disappeared, terrified of what she might see. The hallway was empty. She stumbled and straightened, flattening herself against the wall.

How can that be? She turned back to the light. Then, the thought occurred to her as she saw the room so tantalisingly close.

Do I go in here? It's a trap. It has to be. No, someone must be in there. Zach said a producer was in there unless he or she was dead now. Was that the scream they heard? No, that was overhead.

The choice was to stay in the dark or head to the light. There was no choice.

Skye hurried the remaining way down the hall. The carpet absorbed her footsteps, and then the light went off, and she gasped. It was black, pitch black again.

Another light went on in a room closer to her. Suddenly, anger welled inside her.

'Is this your idea of fun?' She called out, her voice bouncing off the walls. 'Leaf!'

A door slammed on another level. Fearing she would hear another scream or be in the dark again, Skye hurried to the last room, made it, and burst in with relief, not bothering to knock.

Sitting in a glass studio was a man slumped in a chair, blood on his chest, and there, on the floor, was Leaf, staring at her, eyes wide open, frozen. Dead.

Skye screamed and wheeled around in fright to leave. A man wearing a clown mask was standing in the doorway.

'Welcome to the show, Skye,' he sang in a sing-song voice, and she screamed hysterically, backing up and tripping over Leaf. She scrambled to her feet, looking around. There was no exit.

'Don't you want to play?' the clown asked. 'We could be good friends.'

She was crying and flailing in terror as he came closer and closer. Skye fell to the floor on her knees.

All the lights came on, and she looked around, frozen and confused, as the clown seemed to freeze where he stopped. Leaf grinned, rising from the floor. The man removed the mask – it was Zach.

Skye shook, her hands going to her mouth, covering another scream. Tears streamed down her face, and a look of abject fear mixed with disbelief swept across her features.

'That's good to roll,' Zach called, and a voice came in loud and clear as if the walls had speakers.

'Got that, boss.'

Zach was grinning at her, and Leaf hugged her.

'That's your first piece of performance art, my friend,' Leaf said.

'And the viewers will love it,' Zach added.

Chapter 4

Nate rushed up the stairs and stopped dead before the keypad on the entry door. He swore with frustration, but before attempting to punch in the code, Jessica buzzed him in. He raced in, giving her a grateful look and then stopped seeing her hand held up to halt him. He glanced at his closed office door.

'I can't stop. I'm late. What is it?' he asked hurriedly.

'Nathanial, stop immediately,' she said, and he did, wincing at the name that would only be used when he was in trouble. 'Yes, you're late, but so was the Lyons. They've only been waiting five minutes.'

Nate exhaled, relieved. He had been closing a case with a client, but as always, when she discovered her husband was cheating, there were waterworks, and he couldn't just hand her the bill and slip away.

She lowered her voice to a whisper. 'Take a deep breath and enter calmly and professionally.' Jessica dragged out the words to relax him.

He nodded, took a deep breath, pushed a hand through his blonde hair and gave Jessica his best impersonation of calm. Until he whispered, 'What are their names again?'

Jessica rolled her eyes. 'Robin and John Lyons. They are here to talk about their daughter, Sarah, who they think is in trouble, trapped in a cult or something like it.'

'Right, I remember.' He exhaled and nodded. 'Thanks, Jess. Robin and John got it. Where's Adam?' He glanced at the opened office door of his business partner and best friend.

'Prison group session,' she reminded him.

'Oh, of course, what fun.' He took another deep breath, strode to his office, and entered, closing the door behind him but not before shooting Jessica another grateful look in her direction.

'My apologies, Mr and Mrs Lyons. I was held up with a client, and then in traffic, it was a perfect storm.'

Mr Lyons rose and gave him a warm smile and a hand for shaking. 'We had the same problem,' he assured Nate. 'The population has increased and with it, the traffic.'

'So true,' Nate agreed, leaning over to shake the offered hand and Mrs Lyons' hand for good measure.

'Please, it's Robin and John,' Mrs Lyons said.

He acknowledged them and sat opposite at the round table. Jessica had put a pen and paper there for him; the Lyons both had a glass of water and a cup of coffee in front of them. She was worth her weight in gold, dollars, or whatever he and Adam paid her. Nate took full credit for hiring her; he remembered how she managed the department for her boss and all of the officers in his police service days. It was why he was keen to get her on board. When she agreed to come for an office manager interview, Nate easily convinced Adam they need not interview anyone else and hired her that day.

'How can I help? I believe you are worried about your daughter?' Nate started.

John Lyons nodded. 'It's not the first time we've sought help, I admit, but something has shifted, and now, well, let me tell the story from the top.'

'Please,' Nate agreed. He studied the man. He had a warm tenor voice and a kind face, craggy as if stress had taken its toll.

'Sarah is our middle child – we have two daughters and a son. Sarah is a very beautiful girl, and that's not just a father being biased.' John Lyons opened a plastic folder he had brought with him and slipped a photo to Nate, who agreed she was a beautiful young woman. Nate tried to keep his face neutral and not too enthusiastic, but she was a stunning blonde if you like the willowy model type. Like his ex-wife, Erin.

John continued. 'But Sarah is just the type to be sucked into a commune or a cult, whatever you want to call it,' he said pragmatically. Nate liked him immediately, even as his wife remonstrated.

'Well, she is Robin. Let's not beat around the bush here and waste the young man's time. We want Nate to help her, so the more direct we can be, the better,' he told his wife. 'Best we tell the story, warts and all.'

Nate thanked him; if only all his clients were astute, he'd knock off early every day. He recognised the type of man John Lyons was – a man who had always been in charge – sensible, learned, the man of the house. Robin looked a little arty as if she was into crafts and would float off at any moment. Nate suspected Sarah, the daughter, took after her. He wondered if Adam would be impressed by his character readings or would have a whole different take.

'Warts and all are good,' Nate agreed, giving Robin a sympathetic look.

John continued. 'She was always a follower, always looking for an identity. Desperate to get noticed and be accepted.'

'Give me an example, please,' Nate said and saw John look to Robin, who answered.

'Well, for starters, she was into everything but finished nothing, racing from one project to the next. It's like she was desperate to be good at something to stand out and validate herself.'

'The middle child tag really hit her hard, as if she had to prove she was as special as the eldest or youngest and forge her own identity,' John said. 'Being beautiful didn't help, as strange as that may sound. She always drew the eye, and I believe she thought that is all she had to trade on.'

Robin agreed. 'Sarah had all the same opportunities as our other two children, but she never excelled at anything or persisted long enough to do so. If she weren't brilliant straight away, she'd throw it in. It was almost desperate – acting, ballet, art, netball, golf, jazz ballet, debating, singing, and on it went.'

'Were her siblings' achievers?' Nate asked.

'Her big sister was an excellent scholar and won a university scholarship. She's now a doctor. Her brother excelled at rowing and cricket, and as the only boy, he was special in his own way. He's a sports teacher.'

Nate nodded. 'So, she was all about finding herself, and then she found a group who thought she was special.'

'That's what we believe, but she pushed us away for the last few years, saying it was her choice and what she wanted to do. Sorry, I'm getting ahead of myself... she found a man who thought he could launch her modelling career,' John said. 'He wanted her to sign a three-year contract and train with his other actors and models at this camp he ran. I didn't like it right from the start, but she was of age and didn't need my permission.'

'And he promised her the world,' Robin said. 'He told Sarah how classically beautiful she was and that he could make her a screen star. She signed that contract and moved to the camp, and that was nearly two years ago now.'

'She hasn't been home since; we believe they are discouraged from contacting people in the real world and encouraged to focus on their "craft" as Sarah calls it.' John made exclamation marks with his hands as he said the word craft.

'We've seen no evidence of her acting success,' Robin said and sighed. 'No magazine features, advertising appearances, model shoots, catwalks, or television appearances. Nothing.'

John nodded. 'I don't know what training is going on there, but we want our daughter back.'

Adam Murphy returned from his prison therapy group in Danielle's Mazda. Swinging into the car park, he was pleased to find the media party had left, but his car wasn't back yet. He decided it was best not to think about it. *Let it go!* He tried to adopt the suggestion he made to his own patients often enough when they got caught up in the detail of a drama, nevertheless, he could imagine Danielle drinking coffee in the front seat on his leather chair, and distracted while driving, singing along to her music or whatever she did. *Let it go!*

He returned his thoughts to his prison group. Some days, he felt like he had made a difference with the men incarcerated for long-term sentences, but today was not one of them. Everyone was restless; it must have been a Monday thing, even in prison, where every day was most likely the same. There were two fights amongst his group, and several prisoners refused to talk while another refused to shut up. It had him wondering if he should change the session time to the afternoon in the future. Although, he recalled a recent study that claimed patients made more progress overcoming their issues if they had counselling in the morning.

He parked the Mazda, locked it and took the stairs to the office, remembering to pin the code in before barging in – the security was only installed recently, and several times, both he and Nate had bounced off the door, forgetting it needed a code. Entering, he saw Nate's closed door and raised an eyebrow in Jessica's direction. 'He's doing some work?'

'Apparently so,' she said with a smile. 'How did the ruse work?'

'Like a dream, thanks. And don't tell Dan, but the Mazda hatch was pretty good to drive,' he smiled.

'Did you fill-up the tank?'

'Of course. I didn't have much choice; it was about a quarter full. I might not have got back here otherwise.'

Jessica grinned. 'You are a sweety. She'll hug you even more now.'

'Great,' Adam looked less than thrilled.

Nate's door opened with a rush, and Adam was caught in full view of Nate's clients. Nate closed the door slightly.

'Ah, you're back,' he stated the obvious. He lowered his voice. 'Remember I mentioned there might be a project we can work on together?'

'The cult?'

'Yep, in a manner of speaking. Got a minute? I mentioned you to the parents, who are keen to use us both.' He mouthed the words, 'money is no object, apparently.'

'You've got an hour,' Jessica told him with a glance at her laptop diary.

'We won't need half of that,' Nate assured him.

Adam looked from one to the other as they managed him and sighed. 'Give me a minute to drop my files off, and I'll be there.'

'I'll take them in for you,' Jessica said, rising, and Nate smiled, indicating the door. 'I'll bring in some more coffee,' she offered.

Adam followed Nate into his office, feeling like he had been hoodwinked. The back of Nate's head was no stranger to Adam, who was used to following Nate around. He noted the strain on the faces of the mature aged couple; he had seen that look many times in his counselling practice – the war-weary and desperate.

Nate made the introductions, and Adam shook both of their hands before sitting down. They listened as Nate gave Adam a brief overview, inviting the Lyons to interrupt at any time.

'So, we tried to get her out three times before, but she insisted she was happy and wanted to stay,' Robin Lyons said after Nate explained the situation. 'It is supposed to be a wellness camp and acting studio, but it is trussed up like a commune.'

'She didn't look brainwashed,' John Lyons admitted, 'but if it were a wellness camp, we should surely be able to phone her.' He shrugged. 'Although, I have found some of those wellness places want phones handed in at reception so as not to interrupt whatever they are there to do.'

'Let the healing begin,' Nate said.

'Yes, although why an acting studio needs that kind of closed-communication policy is beyond me,' John said with a shake of his head.

'We have no power; all we can do is trust she wants to be there,' Robin added.

'It doesn't sound like a healthy environment for the vulnerable,' Adam said, supporting them, 'and you are right to worry about her.'

'Thank you, that at least is reassuring. Have you worked with cult members before?' John asked as he studied the two men.

'No,' Adam said bluntly. 'But I've worked with many clients who are coerced or manipulated and can't get out of situations because they have lost the ability to be subjective and independent.'

'Good, good,' John said, relieved and nodded.

'There's also only two men there, or so Sarah told us on one of the few times we were permitted to speak with her,' Robin added and gave a little shudder. John looked at his wife. 'I hate to think what might be going on. Why are there so many women if it is an acting studio?'

John patted her hand comfortingly.

'I can't say I've heard of the group,' Nate told Adam. 'They've set up in a rainforest retreat at Tamborine Mountain, just over an hour's drive from here.'

'Right. The name?' Adam asked.

'*The Fidelium*,' John said. '*Fidelium Wellness Camp*, that's what it is called.'

'Fidelium – Latin for the faithful,' Adam said, musing on the name. 'Faithful to what I wonder.' He realised they were all looking at him as he thought out loud. 'I'm guessing the owner or studio boss made her feel like she was valued and her talent would shine with the right training and support.'

'And her money,' John added. 'We gave her $20,000 for her eighteenth birthday to buy a car, and we did it for all of our children. That just happened to be the entry fee for this wellness camp, acting studio, or whatever it is.'

'Do they get thrown out when the money runs out?' Nate asked.

'No, and that's what worries me. What is she doing now to earn her keep?' he said with a glance at his wife.

'So, what's changed? Why do you wish to try again?' Adam asked.

'We've had a spate of phone calls, about five now over the space of two weeks, and the caller doesn't say anything. They just breathe and then hang up after about ten seconds,' Robin said.

John continued: 'We don't know if it is Sarah trying to call and she is afraid to speak or can't speak. Maybe this is the only way she can communicate with us. But we have to know. We couldn't forgive ourselves if we didn't investigate. Will you take it on?' John looked from Adam to Nate.

Nate read Adam's expression and agreed. 'Of course.'

'She doesn't go by the name Sarah,' Robin said. 'Her name in there is Skye.'

'Why?' Adam asked.

'Sarah said they all have an acting name assigned to them. It's odd, isn't it?' Robin asked, 'Especially if they want to make a name for themselves as actors, why change it?'

'Very strange,' Nate agreed.

'And if she still doesn't want to come home?' Adam asked.

'Then I want her to tell us that to our face. For the last time,' John said.

'But I think something's wrong. I feel it in my bones,' Robin said.

Chapter 5

T hen...

Audrey Murphy, 58, slim, tall, sophisticated, and always willing to offer an opinion on all matters topical, was driving in her usual manner – somewhat erratic, sometimes too fast, rarely too slow, depending on her degree of passion for the talkback topic on the radio. Beside her, Adam sat listening attentively, anticipating his grandmother's questions. She liked to test him and ensure he was developing his own opinions and arguments.

In the backseat where Tom used to sit was his new security guard, Charlotte Duffy – or Charlie, as she insisted on being called. She was hot, and Adam knew Nate was madly in love with her, but he rarely got a lift when Audrey was driving, only on the mornings when Charlie sat behind the wheel, and his grandmother stayed at home to prepare for her bridge game.

He glanced back at Charlie, and they shared a smile. Nate was right; she was pretty and super fit. She wore her brown hair in a ponytail, and Nate said she was just like Sarah Connor in the *Terminator* movie. They had watched it a lot since Charlie became his security guard. Adam told his mother he wanted it, and she got the movie for him straight away. Nate couldn't believe it. He wouldn't have been allowed to watch it because it was R-rated, and even if it weren't, he would have had to do enough jobs around the house and save his pocket money to buy it.

Adam boasted to his school friends that Charlie used to be in the army, and Audrey said she was very experienced. He didn't know why she wanted to look after him, but she must be getting paid a shitload, as Nate put it. Anyway, she was nice, he mused, and she seemed happy to be with him, unlike Tom, who had kissed his mother when he thought no one was looking and didn't want to be stuck with Adam or Nate or any kids for that matter. He just wanted to return to the SAS, where he could be a big shot. Adam smiled, remembering how he asked his dad if he could have a different security office after Tom beat up Uncle Allan, and his dad agreed. It was that easy, but that wasn't normal. Only his mother, who was never around, did his bidding quickly and gifted him things to make up for it.

Audrey went past the front of the school and headed towards the sports oval; Adam visibly relaxed. On his 11th birthday, he had struck a deal with his grandmother that he could be dropped off at the side gate instead of right in front of the main school gate where she usually stopped. He was spared the embarrassment of Audrey's regency red 1968 XJ6 Jaguar pulling up in full sight of all arriving students and his security guard, Charlie, seeing him to the entrance. Some of Adam's friends were playing a hit of cricket on the oval before school started. He rushed his farewell so he could join them.

'Thanks, Audrey,' he said, kissing the cheek proffered in his direction and leaping from the car while Charlie exited the back seat. He didn't mind her seeing him in; the boys liked her and thought she was really cool. Several of them waved, and she returned the wave, but not before ensuring that no one in the vicinity looked sinister. She high-fived Adam, and once he was inside the school grounds, Adam turned to see her take the front seat he had just abandoned. He wondered if Audrey had made Charlie listen to talk-back radio and quizzed her about it on the way home.

'About time you're bowling,' Stuart told him, tossing the ball at Adam before he'd barely put his bag down.

'Going to get you out for a duck,' Adam joked, shining the ball on his clean uniform pants.

'Like to see that,' Stuart shot back with a grin.

Adam rearranged a couple of friends where he wanted them in the field to psyche Stuart out and came in for the run. Stuart whacked the ball but missed, and the boys ribbed him. Then he scowled, looking behind Adam and asked, 'What's he want?'

Adam turned to see Griffin Maxwell and his mates coming across the oval. They weren't the sporty types, more cool-like, trendy. Adam would fit right in with his looks and pedigree.

'We're playing here,' Stuart told them, and Griffin ignored him and smiled at Adam.

'You should have come along yesterday afternoon, Murph; it was really cool,' Griffin told him, ignoring Stuart.

'It was super freaky,' one of Griffin's sidekicks agreed.

'Yeah?' Adam asked casually. 'You can join in if you want to field.'

Griffin looked around, taking in Adam's friend, and with a look of disdain, he gave a slight shake of his head. 'No, but thanks. Dad's taking me out on his boat this weekend. You should come,' he offered.

'His dad's a politician,' the sidekick said like that was important.

All Adam heard was that Griffin's father was taking his son sailing. His own father would be working all weekend, as he usually did.

'Thanks, Griff,' Adam said, 'I'm doing something with Nate. Got to bowl.' He held up the ball and nodded in Stuart's direction.

'Catch you in maths, then,' Griffin said and strolled off, his three sidekicks beside him, with their hands in their pockets, looking relaxed.

'Wanker,' Stuart muttered under his breath.

Adam shrugged. 'He's alright.'

'Dad says his dad's going to be the next premier. Like big deal,' Stuart said.

'Yeah,' Adam agreed, thinking of his own father, who owned the media. But Adam liked Griffin and couldn't figure out why no one else did.

Now...

Jessica Johnson took the stairs to the office bearing the lettering on the door:

Nathan Delaney, *BA (PsychCrimnlgyJust)*
Private Investigator
Adam Murphy, *DPsych (Clinical), MSc (Psych), MAPS*
Psychologist

She entered the office with four coffees in a tray. It was well established that Jessica did the morning coffee run for the office team, including Danielle if she was on her way, but after that, they were fetching their own. Unless Jessica wanted another one, then she'd deigned to offer. It was coming up a year since Jessica had joined the boys in their new venture, and she was happy. Adam and his supervisor, psychologist Rob, were likeable, considerate, and kind. She knew from the start what to expect from Nate, from their time working together in the police force, and held no high hopes for his redemption.

'Coffees up,' she called to the men after punching in the pin number on the pad and gaining entry. Nate wandered out of Adam's office with Adam in tow, and Rob appeared in the doorway of his office.

'You know, it's almost the anniversary of my starting date,' she said, handing out their coffees.

'It's in my diary! We'll have to go out to lunch, all of us,' Nate said.

'In your diary? I'm impressed,' Jessica teased.

'Thank goodness you found us,' Adam agreed. 'No regrets?'

'Not for a minute, I love it,' she assured them.

'Well, no one would have seen that coming?' Rob joked, 'Although the premises are nice, and Stones Corner is a good little village to work in.'

'Of course she loves working with us, especially me. That's why you took the job, wasn't it?' Nate teased.

Jessica made a face and hesitated. 'At the time of agreeing to be the office manager, I had doubts that we could work together, Nate.'

His hand went to his heart, and Nate feigned shock.

'You were a pain in the butt during our police administration days,' she said, justifying herself, 'but I was desperate to get out of the city.'

Adam laughed. 'So that was the hook.' He became slightly more serious, 'not keen to work in a high rise then?'

She shook her head.

'You are not alone there. Many people like to be close to the ground and an exit,' Rob assured her.

'It's probably an irrational fear – being trapped, the building burning, and having to decide to die by fire or jump,' she shrugged. Even now, when she waited on street corners to cross at the lights, Jessica would position herself behind the pole in case someone intentionally rammed into the crowd on the sidewalk. Jessica imagined Adam and Rob would have something to say about her fears, but she wasn't one for talking about it.

'Don't worry, if there's a fire, we'll happily push you out the window before us,' Nate assured her.

'I feel so much better,' she said with a smile in his direction.

Hopefully, going to Winsome and Jack's wedding together would not be too awkward. Jack invited her, and Winsome invited Nate, so they decided to go together since they didn't have dates. She liked him. More than as a colleague, she was ninety per cent sure Nate felt the same. The ten per cent missing could be attributed to them not knowing where it would lead, what it would look like professionally, or if it was worth the risk. It was silently acknowledged that the wedding was a date of sorts, a trial run. At least Danielle would be there too as their security detail; that would keep things relaxed. Jessica had spared no expense on her dress for the night and had booked a hair appointment for that morning. After all, she was at Adam's table, the VIP table. She was secretly looking forward to seeing Nate in black-tie too.

Jessica glanced at the clock. 'Speaking of irrational fears, better drink that coffee quickly,' she told Adam. 'You've got *Stressed Girl* this morning, and your drinking might stress her out.'

Nate scoffed, and Jessica smiled at Adam's pained expression. She shrugged. 'Best, I don't use their names, so I have to distinguish them somehow.'

'You want to laugh, and you're just scared to because your supervisor is here,' Nate said to Adam, with a look to Rob.

'Not true,' Adam said, giving Nate a stern look. 'I never laugh at my patients. Out loud anyway.'

'Regardless, it's true, she's stressed to the max,' Jessica said. 'And your other patient, *Hungry Girl*, is easily spooked too. I was having a biscuit with my tea when *Hungry Girl* was waiting for you one day, and she looked truly terrified for me that I was having all those kilojoules. I had to put it in the drawer until she left.'

Nate chuckled, and Rob and Adam smiled with acceptance. They had seen it firsthand and understood the fear.

'Can you put on weight by watching someone eat?' Nate asked.

'Osmosis? Never worked for me,' Adam said, drinking his coffee. 'I've watched Nate scoff down some incredible junk all his life, and look how svelte I am,' he joked.

Nate grinned as they laughed at his expense. 'Yeah, your body's a temple,' he shot back. 'Speaking of which, have we got any biscuits?'

Rob shook his head. 'I hate to think about what goes on here on the days I'm not in the office.'

'Time wasting and bedlam,' Jessica assured him and handed Nate a biscuit tin from under her desk. 'Rob, you have a meeting with *Angry Guy* for the class action.' She turned to Nate, 'Danielle is coming in to see you at 10.30 about the cult case. Can you call it a cult?'

'Gosh, we sound so busy and important,' Nate joked. 'And it's more of a wellness studio, I believe.'

'It's like a 21st-century cult,' Adam suggested, filling Rob in briefly on the case. 'Select people doing workshops with just one or two leaders and donating their money to them while they become stars.'

'Yeah, in the old days of cults, the "workshops" were spiritually based – finding your faith, following gurus, aliens, false gods,' Rob said. 'Now it's fame?'

'Maybe,' Nate shrugged.

'And you have fame right at your fingertips and don't want it,' Jessica said to Adam as if the concept was so foreign.

'Yeah. No thanks,' Adam said. 'I don't get why anyone would want to pose and smile all day and wear different outfits, have to change all the time, have your hair done and re-done, and have people recognising you wherever you go.'

Jessica rolled her eyes. 'Well, when you say it like that, it sounds dull. But I think it would be exciting to model the latest designer clothes and shoes and bags and go to star-studded events and VIP openings and spend your day doing creative things like acting... but I love my job,' she added quickly with a smile, making Nate and Rob laugh.

Adam grinned. 'You're as bad as Dan. She asked if she could get some shots posing with me as my security detail, but she'd have to change a few times.' He laughed at the thought and hurriedly added, 'I said no.'

'Spoilsport,' Rob ribbed him.

'You're getting a haircut before the wedding, aren't you?' Jessica turned to Nate.

'Why?' he looked indignant and ran a hand through his blond wavy hair that needed a haircut. 'Some girls love to run their hands through my hair.'

'Scruffy, just saying,' Jessica mumbled with a smile, knowing he would get a haircut now. 'Anyway, Dan's up for some surveillance of the wellness studio,' Jessica finished.

'I thought we were going to do the surveillance,' Adam turned to Nate. 'Not that I'm not happy to palm it off on Dan.'

'Don't get excited, we're doing it. I know you like the quality time together,' he joked. 'But I thought I'd get Dan doing some research first on the place itself – you know, what access is like, if anyone is coming and going, who's in the house, what sort of acting workshops are going on, how you get a piece of the action, all that.'

'Good thinking,' Adam said, surprised, earning a smirk from his best friend.

'Ever been tempted to join a cult?' Nate asked Adam with a quizzical look on his face.

'Nope. You?'

'Never.'

No one spoke, waiting for Nate to elaborate on why he asked, but he didn't.

'Hmm. Good talk,' Adam said, and Jessica laughed.

'You two are clowns.' She turned to Adam. 'Oh, one more thing... Tom's coming in this afternoon and wants to catch up with you as well.' She waited for his inevitable reaction.

'God no, what's he want?'

Jessica shrugged. 'Wedding security talk, I'm guessing.'

'For the love of God,' Adam grumbled. No love was lost between Adam and his former boyhood security guard, whom his mother had appointed to provide security for her wedding. 'Can't you say I'm out? Until after the wedding?'

Jessica chuckled, and Nate clapped him on the shoulder. 'Price of fame, my friend, you'll just have to suck it up.'

The office buzzer went downstairs, and Jessica glanced at the screen, ready to admit a client. Adam ventured back to his office for his appointment with '*Stressed Girl*', and the group disbanded.

Chapter 6

Adam sat at his desk and glanced at Ellie's file again while he waited for her to come upstairs, pay Jessica for her session, and sit for five minutes before he admitted her to his office. He liked his clients to undergo that routine so they didn't rush in, hyped up and unfocused. Jessica was right; everything stressed Ellie. She was young and beautiful and stressed. He was amazed by how many young patients he saw with the same anxieties. To look at them, you would think they had the world at their feet, but they were struggling to function and so needy of endorsement. The *Like Me* generation, he mused, defined by their followers, crippled by negativity. Adam read over her file and notes from her two visits. Her doctor had referred her after working with another psychologist who no longer wanted to work with Ellie. Adam searched the notes for the reason. Apparently, he was winding back, doing less work with clients, or so he said.

Adam scanned her past. She was an attractive woman who had matured too fast as a young girl. Her history showed plenty of dependencies; from a young age, she moved from one relationship to the next. She seduced her mother's boyfriend and was thrown out of the house. Then, she seduced her carer's husband and was moved out of care, then seduced a teacher. He was getting the picture; she needed a man for security, to make her feel whole and wanted. Throw in a bit of cutting and self-harm, and that rounded off his client's issues. He wanted Ellie to create a life that didn't involve needing a man. Adam was pretty confident now about why the last psychologist had let her go.

He had checked out her social media pages, mainly at her insistence, as she showed him her photos and the positive responses she had received. Everyone loved her and thought she was beautiful, and there were so many likes and comments. So unimportant. Giving up her phone was not an option in the modern world, but could she learn not to use it to boost her self-esteem without relying on others to pump her up? Time will tell. During the last two visits, Ellie seemed rational, but he saw the signs, or maybe he was looking for them now. She was flirting with him.

Ellie Langdon was in love with Adam Murphy; she knew he felt the same. She saw how he looked at her during her sessions; he was so sincere and warm. His blue eyes never left her face. When she got him to smile, it changed how he looked; he'd look away as if he was uncomfortable being caught smiling at work or shy. He was beautiful. She couldn't believe he wasn't online... OMG, he'd have the biggest following, especially given his mother was the gorgeous Winsome Keeley, and his godfather was Jack Bernham. His dad might be dead, but he was still a huge name, too – James Murphy – everyone knew of him. Imagine marrying into that family. She had a rush of excitement thinking about it.

Ellie was convinced Adam wanted to tell her how he felt but couldn't because of his work. But if she opened herself to him, if she admitted her feelings first, they would flood out of him. She would fit so well into his world. For many hours at night, she had gone through the different scenarios of how the scene would play out, how they would both admit their love, and how their future would be. The time had come.

Before entering his office, Ellie sat in the car park, preparing herself.
Today is the day.

She checked her lipstick again. She practised a smile.

He told me he wanted me to be confident and to know just how important I am. I'm sure he meant how important I am to him.

She said a few mantras about her strength and power to boost herself before entry. Taking a deep breath before exiting the car, Ellie made her way to the office and stopped at the entry buzzer, like she had done the three meetings before. The first time they met and the two visits since she felt their bond deepening and their relationship growing. She had missed him terribly the last two weeks while he was away on leave; he must have felt that separation, too.

'Fate,' she whispered. *I was meant to come to Adam, and he was meant to be my therapist.*

She didn't like her other therapist, and she didn't like Adam's office manager, Jessica. She hoped Adam didn't either. Ellie straightened her red dress, took a deep breath and pressed the buzzer.

'Delaney and Murphy,' the office manager said in her professional voice.

'It's Ellie here for my appointment with Adam.'

'Sure, Ellie, come on up.'

The door was unlatched with a buzz, and Ellie took the stairs slowly; she didn't want to get hot and sweaty or ruin her hair. She entered the office when the door at the top of the stairs buzzed, letting her in. She came to the desk, settled her account, and sat in the small waiting room. The other two doors were closed, but she had seen the private detective once and the other psychologist a few times. Once, he arrived with Adam when they were running late. She settled, reminding herself of the importance of today and then his door opened, and Adam appeared.

'Hi Ellie, come on in.'

Ellie rose hurriedly and looked over to give Jessica a smile of thanks even though she didn't like her, but Adam would see how considerate she was to his staff. She entered Adam's office with her stomach whirling with nerves and excitement.

Chapter 7

W hen Nate saw that the visitor downstairs was not for him but a client of Adam's, he returned to his office to avoid encountering one of Adam's patients. He listened, hearing the woman enter and be admitted to Adam's room. He gave it five minutes, stuck his head out again, and, seeing the reception was free of visitors, sought out Jessica in the kitchen.

'Burnsy is on his way,' Nate said, referring to their old colleague Sergeant Matt Burns, who was still in the police service and helped them out on occasion.

'What have you done?' she teased in a suspicious voice. 'Do I need to raise bail?'

'Not this time, but never say never,' Nate said with a chuckle. 'So, he asked you out, huh?'

She gave a casual shrug. 'He might have. He's a really nice guy.'

'Yeah, he is *nice*,' Nate agreed, putting the emphasis on "nice" as if that was everything he was not. A short silence followed while he followed her from the kitchen back to her desk.

'That it?' she asked. 'No inquisition, no agenda?'

'Nope, that's all I've got,' Nate said and leaned on her desk. He looked to Adam's door, often fascinated by the people who sought help. His own mantra was "Get over it".

'If you want to talk with Adam, you'll have to wait until *Stressed Girl* leaves,' Jessica said. 'I think she's in love with him.'

'I saw her on the camera; she looked like she was dressed for a date. She wouldn't be the first patient to fall in love with him. So tall, dark and handsome, so strong.'

Jessica laughed. 'You're an idiot. I suspect male and female therapists often have the same problem with clients falling for them. She's young, vulnerable, he's providing this safe, intimate environment, and he's good-looking.' She shrugged.

'And she's telling him all her secrets,' Nate whispered mysteriously.

Jessica jumped as the buzzer on her desk went off. Nate leaned over, saw Burnsy on the screen downstairs and buzzed him in. 'Your boyfriend's here,' he joked but felt a pang of jealousy. Even if Burnsy hadn't got to first base with Jessica, there was nothing to say he wouldn't try again in the future.

'At least someone wants to date me,' she retorted. Their pending wedding "date" at Winsome and Jack's nuptials hung over their heads like the beginning or end of something good. Nate hoped it would be the former, but he wasn't taking any action until then in case he blew it. Everyone knew a wedding was the perfect occasion for a date, or so he'd been told. So romantic, everyone looking their best, dancing, drinking, general happiness... *whatever,* he'd tap into it, he decided.

Seeing Burnsy at the door, Nate opened it, and Sergeant Matt Burns entered, dressed in his police uniform, which always put Jessica on edge – memories of her years working in the metropolitan police administration. He greeted them both.

'Did I miss something?' he asked, 'you both look tense.'

'We always look like this,' Nate said. 'Jessica is wound up, and I'm constipated.'

'Eww,' she groaned. 'Take your boy humour and go to your office, please.'

Nate laughed.

'I'll move him along, Ma'am,' Burnsy joked, falling into his police role and smiling at her as he followed Nate.

'What do you know about the *Fidelium Wellness Studio* at Mount Tamborine?' Nate asked, moving to his meeting table and asking before they were even seated.

Burnsy groaned. 'That old chestnut. Why are you asking?' He took off his police hat and dropped it on the chair beside him, running a hand through his thinning hair.

'I've got a new client – parents of one of their actors or models who believe she might be captive, even though she's told them twice in the past she's not. She's got a three-year contract for performing, allegedly.' Nate explained the situation.

Burnsy nodded when Nate finished and added: 'The guy who runs it is a nutter, and his friend who is locked in there with him enjoying the spoils of fifteen or more women for two guys, is actually a lawyer; he knows his rights, or rather their rights. Interesting. They call it a wellness studio, or acting camp, or something like that, not a cult, which it probably is, truthfully known.'

'But if this woman has a legal contract to study acting and perform with them, then it's not really a cult as she's not blindly following a leader. Or is she?'

Burnsy shrugged. 'I believe there are enough gullible women of various ages in there that have formed a dependency on the owner; that's a cult in my books.'

'So legally, they can operate below the radar?' Nate asked.

'If no one is strong-armed into being there, yes. It's usually the families that are concerned. I haven't seen the so-called contracts, but I'd like to set eyes on them,' Burnsy's eyes narrowed with suspicion. 'But from memory, I think anyone can leave there whenever they want, even if it means breaking a contract. I'd have to check that out, though; it's been a while since they've come across my desk.'

'Do you think that's the case though, or are women coerced to stay – fear, shame, addiction maybe?'

Burnsy shrugged. 'The parents believe that, don't they?'

'Right. What trouble have you had with them?' Nate pressed.

Burnsy gave it some thought. 'The last time was a few years back. We were called there because of a death.'

Nate sat forward. 'Yeah?'

'In childbirth. It was the woman's choice to have her child there, but she had complications, and by the time the ambulance arrived, she had lost the child.'

'Horrendous,' Nate said and sat back. 'Did she stay?'

Burnsy shook her head. 'If memory serves, once she got taken to the hospital, she never returned to the camp.'

'Was the father of the child the owner of the place?'

'I can't say, but there are only a few men in the place unless she was pregnant when she entered.' Burnsy ran a hand over his jaw while he thought. 'I'd be surprised if they accepted a young actress or model into the camp if she were pregnant, so my guess is she got pregnant there.'

'I wouldn't mind speaking with her. Any chance you'd have a name?'

'I can get it. The story was in the press, and you'll find her name online if she still goes by the same name.' He frowned. 'Come to think of it, I believe her name then was Moondrop or something equally way out there!'

Nate grinned. 'Well, I'll get Dan onto it, but if you can help with some details about Moondrop, that'd be appreciated.'

'I'll put it on my list of things to do,' Burnsy said and sighed. 'I only ever met a few others that came out of there, and they were closed off.'

'Meaning what? On drugs?'

'No, insecure, nervous... I'd almost say too scared to talk. They had money, but maybe it was hush money. I can't say. I've had no grounds to pursue them.'

'So why were these women who came out talking with you then?' Nate asked the obvious.

'I was following up on the death of the child, so I sought them out. None of them would say a bad word about the place.'

'Hmm,' Nate mused. 'While I'm pushing my luck, if you have any other information on the camp, studio, whatever, that you'd be prepared to throw my way so I'm not starting from scratch, that'd be great.'

'Like what?'

'Who the staff or owners are, any names from current and former "students", financial papers showing how they exist, the songlist from their weekly wellness chant,' Nate joked, and Burnsy laughed.

'Leave it with me, and I'll see what's there. Truly, what would you do without me?'

'Perish the thought,' Nate joked and then added sincerely, 'Thanks, I owe you. Again.'

'You can put in a good word for me,' he said, nodding to Jessica outside the door.

Nate winced.

'Ah, not possible then,' Burnsy read him.

'Wouldn't want you to think I undercut you.'

'May the best man win.' Burnsy gave him a grin and rose to depart. Nate hoped he would win Jessica's heart, and the wedding could not come soon enough. He knew Adam thought the same thing for an entirely different reason.

Ellie gave her best impression of a confident walk as she entered the therapy room, and Adam closed the door behind her. He invited her to sit on one of the couches and remained standing until she had sat; he was so charming, she thought. That was just one of the things that made him so attractive.

'Oh wow, you look great,' she blushed as the words left her mouth. 'Tanned, I mean, healthy.'

He smiled. 'Thanks, a few weeks away at the beach will do that for you.' He sat opposite, placing her file down beside him. Two glasses and a jug of water were on the low glass table between them.

She imagined herself saying, 'Why did you go away? Who did you go with? Did you think of me?' But she had planned what she would say and wanted to keep to that prepared script. She was confident of her words then. Adam gave her some tips in their last session on how to reduce anxiety – controlling her mind and preparing for situations she knew she had to face. Today, she had taken his lessons on board; she was prepared.

Ellie opened her bag, checked inside and closed it again.

'Is everything alright?' Adam asked and poured a glass of water for them both.

'Yes, just checking I had... turned my phone off.'

Adam began. 'So, how are you feeling, Ellie? What challenges have you experienced since we last met, a good two weeks ago now?' He sat back, studying her, and she crossed her legs and tried to adopt the same comfortable pose that he obviously felt in her presence. She loved that she must have that effect upon him.

Ellie wanted to say the hardest challenge had been not seeing him for two weeks and wondering where he was and what he was doing. She had read everything she could find about him, printed out all the photos she found online and put them near her bed. She couldn't find any photos of him on his holidays, making his absence even worse. This was love; she just knew it. Stronger, more intense than anything she had ever felt, and that old saying was true – absence had made her heart grow fonder.

Ellie answered Adam's questions perfunctorily. 'I have been fine, just practising everything you taught me. It really helped,' she tried not to gush. She opened her handbag again, looked in and closed it.

'You're distracted, Ellie. What's going on?' he cut to the chase.

She gave a small smile and nodded. 'I'm, sorry I've got a lot on my mind.'

'That's okay. Do you want to tell me what's distracting you?'

Ellie bit her lip. In her script, she was going to tell him how she felt after he told her about his holiday. She thought sharing their stories would be so wonderful, but he had made short work of that, and she had lost her cues; her timing felt wrong. Plus, she hadn't counted on how distracting he was, how awkward he made her feel. Adam was beautiful in his suit. Clean-shaven, his blue eyes even brighter since he got a tan, his dark hair mussed and stylishly cut. He looked like the former prime minister and media mogul James Murphy. She couldn't be sure whose son he was, but it didn't matter; whatever made him happy would make her happy.

'I have something to tell you.' She started bravely and abruptly.

'Okay. You can tell me anything. You don't have to be nervous,' he said sincerely. She loved that about Adam.

Ellie crossed her legs over again in front of him and tried to look relaxed. Coaching herself that she was prepared, she had this.

'I'm falling in love with you.' She said the words softly, then smiled and leaned forward slightly, waiting for him to smile and reciprocate. She knew he would be relieved; he might even reach for her hand – that was in one of her dream scenarios.

But that didn't happen.

Adam's breath hitched, and then he exhaled as if calming himself. He gave a small nod and then showed no other emotion. He was a blank slate. No sudden movements, no surprised expression. It was as if she had said the weather was nice today.

Ellie studied him. Why was he not reacting, not reciprocating?

'Did you hear me?' she asked tentatively.

'Yes. You know, Ellie, that's okay. Those feelings are normal in these sorts of situations,' he said soothingly as if she were distressed. 'It's because we trust each other and share your history.'

'No,' she shook her head. 'This is not a *situation* we are in,' she declared loudly, stopped, took a breath and lowered her voice. This was not going how she had planned. 'I am not one of your patients who is dependent on you or... I'm just not. I know the difference, and I know you feel the same, too; I can tell.'

His jaw flexed for a moment, and then Adam said. 'No, I have a partner. Our relationship – yours and mine – is professional, and I appreciate being able to help you.'

Ellie's eyes narrowed with anger.

'You want me more than your partner. You know it, and I know it,' she snapped.

There was a moment of silence between them, and Ellie realised she would not appear attractive to him if she got nasty. She smiled at him.

'You don't need to feel embarrassed or ashamed, Ellie,' Adam said, sitting forward slightly. 'You are not the first person to feel that way with a therapist, not just me.'

'I don't feel embarrassed. I'm just angry that you are putting your work before your feelings,' she said, hissing the words out between her teeth. 'If you were honest...'

Adam held up his hands in a pacifying gesture. 'Ellie—'

'Seeing you is the highlight of my week. You feel the same!' she said, her voice raising. She didn't want to cry, but she could feel the tears welling in her eyes. She wanted to hit him and kiss him.

Adam cleared his throat. 'Let's step back here. Do you want a break?'

'No!' she screamed. 'Admit it!'

Jessica sat bolt upright at her desk. What the hell was that? A scream? She rose and went to Adam's door and knocked lightly.

There was no response. She knew she wasn't allowed to enter, especially if Adam had an aggressive client; it was too dangerous. She listened again for a little longer but could not hear anything. Jessica turned and hurried to Nate's office and knocked on the door, entering without waiting for an invitation. Burnsy was still with him, standing ready to depart.

'I think Adam's in trouble,' she blurted, interrupting them.

'Has he pressed the buzzer?' Nate asked, rising, his face etched with concern.

'No.'

'Who is in with him?' Burnsy asked.

'One of his female patients.'

Nate breathed a sigh of relief. 'He can handle that.'

'She just screamed.'

'Well, at least he's not screaming,' Nate said.

Burnsy walked to Nate's door and looked towards Adam's office. 'Do you want me to check?'

'Yes, please,' Jessica said.

'What about privacy and all that doctor-patient privilege crap?' Nate asked. 'Can you just go in?'

Burnsy shrugged. 'I'll just knock, announce myself, and ask the question. I won't go in.'

'Thank you,' Jessica said, relieved and followed Burnsy and Nate to Adam's office door.

There was no noise coming from the office, not even voices. All three turned as a figure appeared at the office doorway, putting in the code. Rob entered – Adam's supervisor and an experienced psychologist – back from a meeting.

'Rob will know what to do,' Jessica said, relieved as he entered.

'Thank God,' Nate said on seeing him.

'What's going on?' he asked, concerned as they gathered outside Adam's office. Jessica explained, and Rob moved quickly to the door.

With his hand on the door handle, Rob asked, 'What's his patient's name?'

'Ellie,' Jessica said.

'Best you wait here, all of you,' he said, knocking once, he walked straight in without waiting.

Chapter 8

T hen...

Adam spun around, sensing someone nearby. He was always on alert; his father drummed it into him, especially since his last security guard bashed up Adam's friend, Uncle Allan. His father said Uncle Allan was not a friend or an uncle, but Adam liked him and missed him. Uncle Allan used to come to his and Nate's cricket games; his father never had the time.

Adam swung by the oval to get his cricket bat, which he'd left behind and was late crossing the oval to meet Charlie. He could see her waiting near the gate, scanning the boys for his face. She looked hot, dressed in tight black pants and a black singlet, her sunnies on. Nate was in love with her and swore he'd marry Charlie when he grew up.

Adam didn't see Griffin Maxwell's two friends until they were almost on top of him, too close – Zach and Ben – he hadn't spoken to them much at all.

He stepped back. 'What do you want?'

'Griff wants you to hang with us. He said to let you know you should, or else.'

Adam looked from one to the other. They were about his size; Zach was thinner, but he had a sneer that made him look like he'd do damage. Ben was solid, and he played football.

'Why's he care who I hang out with?' Adam asked and tried to walk ahead, but they crowded him.

'Just 'cause he does, he says you'd fit in, and you're lucky that we're letting you in our group. Lots of people want to hang around with us, and he's letting you. You should be thanking him.'

'I'm hanging out with Stuart.'

'You want me to tell him that?' Ben asked with a grin that served as more of a warning.

A shadow cast across Adam's face, letting him look up without squinting.

'Everything all right here, boys?' Charlie asked. 'Because if you are hassling my friend, Adam, we'll have to talk.'

Zach scowled up at Charlie, which amazed Adam that he'd be so rude to an adult. His grandmother, Audrey, would have a fit.

'Yeah, we're just hanging out,' Ben said and stepped back. 'See you tomorrow, Murphy.' The two boys walked away without looking back.

'Everything okay?' Charlie asked as they walked toward the car.

'Yeah, it's all good,' Adam said casually.

'You would tell me if it wasn't, Adam?' she pushed.

'Sure.'

'Look at me.'

Adam looked up at his sporty, super-fit bodyguard, giving her his best-winning smile. He had seen his father use it with his grandmother when the situation required it.

'I would, Charlie, there's nothing to worry about. Nothing at all.'

Now...

Dr Robert Ware, Adam's supervisor, hurriedly entered Adam's office and closed the door behind him. He read the relief on Adam's face. In front of Rob, a young woman, tall, in a red dress, with dark hair and wearing too much make-up stood by the window staring at Adam. On the floor was a handbag, and in her hand was a Stanley knife – an artist's knife that retracted and had a hellishly sharp blade. Rob recognised the type from his wife's painting hobby, she used the knife to cut canvas.

Adam had blood on his hand, a cut of some sort that was dripping onto the carpet. Rob couldn't see if that was his only wound; the colour on his face was fine, and he wasn't pale or shaking. The girl had no obvious injuries but rocked slightly as she stood in front of the window frame. Rob read the situation.

'Hi, Adam and Ellie, sorry to interrupt.' Rob used a calm and measured voice. 'Ellie, I'm Adam's business partner. I need to speak with him. But are you okay?'

She hadn't taken her eyes off Adam, who stood near the two chairs where they had been sitting.

'We're talking,' she snapped, still watching Adam. 'Leave us alone; we're not finished talking.'

'I imagine you've got a lot to catch up on, given Adam's been away for two weeks,' Rob said and went towards the door with no intention of leaving. He knew Adam would understand what he was doing. Rob opened the door a little and saw the three still waiting. 'Ambulance, sedative,' he whispered, leaning back into the office.

'I'll tell you what, Ellie. You and Adam need some time to talk, some privacy,' he said. 'Why don't you put that knife down on the windowsill, come back here, and sit down.'

He patted the chair opposite Adam that she must have evacuated earlier.

Rob continued. 'I'll get some coffee for you both and tell Jessica you are not to be interrupted. What do you think?'

Ellie flicked the blade up and down the retractable knife, the sound of it clicking as it retracted each time. She needed Adam to invite her to sit down and encourage her.

Adam cleared his throat. 'That's a good idea. We've got a lot to talk about... the future.'

'The future?' she asked, her voice rising with a little hope.

He nodded. 'The future.'

'Leave the knife there then,' Rob said. 'Come and sit down.'

Ellie looked down at the knife and then at Adam. Suddenly, with force, she thrust it into her leg and screamed out with pain and anger.

'Jesus, Ellie,' Adam yelled and ran towards her.

'Adam, stay back,' Rob ordered, pushing him away.

Hearing the yelling, Burnsy rushed in, his eyes appraising the situation in a moment. 'All of you get back,' he commanded, taking over, and drew a taser. They heard the wail of an ambulance, and behind Burnsy, Nate rushed in, sending Jessica back to her desk to let in the emergency services.

'Drop the knife,' Burnsy ordered. Ellie was breathing fast; she had pulled the knife out of her leg but was holding it, still fixated on Adam, bleeding.

'Are you hurt?' Rob asked Adam.

'No.'

'Where's the blood coming from?' Nate asked, seeing it dripping from Adam's fingers.

Adam held up his hand. 'Just a cut.'

'Self-defence wound?' Rob asked, and Adam nodded.

'You promised we'd be alone,' Ellie said between gasps, looking at Rob and then back to Adam.

'Put the knife down now, Ellie,' Rob said, 'and we can talk about it. We'll give you and Adam some more time, but there'll be no meeting with him while you're carrying a knife.'

They could hear Jessica buzzing in the ambulance team at reception. Ellie began to lower the knife and then extended the blade, throwing it full force at Adam. It happened too fast for him to move, his arm going up instinctively to protect himself.

Nate pushed him; the knife flew by, just missing Adam, and Burnsy grabbed the young girl, restraining her. Ellie sunk to the floor in Burnsy's grip.

'We need a sedative here,' Rob instructed the two paramedics that Jessica hurriedly escorted into the room.

'That was fast,' Adam said, surprised.

'We were having our break just up the street,' one of the men explained their hasty arrival.

'You owe me a bacon and egg burger,' the other joked.

'Where are you injured?' one of the paramedics asked Adam, and he held up his hand. 'That it?'

'That's it,' Adam agreed and exhaled, watching Ellie as she was restrained and given a sedative. She never removed her eyes from him – her expression changing from despair to anger to high emotion.

Burnsy spoke to Adam. 'Do you want to file a complaint?'

'No, definitely not,' he said with a shake of his head. 'But thanks for stepping in.'

'Lucky I was on the premises,' Burnsy said.

'And thanks for the shove,' he said to Nate.

'Always happy to push you around,' Nate joked. 'Did you see this coming?' He nodded towards Ellie as the paramedics treated her.

Adam gave a casual shrug. 'I thought last session she had started showing signs of attraction, but I thought the two-week break might cool that.'

'Apparently not,' Rob said. 'Are you okay?'

'Yeah, fine,' Adam said, dismissing their concerns and watching the paramedics in action.

The paramedics guided a sedated Ellie onto the guernsey and strapped her down. They wheeled her out. One of them stopped long enough to bandage Adam's hand.

'I'll have a chat with the paramedics and let the hospital know what to expect,' Rob said. 'Then we talk.'

Security officer and ex-military man, Tom Hartigan, pulled up in the car park of *Delaney and Murphy* and casually observed the ambulance at the front of the building. They were lifting someone into the back, and a small crowd had gathered to watch the unfolding drama. He came out of the car park, locking his car, and then it crossed his mind it could be Adam on the guernsey. He raced over; it was a woman. He walked away, not caring but keen to set eyes on Adam to ensure he was upright.

Once Adam's appointed security detail, even now, twenty years later, his instinct was to protect the guy whom he couldn't stand; the feeling of dislike was mutual. But Adam's model mother, Winsome, still held a soft spot for Tom. They had shared a brief affair while she was married to Adam's father, who was conveniently away on business. Adam had seen them being intimate and was not the forgiving type. Regardless, while he was in Winsome's employ, he would provide the required security for Adam, his partner Kelsey, Nate, and the aged Audrey. Tom needed the work and was happy for it; he knew Adam wished the whole wedding circus was over, they both did.

Then, Tom saw Adam's partner, Dr Robert Ware, talking with a paramedic near the entrance to the office building and the adrenaline kicked in. He raced up the stairs, still fit and fast at 58, pinned in the number before Jessica could let him in from behind her desk where she stood, and raced in.

'Adam!' he yelled.

'Here,' Adam called from his office, and Tom Hartigan exhaled, his hand going to his heart.

'What the fuck is going on?' he asked Jessica as he stormed to Adam's office, not waiting for an answer. He entered and saw the blood trail and bandage on Adam's hand. 'Are you alright? What's happened?' he asked, taking in the scene, ready for action.

'Stand down,' Adam said drily. He was no fan of Hartigan's. 'Just a patient who got a little emotional.'

'She fell in love with Adam and couldn't understand why it wasn't reciprocated,' Nate filled in the blanks.

'And what? She pulled a bloody knife on you?' Tom asked.

'That's about it,' Adam said, looking down at his bandaged hand.

'You didn't press the alarm!' Tom glared at Adam as if he avoided the alarm just to rile Tom.

'I was at the table; the buzzer was under the desk,' Adam responded, 'I couldn't get there.'

Tom Hartigan froze. He closed his eyes for a moment while reining in his anger. He and Adam had been at each other since he reappeared in Adam's life, but he thought they had reached a level of understanding. He was wrong. Tom opened his eyes and spoke slowly.

'You knew I was installing security in your office and home, and you didn't think to mention that you needed it at the coffee table because that's where you met with your clients?'

Adam glared at him. 'If you have ever had therapy...' he started, knowing full well Tom Hartigan had compulsory therapy on his discharge from his military service, 'you would know that the psychologist and the patient do not sit across a desk from each other.'

The two men glared at each other.

'You know what your problem is?' Tom asked him.

'Hell yeah, I've several of them, including you,' Adam said. He heard Nate restrain a laugh.

Tom ignored them both and continued. 'You think you are hard done by.'

Adam laughed. 'Really? I run a prison therapy group; I know what hard done by looks like. You know what your problem is?'

'Oh good,' Nate said and sighed, sitting back on Adam's desk and folding his arms across his chest.

'Free therapy, let's hear it,' Tom said with attitude.

'You don't like yourself.'

Tom's eyes widened with surprise. Adam continued. 'Your self-esteem is shot. It makes you aggressive, competitive, jealous, promiscuous... I don't know why you have no self-esteem when you seem to have plenty of good stuff going on. Just saying,' Adam concluded.

Tom looked from Adam to Nate and back to Adam. 'You've got to be fucking kidding me?'

Adam shrugged.

'Right then, since we've sorted that,' Nate said, rising, 'Adam, you think you are hard done by, and Tom, you've got no self-esteem. So, moving on.'

Tom shook his head and said to Adam: 'I've just got to get you safely to that wedding and home afterwards, and then we're done with each other,' he said through gritted teeth. 'Do you think you could meet me halfway until then?'

Adam thought about it, but before he could respond, Nate stepped in again, moving closer to stand beside Adam at the edge of the desk and gripped Adam's shoulder.

'We can do that. Adam just needs to find clients who don't fall in love with him.'

Jessica walked in, hearing the last line of their discussion.

'That was freaky,' she shuddered.

'Quick thinking though, thanks,' Adam said to her.

'It all came together. Burnsy was in the office, and then Rob arrived back,' she explained.

'I'm organising an alarm for under the coffee table,' Tom said to Jessica, ignoring Adam.

'No more new clients, Jess,' Adam said, and they all snapped to look at him. 'I'm done.'

There was a momentary silence, and Rob could be heard at the door pumping in the code. He re-entered and appeared in the doorway of Adam's office.

'Burnsy's headed back to work. He said he'd call you later, Nate. Adam, we need to talk,' he ventured further in.

'No, we're done here. No more new clients. I'll finish up the ones I've got; that's it.'

'Hold up a minute,' Nate said. 'Don't throw it all in just because one nutcase falls in love with you. God, it always happens to me, especially with the deserted wives.'

'But they don't pull knives,' Tom pointed out the obvious.

'Besides, I'm sure "nutcase" is not the best word to use these days,' Rob suggested.

'I'm not throwing it all in,' Adam said. 'I'm just changing focus; I've been thinking about it for a long while… since Mum started with this wedding crap, and Jess has been overwhelmed with idiot clients trying to get a story or get an appointment.'

'It's okay though,' she assured him, 'I can handle it.'

He shook his head and then saw Nate's stricken expression. 'I'm still working here, just changing tact.'

Nate exhaled. 'Thank God. I've just broken you in, well, there's a bit of work still to be done,' he joked, and Adam grimaced at him.

'What are you going to do then, since I have to protect your sorry ass?' Tom asked, making himself comfortable leaning on the back of the couch.

'It'll be nice and easy for you. I've had a few offers to work in forensic psychology, so I'm leaning that way. We've been doing a bit with our class actions already,' he said with a glance at his mentor, Rob.

Tom frowned. 'Right. So now I'm going to have to protect you from criminals trying to knock you off, so you don't testify against them?'

'Will you still work with me on cases?' Nate asked.

'Are you going to need me for anything then?' Jessica added, her voice laced with concern.

Rob cut in. 'It's actually a good idea, Adam, especially given you've got a profile now whether you like it or not. This gets you behind the scenes and dealing with professionals more so than the public.'

Adam looked at him, pleased for the support.

'What will you be doing?' Jessica asked, 'What will I be doing?'

Rob explained for Adam. 'It's varied work, some of it quite methodical, so you'll be just as busy, Jessica, and it is probably even more related to your work, Nate.' He looked to Tom and then to the group. 'It might include assessing a person's behaviour, mental status, and criminal responsibility.'

'Like when a person is found unfit for trial?' Jessica asked.

'Exactly,' Adam agreed. 'It also could include providing expert testimony in court about what should happen to the defendant, the treatment needed, and the risk of them doing the crime again.'

'Plus, Adam might also provide counselling to the victims of crimes as well as to the convicted. Just different clients, different reports,' Rob reassured Nate and Jessica. 'That's what you are envisioning?' he asked Adam.

'Exactly.'

Jessica's eyes widened with interest. 'Will you have to profile criminals so the police can catch them?'

Adam smiled. 'No, I'll leave that to the criminologists. I'm sticking with mental health.'

Tom stood. 'I can't see how you are going to be any less in danger. You'll go from being with nutcases in your office to being with criminal nutcases. It just gets better,' he said with a sigh.

Adam opened his mouth to fire back, and Nate beat him to speaking. 'You're just the man for it, Tom.' He rose and slapped the private security guard on the back with encouragement.

Tom grunted. 'I'm assuming you've still got some patients coming in until you cure them or handball them to someone else, so I'll get the alarm installed under the coffee table.'

'Thanks,' Adam said, and Tom looked at him suspiciously, waiting for another retort. 'That's it,' Adam shrugged, 'unless you want me to come up with a better reply like I don't give a fuck if you do or don't?'

Tom stepped forward. 'The last thing I want to do is hurt you for your mother's sake, but it's still on my list of life goals.'

Adam laughed as Tom glared at him. Nate groaned, Rob ran a hand over the back of his neck, and Jessica thanked Tom for organising the alarm.

'Why are you here, by the way?' Adam asked.

'Oh, yeah,' Tom remembered his mission. 'The magazine shoot—'

'Not doing it,' Adam said.

'Right, I'll let your mother know.'

'Why doesn't she ask me? Why is she calling on you to ask me?'

'Because she knows you'll say no,' Tom said, 'so she's hoping I'll persuade you to do it.'

Nate scoffed in the background.

'What does that persuasion involve?' Adam asked, curious as to how his mother thought Tom would talk him into anything.

Tom spoke to Jessica, ignoring Adam. 'I'll get the security team here tomorrow at 10am to put the buzzer under the coffee table unless Adam has a client.'

'I'll check. Follow me.' Jessica led the way out of Adam's office, and Tom gave them all a glance, a brief head nod, and an unceremonious snort in Adam's direction and departed.

'Do you have to bait him?' Nate asked, lowering his voice after Tom had left the room. 'You of all people, it's beneath you.'

Adam looked at his friend, surprised. Nate had never judged him before.

'I thought you knew me,' Adam said.

'Yeah, I don't know why I said that. It was stupid,' Nate said and gave a shrug. 'Jessica said it to me the other day when I complained about a client, and I thought about it a lot afterwards. But you're right, nothing's beneath us.'

Rob laughed at the pair, relaxing now the tension had eased.

Adam grinned. 'At least not where Tom Hartigan is concerned. I've only got a few weeks left to annoy him, and I want to enjoy it as much as possible.

'That's something I'd say. I've really rubbed off on you.' Nate patted his friend on the back like he was proud of him.

'I've got to go,' Adam said and turned to his desk, grabbing his keys and phone.

'Wait up, we need to talk,' Rob started.

'Can it wait?'

Rob hesitated. 'Okay.'

Adam thanked them both and left in a hurry, as Jessica called after him, 'I'll clean up the blood before your next appointment. It's not good for business.'

Chapter 9

S kye finished her hair and make-up and put on the white dress. Today was her Marilyn day. Each day she had a theme from film to fantasy, bad girl to good girl, whatever it took to make good content five days a week. She had two days rostered off to take acting instruction and see to her grooming – nails, hair, tanning and the wellness part of the wellness camp.

In her monthly review meeting, Zach had told her that she was a big earner, up there in the top three of the most popular actresses and models in the camp's history, and Griffin was proud of her. To reward her, Griffin had commissioned a photographer and printed a life-size portrait of Skye that featured along with some of his other star ladies on the walls that lead to the studios – five sound-proof white rooms with a studio desk set up behind glass. It still gave her a buzz when she passed the portrait, she had never looked so beautiful.

She knew only one of the ladies featured on the wall, and the others were no longer working at the camp. Served their contracts out, she imagined. Although there were a couple of ladies who remained after their three years and kept working. It wasn't a bad life if you had nowhere else to go, but it wasn't Sarah "Skye" Lyons's dream job or how she saw her acting dreams playing out. She thought she would be on television or in a series, even on the big screen. A laugh bubbled inside her as she remembered that dream; it quickly turned to despair.

It was different when she was in love with Griffin, the one he came to at night and the top girl, she no longer held that title. Now, she had followers and a sizeable bank account but was just another pretty face. It should be enough, but it wasn't. Skyre realised some time ago, in a moment of clarity, that it was a great life for a working girl – luxury surroundings, safety, the chance to build a great income for themselves and Griffin, and sex if you wanted it. No romance, no future husband or family, but for some of the girls whose stories in the real world had been brutal beforehand, the *Fidelium Wellness Studio* was nirvana.

Her success meant she was moved into a large private suite with views and a luxury bathroom. She could see from her balcony the rooms where the young actresses lived, where she once resided and envied the girls in the luxury wing on the hill. Her new status also gave her priority to the wellness services, and the younger girls looked up to her with something akin to worship until the realisation kicked in of what acting they were doing, then the disillusionment was evident in their eyes.

She remembered when she signed up, she was so overwhelmed with it all, so excited. Her timetable included acting classes, studio work, script planning, dress and costume fittings, and hair and make-up sessions. She felt like she had made it. It also came with the discipline of the weekly weigh-in to ensure she was not putting on or losing weight, the compulsory exercise classes and private sessions with Griffin.

Then, Griffin had wanted her and her only. He couldn't get enough, seducing her in costume the moment she finished in the studio and again that night. Some mornings, he would arrive before she was out of bed and have her then and there, sleepy and tousled. And then, one day, there was another new girl. Now, Skye was made available to Zach if she was open to his advances, and it was in her best interest to be so.

She knew of actresses that had been let go. Griffin terminated their contract – their classes were done, they weren't attracting clients, and they were free to go out on their own to try their luck in the world. But the ladies like Skye, who still had plenty of potential, were not going anywhere, and Skye feared that meant even after her contract was up.

She entered the all-white studio booth to find Zach waiting, along with the technician, Alex Narula – a guy in his late twenties who did a great job of not looking like the content excited him. Perhaps he was gay.

'Looking beautiful as always, Skye,' Zach said, his eyes roaming over her and the low cut of the white "Marilyn" dress. 'What will you be performing today?'

Skye hid her smirk. *Performing.* To a group of people who paid to see sex content – faceless, nameless, cash cows, all waiting for a glimpse of skin.

'I'm going to be doing a scene from *How to Marry a Millionaire.*'

'Righto, plenty of bending over towards the camera, lick your lips, wide eyes, you know the drill. And for the VIPs?'

'Offer me singing "Happy birthday" in my Marilyn outfit. If you have any private room takers, I can sing their name if they are willing to pay.'

Zach grinned. 'Excellent. Let's go then. Positions,' he called even though only she and Alex were present. Alex turned on the camera, ensured the content was streaming and then did the same in the next four rooms where girls prepared to deliver their performances.

Zach waited until Skye's performance began and departed for the next studio. At the end of her session, she looked pleadingly at the tech, Alex, who nodded and passed her his phone. Skye gave him a grateful look, punched in her parent's phone number and heard her mother's voice when she answered. She couldn't ask for help; she had told the tech guy she only wanted to hear their voices. Skye couldn't be sure how loyal he was to Zach or Griffin, and she didn't want him to lose his job. So, she breathed and then hung up, handing it back.

'Ready to roll again?' he asked, and Skye nodded, blinking back the tears.

'Thank you,' she said in her breathy Marilyn voice, and she began her performance just for the VIPs. She couldn't do this for much longer. Even if it meant doing something extreme, and that time was coming.

Then...

Nate's parents allowed him to have two birthday parties and invite his friends over in grade four when he was eight years old and again in grade seven when he was eleven.

Adam's parents didn't want children around their home, and children's parties were not discussed or encouraged. But Audrey talked them into allowing Adam to have a birthday party – a rite of passage for every child. Given that Winsome and James were away the month of Adam's birthday, Audrey advised that she and Charlie would manage the event. Aged 11, Adam had his first birthday party with friends at his house. Extra security was hired, including a lifeguard for the pool – Winsome's idea as she was frightened of water – and an events person to organise the party. Adam just wanted to invite his mates around, play cricket, swim in the pool, and eat a lot of junk food.

The cars rolled into the driveway – the prestigious to the working vehicles. Even at eleven years of age, Adam knew there was a clear divide and something brewing between Nate and his after-school friends and the boys from his private school.

One vehicle in particular stayed. Griffin Maxwell got out of the passenger side of the sleek black limousine and gave Adam a wave.

He carried a medium-sized gift; Adam could see the silver bow on the wrapping paper. His father exited at the same time and indicated to his son the location of the gift table near the front entrance; it was overflowing with gifts. Mr Maxwell said a few words to the driver who remained in the car. Adam watched as Griffin's dad and Audrey exchanged cheek kisses on both sides. They spoke for a while. How did his grandma know Griffin's dad? She loved her news and politics, and he was a politician; maybe they met that way. Then, Mr Maxwell wished Adam a happy birthday, got back into his car and departed as Audrey waved him goodbye.

'I will check on the catering, birthday boy,' Audrey said, planting a kiss on his head in front of everyone. Not that anyone was looking, but to an 11-year-old, he was sure his school friends saw it. How embarrassing.

Adam turned to find Griffin approaching.

'Happy birthday, Murph,' he said. I hope you like the present.' He nodded towards the table of gifts. Adam's invitation had said no gifts were necessary, but everyone ignored that.

'Thanks, you didn't have to bring a gift.'

Griffin shrugged. 'My dad and your grandma know each other. You should come and crash the night at my place soon, sleepover one weekend. Dad was going to suggest it to your grandma. Dad's not home much, so we could stay up really late, and he'd never know.'

Adam smiled, happy at the thought. He didn't have a lot of friends with parents like his – rich, powerful and absent. Maybe Griffin would get him. Maybe they really were alike.

Then Nate called out. 'You're up, Murph.'

'Got to go bowl,' he said with a casual shrug. 'You play cricket?'

'Nuh,' Griffin said. 'I'm going for a swim. I'll beat you in the diving game,' he teased.

'Doubt it,' Adam laughed. He was only joking; he wasn't great in the pool.

Adam moved away, and Griffin found some of his friends from school. When Adam looked back, Griffin was still watching him.

At 5.30pm, the last of the party guests left, except for Nate, who was spending the night. The lifeguard went home, Charlie clocked off for the evening, and Adam and Nate picked on leftovers in the kitchen.

'Did you enjoy it, darling boy?' Audrey asked, hugging him.

'I did thank you, Audrey, for letting me have a party. Thanks for talking Mum and Dad into it.'

'My pleasure. Now don't make yourselves sick on cake and cheerios,' she warned, looking at the now cold small sausages and leftover cake. 'I don't want to explain to your parents, young Nathaniel, why I'm bringing you home green.'

The boys laughed at the thought.

'You could tell them I transformed into the incredible hulk!' Nate said, excited.

Adam laughed. 'Don't worry, Audrey, we won't get sick,' he assured her, and when Nate went to call his Mum to tell her he was fine and was still sleeping over, Audrey studied her grandson.

'I like that young man, Griffin Maxwell,' she said. 'His father and I have met on several committees. You might do well to make friends with him.'

'He's alright. He has a lot of friends already.'

'He is like you, young man. He has charisma.'

Adam wasn't sure what that meant or why they both had it, but he brightened as Nate returned to the room, and the conversation was dropped. 'We're going to open the presents.'

'Yeah. Mine first though, you'll like it,' Nate promised.

'You weren't supposed to bring one.'

'Mum said you can't go to a party empty-handed.'

'Quite right, Nathaniel dear,' Audrey said. 'Your mother is teaching you well. Boys, I shall leave you to it then. I'm going to make a pot of tea and retire to the lounge room with my book. All you young boys have worn me out. Do call if you need me,' she said.

The boys watched her depart, and each grabbed a bowl of leftover party food and headed to the gift table.

'One each at a time,' Adam said. 'Select anyone you like.'

'But they're your presents.'

'It'll be more fun this way,' he said, searching for Nate's present, finding it and reading the card.

'Don't worry about the card,' Nate said impatiently. 'Mum wrote it.'

Adam nodded and began to tear the paper off. He laughed. 'That's great, thanks.'

Nate grinned. 'Now we're matching,' he said, looking at the BMX bike racing top in Adam's hand. Nate reached for one of the presents, and then he saw the gift from Griffin – the medium-sized box wrapped extravagantly with shiny paper and a silver bow.

'That'd be right,' Nate said, passing it to Adam. 'Thought he'd buy you something huge like a new bike.'

Adam shrugged and opened it, pulling aside the tissue paper.

'A camera!'

'That's cool,' Nate said almost begrudgingly.

Adam stuck it back in the box and put it back on the table for now. He didn't want to get Nate angry and ruin the night just because Griffin Maxwell thought he'd be a better best friend than the one Adam currently had. Now Audrey appeared to think so too. In his gut, he knew something wasn't right, and his gut told him Griffin Maxwell would have his friends force them to be mates. Whether he liked it or not.

Chapter 10

N ow...
Adam needed to see Kelsey. He couldn't explain why... but it was like the perfect storm had come to a head. An unbalanced patient stabbing herself and declaring her feelings for him, the building pressure of the spotlight with the celebrity wedding, and his voicing his decision to change his work focus out loud... all those things rolling over him at once. Plus, they had just come back from two weeks away, and he wasn't ready for reality yet.

He saw Kelsey before she saw him. He waited near the library entrance, watched her as she served an elderly man, and laughed at something he said. Her smile was so gorgeous, her pale grey-blue eyes alight with humour, and her long red hair plaited loosely made her look so feminine. She was his, perfect for him in every way, and so different from his ex, Stephanie, who would also be at the wedding. The thought made him sigh again; he'd been doing that a bit of late. *Just get it over with!*

Adam entered through the door as the customer bid Kesley farewell and exited.

'What are you doing here?' she exclaimed with a surprised and happy look.

'Taking you out for lunch, hopefully, or to the park?' He didn't attempt to kiss her at work; he knew she wouldn't like that.

'I guess I could share my sandwich with you,' she teased. Then she saw his bandaged hand, and a look of concern swept her face. 'What happened?'

'Nothing to be worried about. A small nick, I'll tell you at lunch.'

'Okay.' She appeared unconvinced. 'I'll just see if Roxy is good for me to take lunch now.'

Adam nodded as Kelsey disappeared into the office, and he occupied himself by looking at the magazines near the door. Two women's magazines had an inset picture of his mother and Jack. He moved his gaze to the men's magazine and was pleased to see his mother and Jack had not graced those covers. A cover in the celebrity section caught his eye, and he grabbed it.

'What the hell,' he muttered under his breath as he saw the headline, *Married to the It Girl's son*. He stuck it back in the rack, cursing his ex-wife, who craved the attention for herself and her business.

He turned as Kelsey returned with a lady beside her, smiling brightly at him. She was a large woman, wearing a very loud orange dress, and he noticed a thin gold wedding band. He guessed she was in her late thirties with kids – she had ruffled clothes, a small stain on her dress, and her brown streaked hair was tied back in a ponytail as if personal grooming was a second thought.

'We're good to go,' Kelsey said. 'This is my manager, Roxy.'

Adam smiled and shook the offered hand.

'So, you're the man our Kelsey is in love with that we've heard so little about,' Roxy teased and then laughed, seeing Kelsey's smirk. 'She keeps you close to her chest,' Roxy said, and Adam was pleased she didn't seem to recognise him.

'It's just where I like to be,' he joked and smiled at Kelsey, who reddened at the inference. Then, he saw the recognition dawn on Roxy's face, but she masked it, her eyes narrowing slightly as she studied him.

'I'll have her checked back in right on time,' Adam assured her, and Roxy laughed.

'Kelsey rarely takes a break, or as long as she is supposed to take it, don't hurry back. And, good to meet you, Adam.' She turned to the self-checkout machine to help a customer struggling with mastering it. The pair escaped.

'Are you okay,' Kelsey asked as she linked her arm through his, and they crossed to the gardens across the road with the café within to grab a coffee. 'Tell me what happened and why you are here?'

Adam knew Kelsey worried more not knowing the full story, so he told her about his patient and that he had made public his decision, stopping only long enough to order their coffees and collect them when ready. She did not speak throughout Adam's recounting of his morning. When he finished, they were seated, and Kelsey offered him half her sandwich, which he accepted.

'Do you think we should go away?' he asked.

Kelsey didn't react. He loved that about her. Everything was considered calmly, a measured response. No hysterics, no performances.

'I had thought the same myself, but I didn't want to deprive you of seeing your mother and Jack married. There is a duty with family.'

He nodded. 'Yeah. You are right. Besides, it's only four hours, which seems to have stretched over six months.' Kelsey laughed at his description, which brought a smile to his face. 'Besides Nate, Jess and Dan will be there, so we'll be amongst friends,' she said.

'We will, and hopefully, all the focus will be on Winsome and Jack.' They both knew that wasn't quite true. Kelsey changed the subject. 'You know I think your work decision is a great idea and timely. How did they take it in the office?'

'Nate had a meltdown because he thought I was packing it in and moving out. Jessica did the same because she probably realised she'd be left alone to manage Nate,' Adam grinned at the thought, 'and Rob knew I'd been thinking about it and thought it was a good time to enact it. I'm due for a change.'

'Well, you've been offered that work before. You can let your networks know you are now free to do it.' Kelsey took a bite of her sandwich, chewed and swallowed before asking, 'Did she freak you out? Your client.'

'More so when she stabbed herself. It was like she couldn't feel it, straight into the leg,' he shook his head.

'It's happened before, hasn't it? Your patients falling in love with you?'

'It happens to a lot of psychologists. But I'm particularly irresistible.' He said it with a straight face, and she laughed and playfully hit him.

'Sure, you are.'

Adam grinned and turned the conversation to her work. 'You didn't tell Roxy who I was?'

'No.'

He nodded and focused on his sandwich. They ate in silence for a moment, enjoying the park's green aspect and people-watching. Once swallowed, he asked, 'Are you ashamed of me?'

She whirled to look at him. 'Of course not, never, don't say that. You know I'm not.'

He nodded, accepting her protest and knowing it was strange to say, but he was feeling strange.

Kelsey pushed him. 'What's wrong with you?'

'Nothing. I'm struggling to return to work after our holiday.' He forced himself to smile and relax. 'It made me revisit things in my life, and I don't welcome being disrupted by Mum and her circus again.'

'I know. Hopefully, after the wedding, we'll all be old news.'

'Tom is at me every time he sees me to get us to move into the family home; apparently, it's easier for him to maintain security that way.' He sighed at the thought. They had been there a short while ago when Adam found himself with a stalker but moved out straight after.

'But no one has discovered us yet,' Kelsey protested.

'I tried that argument, but it is probably only a matter of time, and if they did, we've got no protection at home. At least the family home is gated. Nate said there have been media circling outside the gate of the river wing, he can see them from his room. Audrey said the same from her wing, and it will be worse when Jack and Winsome arrive.'

'It's only a week. We could go back there this weekend,' Kelsey suggested.

'Probably best.' Adam turned to face Kelsey. 'I'm worried that you're wondering what you have gotten yourself into.'

She nudged him and smiled. 'I love being us,' she reassured him. 'And for the record, I felt the same this morning after returning from holidays. We should have come back on a Tuesday instead of a Monday.' She sipped her coffee. 'I didn't tell Roxy who you were because I'm protecting us. You know I don't want the celebrity life.'

'I know. Neither do I, you know that,' he quickly added. 'But it's going to get worse before it gets better.' He studied Kelsey, who looked away as she drank her coffee. Then, she surprised him.

'That's fine, we're up for this.'

He straightened and studied her. 'We are?'

'I'm a little tired of hiding, and I'm not a pushover. Neither are you,' she added.

'Okay,' he said and smiled. 'Can't say I've seen you like this before, but it's hellishly sexy.'

She smiled and shook her head at him before adopting a determined look. 'Well, I say enough. Women throwing themselves at you and throwing knives at you, the media trying to get in your face. They can all back off!'

'Yeah, team Murphy and Bickley! It'd sound much better if we were just Team Murphy. You should hurry up and marry me,' Adam said, sounding her out and giving her the winning smile that he'd learnt from his father.

She narrowed her eyes at him, her lips twitching in a smile even though she tried to appear serious. 'I'll give it some thought.'

'That's the best I can hope for then,' he agreed and looked away pleased.

'I'd want a proper proposal when the time comes. Just because I'm laid back, don't think you can get away with throwing me a line and giving me that sexy smile.'

He hit his heart. 'Ah, you saw right through me, and here I was thinking I'd charm you.'

'This is the new me,' she said. 'The lion king... or queen, rather.'

'I'll step up,' he assured her and leaned over for a kiss. 'I like this lion queen. Does it translate elsewhere?'

She gave him a purr, and Adam realised it was a good day after all.

Returning to work, Kelsey had just set foot back behind the checkout desk when Roxy joined her, smiling.

'Well, you are a dark horse, young lady,' Roxy grinned. 'The very handsome and charming Adam is Adam Murphy and very wealthy, might I add. Why didn't you say that was who you were seeing? If it were me, I would have been boasting for months.'

Kelsey gave a small shrug. 'We like to lay low. Please don't mention it to anyone, Roxy, especially now that his mother's wedding is coming up. It's for his security and mine.'

'Really? I thought it would be fun with all the attention.'

'Not for him when he works as a psychologist. It puts his life on hold and puts us both at risk from unbalanced clients.' She told of this morning's stabbing incident.

'Good grief!' Roxy proclaimed. 'My lips are sealed. But Winsome Keeley. Imagine having her for your mother or mother-in-law,' she said to Kelsey with a raised eyebrow but didn't wait for a reaction. 'And I just love Jack Bernham. What a pairing. I saw Jack in a concert last year. Is he nice? Have you met them both?' Roxy stopped to draw a breath as Kelsey winced. This was why she didn't speak of Adam.

'I've spoken with Winsome on the phone and met Jack a couple of times. They are both really lovely.'

'You're going to the wedding then? What will you wear? You and Adam will be centre stage, after the married couple.'

'We'll be with friends and family; it should be a nice night. I've brought a silver dress.'

'Friends and family! I heard all the VIPs are going,' Roxy raved on with excitement as Kelsey rearranged several things on the desk. 'I would be making plans galore and lining up my hairdresser, dressmaker, you name it.'

Kelsey grimaced. 'I just want the prize without the package.'

Roxy laughed. 'You have that for sure. He is gorgeous, and I wish I had asked him for a photo with me.'

'Roxy, promise me you won't tell anyone?'

She sighed dramatically. 'Fine then, my dear, but if you transfer out or resign, I am broadcasting it immediately.'

Kelsey chuckled. 'I can live with that.'

She was pleased to have a customer to serve. If Roxy leaked the story, there would be photographs of Adam's girlfriend working at the local library. To them, she'd be the girl from the asylum, the girl who was abused by her mother's boyfriends and the runaway. He would be the golden boy son of James Murphy and Winsome Keeley. Too good for her, the girl from the wrong side of the track. The girl that had nothing to offer him. But Kelsey didn't think like that anymore. She had survived more than most. She was the girl who won the prize, and Kelsey intended to protect it.

Chapter 11

S kye Lyons closed her eyes and enjoyed the sun on her face and the breeze on her skin. She could almost hear the earth talking to her – the hum of the dirt, soft and moist beneath her, the insects buzzing around, and the bird calls from the trees surrounding the wellness camp.

She saw the young girl – christened Dawn – arrive this morning; she was so excited like Skye when she arrived two years ago. Dawn was now the seventeenth woman in the camp, with two men and three children on the premises. No one would tell Dawn what to expect – there were hefty fines for doing so, and Skye worked too hard to lose money to save an innocent who'd soon learn the ropes anyway. Leaf was again partnered with the new girl, playing the role so well that no one would ever know she had been in the camp for years or suspect what would come at the end of the first week.

Next would come the roster of content – acting in sexy roles, posing in sexy lingerie, and the options rose in value. If she wanted to make the big money, Dawn would opt for the VIP House and pleasure real customers. The top dollar could be made in the submissive rooms, but Skye passed on this option – she was not a prostitute and had no intention of becoming one. Some of the girls earned four times what she earned by "servicing" clients there. In her mind, it was bad enough that she had become more promiscuous with her content, agreeing to do sexual acts and threesomes while filmed if her face was hidden or if she could be masked. Again, there would have been more money if she had shown her face. It was a smorgasbord that favoured the porn workers and knew how to punish those who didn't play the game.

But it didn't end there. Dawn would be subjected to the occasional moments of terror, recorded live for the subscribers who got off on seeing real fear. That paid really well, and no one had an option of whether to participate or not. Griffin called it unsurpassed acting training – real emotions that would put his actors in good stead for roles once they left. It was mainly afflicted on first-year girls, who lived on tenterhooks, day in, day out, because there was no preparation for the unknown, and adrenaline spiked whether you were exhausted, wary, or already a nervous wreck. By the second year, you were dropped from this roster because you were becoming jaded, and the customer wanted genuine reactions. Thank God, Skye thought.

On her day off, with the sun filtering on her, she forgot she was miserable for just a moment and enjoyed being in the moment like she had practised. The friend she was closest to was leaving – Rain's mother was ill, and Rain was required to care for her, promising the producer, Zach, she would be back as soon as she could and with an inheritance. Skye had no such excuse to depart, and there was a year still left on her contract.

She didn't want to be called Skye anymore. She wanted to be called by her real name, Sarah Lyons. Only yesterday, while in the acting studio, she had broached the subject with trepidation, clearing her throat lightly before she began.

'Griff, I wanted to talk with you about two things.' He raised an eyebrow with interest, and she hurried on. 'I want to go back to using my real name, and I think my time here might be coming to an end.'

There was silence, and she waited while Griffin Maxwell finished studying the recorded version of her performance and looking at the number of voyeurs, or rather, subscribers that tuned in. He tried to spend a little time with each of his girls every day in the studio. It took several minutes until he replied in his usual calm, deep voice, asking Alex, the recording technician, to leave the room. Now, her heart rate jumped.

'I prefer you have these conversations with Zach or me in private.'

'Sorry,' Skye said, hoping she would not be punished for that slip in judgement.

'You have a contract to serve, or have you forgotten?' he asked, turning to study her. 'I believe you owe me another year unless I've miscalculated?' His question mocked her.

'No, you are right, but there's a clause. You said it was possible to review and renegotiate halfway through, and we're past halfway. Three years is a long time.'

'Is it?' He turned his chair to face her full-on now, and she kept her eyes on him, even though he terrified her at times. It hadn't always been like this; she was confident once and sure of her talent. But Griffin Maxwell was charismatic and powerful. He had a way of bending her to his whim, and she wanted to be at her strongest for this conversation. Skye put her chin up, gave him a small smile and called on her acting skills to fill the shortfall in her bravado.

'If I remember,' he started, 'you were desperate to be a star. Desperate to be famous.'

'I'm still not a star or famous,' she answered and hadn't expected his reaction. Like lightning, he leapt up, grabbed her dress, pulled her up, and slapped her, the sound ringing through her ears, her face stinging. He dropped her back down just as quickly. It happened so fast; if it had not been for her burning cheek, Skye might have thought she had imagined it.

'You are the most famous of all my girls and with the biggest following,' he hissed. 'You've made a small fortune. When you finish your three years, you'll not only have a huge following and be allowed to use your name

"Skye" and keep your fans, but you'll also have your six-figure earnings to take with you. Don't forget that.' His eyes glared at her.

She nodded hurriedly. 'I didn't mean to appear ungrateful.'

He held up one hand for her to be silenced, closed his eyes and took a deep breath, calming himself before going on. It took all her self-control not to cry in front of him. Her cheek was stinging, and adrenaline and fear were coursing through her. His unpredictability frightened her, and she had seen other girls punished by his hand. Skye waited, breathing shallowly and hoping that he would leave now. It didn't bode well to anger Griffin Maxwell, and she knew there would be repercussions.

He opened his eyes, dark and soulless, and cleared his throat. 'I don't care if you want to use your real name around the camp, but online, you remain Skye. Clear?'

'Yes.'

'Skye is your name; Skye is who you are. It is a gift from me to you and a beautiful name full of fantasy and hope for the clients who watch you perform. You are a goddess to them, your true fans who pay to watch you every day. Don't you think every one of those men, and even women, are at home wishing they could reach for the sky, reach for you? The nearest they can get to their dream is the time you are live in their rooms on their screens. You are a star to them, like Marilyn Monroe and Jean Harlow. Classic, sexy, beautiful.'

His words washed over her as she sat opposite him, meaningless now that her ego did not need them and stardom had faded. She wasn't sure when the worm turned, but her parents had stopped trying to contact her a year ago, and now Griffin had another pretty new toy, and it wasn't her. It was rarely, if ever, that he visited her room these days. Sarah Lyons was seeing things with eyes wide open, and she was trapped. She wanted to go home, but nobody was coming for her anymore. Months and months of repeatedly telling them to go away had finally worked. They had given up on her.

And from what she had gleaned, nobody had ever left the wellness camp before their contract finished unless Griffin was done with them.

Nate dropped the file like it was burning his hands. He couldn't believe what he was reading. Burnsy had not remembered the name of the owner of the wellness studio, but there it was, written in black and white. Griffin Maxwell. That full-of-himself, entitled, arrogant… he stopped coming up with names just long enough to buzz Jessica.

'When is Adam back?'

'Any minute,' she said. 'He's got another client in thirty minutes.

'I need to see him urgently, and before Rob grabs him. Can you give me the heads-up?'

'Will do, but Rob asked the same,' she said in a sing-song voice.

'This is urgent, work-related, Dan's out there on surveillance…'

'Okay, you first,' she agreed and hung up.

He couldn't concentrate on the file but looked at the photos and found several of Griffin Maxwell. He looked slick and stylish like a man trying hard to stand out. Adam was never that. He could have been, even when they were kids. He had something about him. He was his father's son, and as they grew older, Adam commanded silence; people noticed him, and he had a presence, all of which Nate never had and Griffin Maxwell fabricated. Yep, it had been a long time, but surprisingly, Griffin Maxwell hadn't changed much since Nate knew him from Adam's private school. It was no surprise to him that he'd end up doing something involving fanaticism.

He jumped as his phone buzzed, bringing him back to the now, and Jessica announced Adam was on his way up the stairs. Nate looked out of his office just in time to wave Adam into it.

'I know you've got a client soon, and Rob wants to read your head, but you are not going to believe this.' He moved behind his desk and ran a hand over his mouth.

Adam shifted and looked uncomfortable. 'What's happened?'

Nate looked at him a moment and suggested they both sit. He slid a photo across the desk.

'Who's this?'

'Griffin Maxwell!'

'Griffin... seriously? Wow, this is him,' Adam studied the man he last saw at the age of eleven. 'I haven't seen him since he was pulled out of school – there one day, gone the next.'

'Yeah? I thought he might have tried to contact you.'

'His family took off overseas. I vaguely remember Charlie or Audrey telling me that.' He looked at the papers Nate slid across to him. 'You're kidding me?' Adam snapped to look at Nate. 'He owns this wellness studio place?'

'Apparently so. Kind of fits.'

'Hell, I didn't see that coming,' Adam puffed his cheeks out as he exhaled. 'I haven't given him a minute's thought over the last decade or so except to wonder where he ended up.' Adam answered Nate's expression and added, 'No, I'm not keen on rekindling a friendship.'

Nate smiled. 'I didn't think so after the unusual gift.'

Adam shook his head at the memory. 'I should have told Dad earlier about the birthday present, but, you know,' he shrugged. 'It's not like I saw Dad that often, and it was like this big secret. Until it wasn't.'

'Your Dad covered it up well.'

'He owned the media.'

'But he didn't owe anything to Griffin Maxwell's father.'

'I think it was more complex than that,' Adam said. 'I never really asked Audrey about it, but her take on it would be interesting.'

Adam picked up the photos of Griffin and shuffled through them. 'He's doing his best to keep that cool vibe going.'

'He's had years to cultivate it. I recall he wanted you to be his bestie in the cool group.'

Adam frowned. 'Weird guy.'

'Yep. Well, the apple doesn't fall far from the tree,' Nate said, tapping on the file. 'If Griffin is filming those girls in a way that's got nothing to do with professional acting classes, then Skye's parents are right to be worried.'

Adam looked up at Nate, then at the clock and back to Nate.

'You've got to go, I know,' Nate said.

'The girls have a contract, so I wonder what is in the fine print?' Adam mused. 'Does it include porn or online acting for subscribers only?'

Nate studied him. 'You mean like peep rooms online.'

'More or less.' Adam rose and walked to the door. 'Jess got a minute?' he called.

'What's up?' she asked, hurrying in.

He leaned on the chair in front of Nate's desk. 'You don't have to confess to being a subscriber, but do either of you know of any of those exclusive fan content sites?' Adam asked.

'Ah,' Nate caught on. 'Like the influencers have with subscription content.'

'Yeah. Those sites are perfect for women wanting to produce their X-rated content, get their own audiences and income.'

'Non-contact sex content without a pimp,' Jessica said.

'In some cases,' Adam agreed. 'A safe option for an independent income, and many ladies are making huge money.'

'How do you know this?' Nate asked. 'I'm clearly missing out.'

Adam smiled and shook his head. Jessica rolled her eyes, and Nate laughed and added, 'I was just joking.'

'I had a client or two that ran their own private content businesses,' Adam explained.

'And just when I thought I knew everything about you,' Nate shook his head. 'Why were they after therapy?' Nate sat back in his chair, keen to hear the story.

'One of the ladies was attacked when she worked in a club, so she was getting over that,' Adam said, 'the other, from memory, had relationship dramas with everyone in her life; the therapy wasn't about her work.'

'But they could both pay the bill?' Nate said, impressed.

'Oh yeah,' Adam said. 'Not all content makers can make a good living, but one of them told me if you work hard, at least until you establish yourself and build a following, you can make big dollars. I don't know what the host companies for these sites are called.'

'There's FansForEver and LockedUp, and PayFan, off the top of my head,' Jessica started.

'How do I not know this?' Nate looked genuinely stunned.

'You need to get out more,' Adam said and grinned. Nate saw Adam glance at the clock again.

'Okay, go. Come back when you can,' Nate dismissed him.

'I'd better.' Adam headed to the door, 'but if you two have time, or get Dan on to it – start looking on some of those sites for private subscription content for *Fidelium Wellness Studio* or Skye Lyons or Sarah Lyons.' He shrugged. 'It's just a hunch.'

'Yeah, a good one,' Nate said.

'Let's try and find out through the back door, so to speak, what might be going on in that place.' He disappeared back to his office.

Jessica turned to Nate. 'What makes you think they are doing that at the studio? Has something happened?'

'Yeah, we just discovered who the owner is,' Nate informed her, 'and porn, persuasion and manipulation are right up his alley.'

Chapter 12

G riffin Maxwell pulled his shoulder-length black hair back and, taking a black elastic tie from his wrist, bound his hair off his neck. He ran a hand over his jaw and was satisfied with his grooming. He had something that many had tried to define. His ambitious father had seen it and tried to push his son into politics, claiming he could be the Kennedy of a new generation. But Griffin considered himself lucky; his father died suddenly, leaving him a sizeable inheritance and considerable property. Now, he could do what he believed he was best at – finding out what people needed and supplying it at a price. He liked to call it sexual enlightenment and take as many as possible on the journey with him. He was beautiful, rich, powerful, and the single most important person in everyone's life who lived at his wellness studio. As it should be.

Today, however, he was not happy. The anger lingered; Skye wanted to leave; she wanted to leave *him*. God knows he had wanted to desert them all many a time, start again somewhere else, but every morning, as he looked upon the adoring faces of his group, he felt renewed and understood they needed him. As did those who paid for their subscription and expected their content and daily fix. Griffin provided for all the girls' needs – love, security, shelter, and, more importantly, he helped them realise their dreams as he fed their ambitions and stroked their egos. And this is how Skye repays him for his patronage.

First Rain, now Skye. He had to think about this. Maybe he wasn't giving Skye enough attention. It had been a while since he bedded her; women were insecure and needy, each of them vying for his attention. But the new admission, Dawn, was sweet and naïve, fragile even, and she needed his help to settle in. He had named her so perfectly. Griffin thought about her willingness before his thoughts returned to Skye. Maybe Skye needed a child to focus on, or perhaps it was time to move her onto the next phase of the program. A sharp rap on his private office door got his attention.

'Enter.'

'Just me,' the only other male on the premises, his childhood friend and now lawyer, Zach Crowder, dressed sharply in a dark suit, entered. The same age and similar height, Zach's closeness to Griffin as the right-hand man made him more attractive to the women he lived with and was allowed to share. He was powerful in his own right and bestowed his own favours. The women were encouraged to "service" Zach if they were not chosen to spend the night with Griffin, and things went better for those who did. These women got clients who paid more online and tipped bigger, and they were assured more followers. They were given priority for beauty services, and their stardom was celebrated, at least in their online world.

'You have news, Zach?' Griffin asked abruptly as he stood near the window, webbing his fingers together. He had full faith in the man before him; Zach was among the first to become a follower when they were schoolboys, and his loyalty never waned. He was smart enough to know a good thing when he saw it, and Griffin looked after him better than any legal job ever would. There was only one boy at school that Griffin had targeted who did not join their group.

Adam Murphy.

Thinking of his name further enraged Griffin, who was already fuming. Zach nodded and closed the door.

'I've got the information you wanted on Rain.'

'Good,' Griffin said. 'Just in time, she leaves tomorrow. Maybe. Is it the truth?'

Zach smirked. 'Her mother is not ill, nor does she need her daughter's assistance, mainly because she's already dead.' His sneer became more defined. 'Died nearly five years ago. Her father had already cleared out, remarried, and had a couple more children. Whoever she coerced into sending that urgent message saying she needed to go home must be on staff; she doesn't have any regular clients she could access without me knowing.'

'Poor little rich girl that nobody wants,' Griffin said, remembering when Rain first came to him, the child of divorce, and both parents had moved on.

'Rain has created a story to exit,' Zach concluded.

'Why?' Griffin hissed, slamming his hand against the glass window and making Zach flinch.

'She doesn't know how good she has it,' he answered loyally. 'She's forgotten what the real world is like, how few people really care for her out there. Maybe she needs a reminder.'

'Bring her to me tonight. Tell her since I won't see her until she returns from caring for her ailing mother, I want one more night with her. Do not let on that we have found out the truth.'

Zach nodded.

'I'll explain to Dawn that I have business to attend to tonight. Don't touch her; she's mine for now.'

'Understood,' Zach said. 'What will you do about Rain?'

'What I always do. But I want to enjoy seeing her expression when she finds out I know the truth and she hasn't won.'

Then...

The only birthday present still in its box was the gift from Griffin Maxwell, which Adam had slipped under his bed. He didn't want to open it or play with it around Nate, who acted weird whenever Griffin was around or Adam mentioned his name. But now that he was alone – except for Audrey, who was downstairs watching *A Current Affair* – he could check it out properly. He opened the box and unwrapped the gift properly.

'Cool!' Adam read the box – a Polaroid Sun 600 LMS. Griffin had got him an instant camera; he'd never had one before. Unpacking it, he studied it with fascination, then stood, went to the corner and took a photo of his room. The camera whirred and out came a white photo. Adam pulled it from the camera and looked at it quizzically.

Well, that didn't work, he thought, picking up the box to find the instructions. And then he saw the image start to appear. He placed the white photo down on the bed cover, watching it, and in minutes, his room was captured on film in full colour. Adam grinned. He and Nate could get some cool shots with this. He'd have to thank Griffin.

Adam returned to the box and, moving tissue paper out of the way, found a card that said nothing except "Happy Birthday from Griffin." Also in the box was a packet of extra film to put in the camera, and underneath that was an envelope marked "For Adam's eyes only – confidential" in spy-like red writing, with sticky tape sealing it at the back.

He sat on the edge of the bed and opened it. It was a packet of photos, the same sort of photos that his new camera turned out – square in shape with a white frame border and heavy black backing. Weird, but maybe Griffin wanted to share some of his best pics. Adam's breath hitched; his eyes widened at the photographs in front of him. It was images that an

11-year-old boy would not have seen and shouldn't have seen. He couldn't look away but didn't always understand what he was seeing. Acts that he had no idea adults did with each other. Parts of the female anatomy that he didn't know existed and what they looked like. People with strange costumes.

Despite everything his grandmother had done to protect him and make his life as normal as possible in a world where nothing was normal, Griffin Maxwell's birthday present marked the end of his innocence.

Chapter 13

Now...

Ben Solomon had started on the slippery slope of seeking pleasure that became more and more unconventional. His wife didn't need to know; she was content with vanilla sex, and his job lent itself nicely to his alibis. As an I.T. expert, Ben built programs for clients, and in the case of his old school friend, Griffin Maxwell, loyalty paid off. Ben hated his job; Griffin arrived back in town with an idea for a content site and became Ben's first client. He quit his job, started his own business and built the *Fidelium Wellness Studio*'s entire system from the ground up – from online rooms to security cameras on the site. Griffin was a huge client; Ben could live on Griffin's work alone, and those systems could not break down... an audience was always waiting.

The callouts to the site and the regular after-hour maintenance so as not to interrupt the business happened occasionally, but as far as Ben's wife knew, they were a regular thing. That's I.T., for you. Everyone wanted to be up and working right now. And, of course, back-ups had to be done out of business hours, or so he told his wife.

Ben drove up the dark road to the large house with glazed windows hidden between the trees on a back road on Tamborine Mountain and turned into the undercover car park. There were a dozen other cars there, but privacy was assured at the VIP House – no cameras except in select areas on the second floor where the reality fear scenes were enacted and filmed. Ben exited the car and made his way to the elevator, pressing the button.

'Good evening, your name please,' a smooth, sexy female voice answered.

'Ben Solomon,' he announced.

'Mr Solomon, we're expecting you. The code is 145. Please come in.'

Ben entered the lift and punched in the code. The lift accepted it, and he pressed the reception floor – the only floor guests could enter unless they were given a special code. He had set that system up as well, and it worked nicely.

He entered the private club, which had marble counters and flooring, chandeliers, and rich fabric chairs and curtains.

'The black room, Mr Solomon?' The owner of the sexy voice said, giving him a welcoming smile from behind the reception desk.

'Thank you, Miss Carter,' Ben nodded.

Miss Carter was the hostess for the evening, and all the hostesses were addressed similarly. It was his standard booking, and she rose and led him down the hallway to a room with a large timber door. The hostess opened it, wished him a good night and departed. Inside, Ben relaxed. Griffin knew how to do things with style; the black room was one of his favourite experiences. He liked to dominate; it allowed him to let off steam, and he also liked to be dominated. He'd have a drink before he showered. It was required of guests, and their "model" did not join them until they rang reception to say they were ready. Ben opened the bar and poured a top-shelf scotch. After his session, he would join Griffin and Zach for another drink over at the studio. His job was like that; it was so unpredictable, and there was no knowing how long tonight's maintenance might take.

Griffin occasionally visited the VIP House, but his needs were more primal. Unlike his father, he didn't get off on the weird. He liked the innocence and adoration of the new models, and he liked to occasionally visit his regulars just to see the lust in their eyes. It was his duty, he believed, to satisfy them when they were not encouraged to leave the premises unless it was their allocated holiday period, and many chose to stay and work. They were all there for a purpose and had three years to achieve their goals – and Griffin's.

'How was it?' he asked later that evening, offering a beer to Ben and Zach as they sat on the large veranda of Griffin's suite overlooking the dark valley. He took a seat, clinked his bottle against theirs and sat back.

'Excellent as always. A first-class experience from the moment of entry to the finish,' Ben said and chuckled.

'And aside from your orgasm?' Zach joked.

'The rest was perfect, too,' Ben added, raising his bottle to Griffin. 'As expected.'

'A couple of the girls will finish up in the House next month. Their contracts end. One wants to stay on, but I'm moving her out,' Zach said.

'Not Leaf? She's my favourite,' Ben protested.

Zach shook his head. 'Leaf's got a year to do yet; she wants the money and likes the hours. She studies during the day, goes to classes... nursing.'

Ben huffed with surprise. 'Yeah, her skills in the House won't be much help when she crosses over to a nursing career.'

'I suspect they are both nurturing careers in one way or another,' Griffin joked. 'I want to get some girls in who know what they're doing and offer some darker services, move away from the modelling and actors.'

'Yeah?' Zach asked, surprised.

Griffin shrugged. 'It's one of my ideas. I've got something else on the boil, too, but I'm not in a position to discuss it yet.' He saw Zach's look of displeasure. They usually discussed all business decisions, but this one required Adam Murphy to play a part. It would also mean the end of his involvement in the wellness studio.

Griffin continued, 'I'm thinking of changing the contracts to two years instead of three.'

'Why? It means higher turnover, more work,' Zach asked, alarmed and then saw Griffin's expression and hurriedly answered, 'but you know your business best.'

'There's some discontent amongst the women, and I don't want women here who are infiltrating the ranks with their negativity. Plus, they'll work harder to make their money in two years than they will in three.' Griffin smiled and looked at the men. 'I want the turn-over of fresh flesh more often too. I want more testimonials on how it changed their life.'

'Here's to that,' Zach raised his glass in a toast, and the men drank.

'What about the ones that are currently on three-year contracts?' Zach asked.

'They can renegotiate,' Griffin said.

'You've given this some thought then,' Ben said.

Griffin nodded and looked at Zach. 'Can you re-draft them with your legal speak and show me an amended contract next week?'

'Sure,' Zach said. 'We could offer the girls with three-year contracts the chance to work their last year in the VIP House where they can earn a hell of a lot more.'

Ben pursed his lips in thought. 'What if they don't have the skills needed for the House? It is a speciality area.'

'Then they'll learn quick smart or lose the opportunity,' Griffin said. 'I'm sure Zach will enjoy taking the lessons.'

Zach laughed. 'Perks of the jobs, boys, perks of the job.'

'It's a win-win for all of us,' Griffin said. 'I want girls that are just legal.' He looked at Zach.

'I'll make it happen.'

'I knew you would,' Griffin said.

Chapter 14

It was a nice morning to be out of the office, and Danielle figured a couple of hours of surveillance of the *Fidelium Wellness Studio* in the comfort of Nate's new Audi was a fine idea. It was an hour's drive either way, and she hit the highway, enjoying the power and comfort of his car. She just hoped there was an area where she could watch without being seen. She sipped her coffee and put it back in the Audi's cup holder area. Nate grudgingly allowed her to drink in his new car; Adam wasn't keen on it in his Mercedes, so she had to do it without his knowledge. Boys and their toys, she sighed, thinking of them both. But the Audi was an amazing gift from Winsome. Danielle thought Adam's mother might not win Mother of the Year, but she's up there when it comes to gift-giving.

Danielle was looking forward to the wedding and seeing Winsome in the flesh; she might even get to meet her since she was on the security detail for Adam's table. She couldn't think of two more contrasting childhoods – hers in Darwin with her mother and brother, her parents surviving on the basic wage, happy, not wanting for much because you don't miss what you don't know, and besides, it was all there – family love, the water, swimming, fishing. And then there was Adam's ivory tower life in the mansion on the river with his ritzy parents, security guard, and private school. A life that she sensed Nate still envied on some levels even though he was living in that very house now with its large tennis court, swimming pool, river views and security. Which made her think again of Winsome's gift to Nate, the Audi.

'Yes, very cool,' she said and grinned as she held the steering wheel and smelled the new leather smell, settling in for the drive. She was amazed Nate agreed to lend it to her, but since he was office-bound for the morning and she was doing research on his behalf, the faster her getaway car was, the better, or so she convinced him.

En route, she listened to a podcast on cults and their characteristics. It was nothing she didn't know or hadn't seen in movies or on television – a strong and charismatic leader, weak followers in need of saving, usually more women and fewer men, and many liberties were taken under the guise of self-development. In this case, acting and modelling development. *What a crock*, she huffed.

Danielle's phone rang and cut into her podcast. She momentarily looked to the dashboard to see what button to press to take it hands-free and hit the right one. She didn't notice the caller ID while keeping her eyes on the road.

'Danielle Walters,' she answered.

'Nathanial Delaney,' Nate answered back, and she laughed.

'Checking up on me, boss?'

'Just wondering if you've had any breakthroughs yet.'

'Get real, I'm not even there yet! Admit it, you're checking on your car?'

'Don't be ridiculous. Is it alright?'

She laughed. 'We're getting on just fine, and the podcast on cult leaders I was listening to before you cut in put me in the mood. So, what have you learned about the wellness or acting freaks? Jess said you were looking at subscriber sites. Hope you didn't find my account.'

'What! Seriously?'

'No, but it's not a bad idea. I just can't think of anything interesting to do that anyone would want to pay to see,' she sighed.

'I suspect the content we're looking for doesn't require too much thinking up or creativity. But in terms of what we've found, not much,' he admitted. 'Jess and I are still working through fan sites, and other than Burnsy's files telling us who is running the joint and the few incidents there in the past, that's it. There are no complaints, no charges laid, and nothing for us to be worried about except the hearsay of Skye's parents.'

'So, everything they are doing is legal?'

'Looks like it so far. The actors all have legal contracts, allegedly. While they might be weak or persuaded to do things, if it is a cult in nature, I suspect they'd do it to make the leader happy. In return, they've got shelter, security and a career of sorts.'

'What do you know about him, the owner?' Danielle asked as she took the turn-off to go up the mountain.

'Glad you asked,' Nate huffed. 'We know shady is his middle name – Griffin Shady Maxwell.'

Danielle chuckled. 'Sure, it is. It's probably John.'

'Adam and I actually know him,' Nate admitted.

'Really? How?' She stopped at the lights, checked out the guy in the car next to her who was checking her out looking good in the latest Audi and took off when the green light came on, leaving him behind.

Nate hesitated. 'He went to school with Adam.'

'No way! Did Adam know him, or was he in a different year?'

'Same class, the same year. He arrived from another school he was expelled from, and it didn't take him long to build up his own gang. I met him a few times – at Adam's birthday party and when we were playing cricket. He was a dickhead then and probably still is.'

'Wow, interesting. What does Adam think of him?'

Nate hesitated. 'You'd have to ask him because I suspect his answer would be different to mine. But I think Adam was coerced into being friends with him when he wasn't looking for a friend. Griffin's father was a politician with ambitions to be the state premier, and Adam's father owned the media.'

'A marriage made in heaven.' Danielle slowed to negotiate the winding road up the mountain.

'If you are allies,' Nate agreed. 'I suspect Griffin's father wanted his son to foster the relationship, but it was more than that from where I stood. Griffin had this group of followers, and he was one of those kids who was too cool for school.'

'And Adam had the pedigree to be his equal, and Griffin thought he should be hanging with him?'

'Exactly,' Nate agreed. 'Ask Adam for his take and report back. I'd be interested to hear it.'

'Won't he tell you?' Danielle asked, confused.

'He never says much about Griffin around me; he can read my dislike of him. But I believe Griffin thought he and Adam could be the most powerful kids in class if not the school, and Griffin couldn't understand why Adam didn't want to be in his clique.'

'So, why didn't he?'

'Again, ask him. Adam had his own established school friends and then me after school and at weekends. Plus, some of Griffin's friends were idiots.'

Danielle chuckled. 'So now he's running this business. Kind of fits.'

'Sure does.'

'It's strange,' Danielle mused as she negotiated the turns in the road. 'Usually, there's an escapee who does some sort of expose and tells their sordid stories. Maybe it is a good place. Maybe they are learning some acting and modelling skills, being put through their paces and going on to lead fruitful lives.' She laughed at how ridiculous that sounded.

'Maybe people are too scared to say anything when they leave,' Nate suggested.

'Maybe no one had ever left,' Danielle said in a spooky voice, and Nate chuckled. A voice cut in.

'What was that?' Nate asked.

'Navman telling me to turn left, and I am here. Got to go.'

'Be careful, Dan. Try to get some photos, even if no one is in them, so I can get the lie of the land. Thanks.' He hung up, and the podcast cut back in.

Danielle scanned the area and smiled. 'Perfect.' In the distance, she could see several buildings – sprawling white farmhouses that all looked alike, like a country wellness resort, and then closer to the back of the property, near a row of trees, a darker building that looked like a three-level office complex but with heavily glazed windows. The road she was on did not seem to go that far; she assumed another entrance might run straight to it. There was some money spent on the place, no doubt about it. She contemplated the budget needed to run such a place and concluded Griffin Maxwell must be making some decent money.

There was a small sign at the entrance and a tall, iron, locked gate. Danielle couldn't see a surveillance camera, so she hurriedly snapped a photo of the sign, which read – *Fidelium Wellness Studio, Private Property. Entrance by appointment.* It listed a phone number underneath. Danielle drove on, stopping beside a wall of trees that would hide Nate's car nicely. She pulled over, staying as close as possible to the service road that linked to the highway home, just in case a quick exit was required. Cutting the engine, Danielle grabbed her camera, checked around her once more just to be safe and settled in with her binoculars to observe.

Then...

Charlie leapt from the backseat of Audrey's Jag to check out the area before Adam exited to enter the school grounds. She only had a few moments to do so while Adam said goodbye to his grandmother, giving her the customary kiss on the cheek. He exited the car, and they walked together to the gate.

'See anyone you don't like?' she asked, scanning the playing field. She saw Adam's surprised look as he glanced at her and then to the grounds.

'Nuh, maybe,' he shrugged.

'Is there anyone you want me to move along, rough up a bit?' She teased, trying to keep it light and knowing what his answer would be, but she had to ask the question.

He smiled up at her. 'No, but thanks. Maybe my teacher.'

She laughed. 'Adam, you are developing your father's charm. It will take you a long way. Now, you know to get your teacher to call me anytime you need me.'

'Sure.'

'Alright then. As your grandmother says, enjoy your day of learning and fun, my darling,' she teased him.

Adam grinned, and she smiled as he reddened at her term of endearment. He thanked Charlie, and she watched as he headed into the schoolyard waving to Stuart on the other side of the grounds before waving back to her before she rejoined Audrey in the vacated front seat.

'Mrs Murphy, I am worried about Adam.' She belted up and prepared for Audrey's erratic driving.

'Why?' Audrey hurriedly asked. 'What has happened?'

'Nothing to be concerned about, I think. It's just instinct that tells me something has shifted with him. I found a few boys bullying him, and he assured me all was okay.'

'Just like his father – impossibly hard to read, and they don't want you involved because it might make it worse,' Audrey said, driving back to the river mansion where Charlie's car was also parked. 'Adam will need to fight his own battles with boys his age, and it's a good lesson for life. Don't be too concerned.'

Charlie nodded. 'You are right, of course. But he's looking at me differently, too. I caught him studying me a few times and looking away just as quickly. As if he is awkward or has a confession but can't bring himself to say it.'

'Perhaps he has a crush on you,' Audrey suggested, smiling at the thought.

'No, that's Nate's thing. He brought me a Valentine's Day card and chocolates.'

Audrey laughed. 'That boy. He'll do all right, and his parents have good heads on their shoulders. I couldn't ask for a better friend for Adam, even if he is a bit wild and Adam follows him into mischief.'

Charlie smiled at the thought of the boys up to their antics. 'The party was a success, wasn't it? Nothing untoward happened that I don't know about?'

'No. I believe he had a wonderful time, just like all eleven-year-old children should on their birthday. Thank you for working on that Sunday.'

'My pleasure,' Charlie answered. The salary was double time for the Sunday shift, so she wasn't complaining, even though the arrival of twenty-five parents or more, along with caterers and entertainers, lifeguards, and Lord knows what coming and going, was a security nightmare. Then, a thought occurred to her. 'He's had the talk, hasn't he? Not that it's any of my business,' Charlie hurriedly added.

Audrey tapped the steering wheel as she thought. 'Good question, Charlotte.' Audrey always addressed her by her full name, as she did with Nate on most occasions.

Audrey continued, 'His father comes and goes so much. Perhaps he hasn't had the sex talk with Adam yet. He is only eleven, but it's timely. Is it that sort of look he's giving you?'

'It's more curiosity, but he actually flinched when I went to place my arm around him the other day. He's never done that before. I don't know what he thought I was going to do.'

'I will get James on to it immediately.'

Charlie nodded. 'Thank you. And don't worry, it might be nothing. He's soon to be a teenager, and we can expect some changes.'

'Sadly, yes,' Audrey agreed and sighed as she swung the Jag into the river estate.

Chapter 15

N ow...

'Tom, we need you,' Nate called out, and Adam's fit and muscled security guard raced from Adam's office, where he was fitting an alarm buzzer under the coffee table, into the kitchen where the two men were.

'What's wrong?' he asked, looking around and assessing the scene, his eyes landing on Adam, who looked well enough.

'We can't open the coffee jar,' Nate said, handing it over and trying to keep a straight face.

Tom said some colourful swear words, grabbed it from him, twisted the lid and handed it back. 'You're a bloody idiot.'

'Do you want a coffee?' Adam asked, and Tom's eyebrows shot up in surprise before Adam added, 'Nate's making.'

'What I want...' Tom said, leaning back across the counter, folding his arms across his chest, 'is for you and your girlfriend to move back to the river house.'

Adam grimaced, not letting on that he and Kelsey had already decided to move on the coming weekend. Neither man liked to give the other an inch. 'If no media are circling my house and they are already circling at the river house, what would be the point? We're below the radar where we are, and they can snap all the photos they like of Nate arriving and leaving in his Audi.'

'I'm surprised I haven't got my own fans appearing at the fence,' Nate added, making Adam laugh.

Tom ignored them and spelled it out. 'You should be back living there until after the wedding because if anyone – be it the media, fans, weirdos, stalkers, desperate DNA grabbers – discovers where you live, then you have no security, high fences, and no real escape. And let's face it, you attract them.' Tom did not have to mention the stalker recently locked away who tried to kidnap Adam as a boy, but the inference was there. He nodded to Adam's bandage hand as more evidence.

'I'll talk with Kelsey about it,' Adam said in a conciliatory manner, which surprised both men.

'Can you do it before the wedding?' Tom asked with a smirk.

'This weekend, we'll move back in this weekend,' he said, ignoring Tom's look of surprise. Adam changed the subject. 'You weren't around when Griffin Maxwell and his father were on the scene, were you?' He accepted a cup of coffee from Nate and thanked him.

'The politician?' Tom asked.

'Yeah, his son went to school with Adam. Came to his 11th birthday party,' Nate said.

'No. That was Charlie's shift; I was gone by then,' Tom said. 'I remember the name, though. Didn't he resign from office hurriedly for health reasons or to spend more time with his family, as they all say, and take off? Left the country?'

'That's him,' Adam agreed.

'Why are you asking?' Tom's eyes narrowed.

'His son, who was in my class at school, is running a Wellness Studio that we think might be a cult of sorts, and Nate's clients want their daughter back. I was thinking a reunion with Griffin might be in order so I can sus out the place,' Adam said, trying it on.

'Over my dead body,' Tom said, his jaw locking.

'I'm okay with that,' Adam shot back, taking a sip of his coffee.

'It's a week away, the wedding,' Tom said as if he was telling Adam something he didn't know. He accepted a coffee from Nate and put it down just as quickly so he could continue to fold his arms and look menacingly at Adam. 'All I have to do is safely get you, Audrey, your girlfriend, and your mates to the wedding and home. The next day, you can visit as many cults as you like; you're out of my hair.'

'How sad when you've just been reunited,' Nate joked, looking from one man to the other and receiving a look of derision from both.

'It's actually a good time to investigate it,' Adam continued, 'because you're on hand if anything goes wrong. Mum will get her money's worth out of you since you're not giving her any extra benefits these days.'

The room stilled as both men glared at each other, and the memory of Tom having an affair with Adam's mother loomed over them.

'Right then, back to it,' Nate said, indicating the door.

'What are you intending to do at this cult?' Tom asked, continuing to block the doorway.

'We haven't thought that far ahead yet. Maybe keep it simple... call Griffin, say I just came across his name and heard he was running a cult, could I join?' Adam stirred Tom.

'You'd be the perfect contender for it,' Tom retorted. 'Poor little lost rich boy.'

Adam went at Tom so fast Nate didn't see it coming. His coffee cup flew from his hands, splattering coffee everywhere and shattering. He yelled out to Rob, who tore in just as quickly, and the men pulled them apart.

'For the love of God, what is going on?' Rob asked, seeing the angered state of both men. 'Calm down, both of you.' He studied Adam, incensed, locked jaw, blood pumping hard and short-breathed.

'This is not going to work. You need to leave,' Adam hissed through clenched teeth. 'I don't care if you keep the job, but protect Audrey, Mum and Jack, just not me.'

'We can work through this,' Rob said in a calm voice.

'I don't think we can,' Nate said, shaking his head with a seriousness that was out of character. The two old friends shared a look.

Tom rubbed his jaw where he had taken the first blow. 'I'd say we're even. Let's just move on from it,' he said in a gravelly voice.

'Can you do that?' Rob asked Adam, still standing between the two men for fear the fight would erupt again.

Adam gave a curt nod, and Nate visibly relaxed and muttered something that sounded disbelieving. Tom turned and left as Jessica entered.

'Look at this mess!' she wailed.

'Adam made me do it,' Nate said, giving his best friend a small smile.

'Yeah, how many times have I heard that before,' Adam said with an eye roll.

'What was the fight about this time?' Rob asked

'Just the usual,' Adam said with a sigh. 'We can't speak unless we push each other's buttons.'

'Can you work on it?' Rob asked, frustrated. 'You of all people, Adam.'

'No, and there's not much point,' Adam said, his voice low. 'The wedding is in sight, and then Tom won't be.' He leaned down and started picking up shards of the coffee cup with the hand that wasn't bandaged as Nate asked Jessica where she kept a mop.

'You two go,' she said and sighed dramatically. 'I'll clean up and then do a coffee run for all of us. Clearly, you need it.'

'You are too good to them, Jess,' Rob said, smiling at her as he departed.

'I'm sorry about all this,' Adam, looking embarrassed, said to Nate and Jessica.

'Don't worry about it,' Nate clipped his shoulder. 'Adds a bit of excitement to my day. And I don't think your plan is a bad one. It's just determining how we make the introduction... how you can convincingly say you came across his name.'

'Yeah. I've been giving it a bit of thought since I found out he was the owner. It might be the only way to see first-hand what is going on in there, assuming Griffin wants to boast and take me on a tour.'

'I could go in pretending to be an actress wanting lessons,' Jessica offered. Both men answered at once.

'—definitely not.'

'—worse idea ever.'

She smirked at them.

'Trust me,' Nate said, 'you'll be learning more than how to act.'

'I wasn't going to stay, just get a contract and get out of there. Speaking of acting, I've found something you should both see. Sorry, I had to spend just over $100 to access fan content.'

'It can go on John and Robin's account,' Nate said. 'Does that mean we have access anytime now?' he asked with interest and grinned at the look Jessica gave him.

'So, you've found something?' Adam asked.

'You could say that. Quite an eyeful.'

Skye felt sorry and disheartened for Dawn; her bubble was about to burst. The beautiful, fragile young blonde who, like herself two years early, was sure she had been discovered and was on the way to stardom, but she was just about to have her "reality" moment. That's what the senior girls called it when the newbies were given their first taste of dramatic terror. Skye could still remember her fear from two years ago when she thought a madman was on the loose and had killed Leaf, and she was next. Griffin had welcomed her to his bed and comforted her, but she had never really recovered, never relaxed again. Believing you are so close to a horrific death had that effect on you. In time, they all became nervous, weaker, and needier, and Sarah Lyons hated the person she had become.

There was also the betrayal. Leaf's preparedness to play her part in Skye's terror – and do the same for every other new recruit – was hard to forgive. And now she and another girl, Wren – named for the blue stripe in her hair – were about to be complicit in Dawn's fall. The four ladies made their way to the creek to swim – Dawn, Leaf, Skye and Wren. They knew to keep up the happy banter, to give no inkling of what was going to happen. They were fined and punished if they did, which was not worth it. Principles died hard in the camp.

The creek was part of the acreage Griffin owned around the Wellness Camp, and the girls often visited it on their days off. Today, it was also an outdoor film set – three cameras were hidden in place; audio was wired, and Dawn was none the wiser. Skye tried to keep up with the conversation, but she felt sick at the prank that was soon to be played just for those subscribers who paid a fortune to get off on real-life anguish.

'Perfect day for a swim,' Leaf said, looking skyward and smiling. Arriving, she turned and spread her towel across a large, warm rock. The creek was glistening, cicadas kept up a steady hum in the bushes nearby, and the scene could not have been more perfect for a swimming outing.

'The water will be freezing,' Skye added, doing her best to appear natural and relaxed, knowing Griffin and Zach would watch the video. She dipped her toe in the water and laughed. 'Yep! That's the best about fresh creek water; it makes you feel alive.'

'I not a great swimmer,' Dawn said with trepidation. She had listed a fear of water on her enrolment sheet so she would not be given water-based roles, but it would be used against her, as Skye's fear of the dark was turned on her.

'Neither am I,' Wren added, 'but I don't think anyone's ever got into trouble here. It's not that deep – maybe a little over our heads at its deepest, and the bottom is more like small pebbles and rocks. You can find your feet easily.'

'Up north, people die at freshwater creeks all the time,' Leaf said, stripping down to a skimpy bikini. The other ladies did the same – a bonus for the potential viewers. Skye was sure the cameras would manage to zoom in on their various stages of undress.

'How do they die?' Dawn asked, nervousness edging into her voice, as planned by Leaf and Zach. The small piece of dramatic film was building up nicely – four beautiful women swimming at a creek, stripping off, and danger looming.

'They either get taken by a crocodile or get trapped... you know, jump in, get snagged on something, or knock themselves out and drown,' Leaf said and shrugged casually.

'There's no crocodiles in here, are there?' Dawn asked.

Wren laughed. 'No. It would be a very long way for a freshwater crocodile to travel from North Queensland to here.'

Skye shook her head. 'Not so. Zach told me they had been seen in the Logan River. That's not far from here, but that's a river, and this is a creek, and the last sighting was a long time ago.' She was given the fact to add should the conversation move that way.

'It was probably someone's pet that got away,' Wren said, laughing, as she entered the water. 'Come on, let's swim, and then we can sunbake on the rocks.'

The girls followed her in, Dawn going in last and not as confidently. After a short while, Dawn began to relax. They played in the water for the cameras, splashing and swimming, and then the acting began in earnest. Skye and Wren positioned themselves closer to the small rocks where they entered, while Leaf and Dawn remained in the middle, paddling, immersed, their heads and arms above water.

And then Leaf disappeared.

Dawn looked to where Leaf had been but assumed she had just dunked herself. But turning, Skye and Wren's eyes were wide.

Leaf appeared spluttering. 'Get out! There's something in—' she disappeared again.

Skye and Wren panicked, scrambling up the rocks, and Dawn screamed, paddling towards them.

Leaf surfaced nearer to Dawn and grabbed her. 'Help! Oh my God!'

She was dragging Dawn down with her, and Dawn screamed in panic. She tried to push Leaf away, to loosen the other woman's grip, but she went under with her.

When Dawn surfaced, Leaf was swimming to the edge, still screaming, 'Get out, get out.'

Dawn screamed, flayed in the water, and then disappeared. She surfaced, screaming and crying in terror. On the edge, Skye and Wren held out their hands.

'Take my hand!'

Leaf reached them first, and they pulled her in. Dawn was almost there when she was grabbed by her leg and pulled below again. She surfaced moments later, spluttering, panicked and grabbing their hands, and was pulled to safety.

Hysterical, Dawn ran further up the rocks. She leaned over, crying, her body shaking, and then she collapsed to her knees. Skye and Wren were told not to go to her, to let the camera catch her reaction raw and without obstruction. But for Skye, it was painful and ugly to watch her terror subsiding.

And then, as always, they heard a male voice.

'Cut,' Zach said, appearing from behind a rock enclave. 'That was bloody perfect,' he said and laughed. 'Well done, girls, well done. Thanks, boys, you can pack up.'

Two men emerged and began unhooking cameras and microphones placed around them.

Skye looked at Dawn with sympathy, but she saw the range of emotions on the new girl's face – shock, disbelief, anger, and betrayal.

Leaf laughed and then applauded. 'Bravo, Dawn. That's your first piece of performance art, and you did a great job. Griffin will want to see this and see you after, no doubt.'

The gleam of excitement dulled in Dawn's eyes as the reality of the situation hardened her.

Skye picked up Dawn's towel and moved towards her, wrapping it around the young girl; Dawn stiffened at Skye's touch.

'Welcome to *Fidelium Wellness Studio*, Dawn. Believe it or not, I am your friend,' Skye whispered and understood when Dawn pulled away and walked off, not looking back at any of them.

Chapter 16

Nate sat in the passenger seat of Adam's Mercedes and gave him a quick briefing on the lady they were meeting. 'Her name is Tania Anderson. She's 25 now, and she's been out of the Wellness Studio for three years.'

'So, if she worked a three-year contract, she went in at 19, left at 22.' Adam did the calculations.

'Except she didn't serve out the contract because she lost the baby in the hospital and didn't go back, according to Burnsy. I don't know how many years she did there before it all went pear shape,' Nate admitted. 'But it tells us that he's been running this studio for at least three years, probably longer.'

'What does Tania do now for work?' Adam asked.

'She's a beautician, works part-time and is studying nursing.'

'Ambitious,' Adam said. 'Good on her. It sounds like she's given up the modelling acting dream then.'

Nate agreed. 'But nothing is stopping them from coming out and setting up their own fan sites unless the contract says otherwise.'

'I hope she's still got her contract; I'd love to set eyes on it.'

'Next left,' Nate directed. 'This is the street.'

'Right, so anything else I need to know about Tania?' Adam got back to business.

'In a nutshell, she's single, got a boyfriend who won't be present because he doesn't know anything about that time in her life, and she wants to keep it that way, and she's happy to talk with us, but we're not to record the conversation.'

'Fair enough.' Adam entered the street filled with units and just as many cars on the street. Nate looked for the street number.

'Keep going, your side about halfway up, I'd say.' He pointed out a street car park. 'I hate these high-rise choked streets.'

'Better that they are all together though than ruining a character street,' Adam observed. He navigated into a tight car park and cut the engine.

'You're just saying that because you have a character house.'

'Exactly.'

Nate left his jacket in the car, but Adam didn't. He glanced back to check Adam was following him. Arriving, Nate found the number on the buzzer, announced them, and they were in a neat unit on the second floor not long after.

'I've made coffee,' she offered, which they accepted.

Nate studied Tania. She was a beautiful-looking woman with light brown hair loose around her shoulders, a small face, and expressive brown eyes. She was not unique or special but attractive enough to consider a career in modelling. She had a bit of weight on her, which looked healthier than some of the models he'd seen in campaigns. There were a couple of photos on the wall of her with a clean-cut guy who looked nothing like Griffin Maxwell.

'My name was Harmony in the camp,' she said, sitting with her coffee after serving the men. She gave a small laugh. 'Ridiculous. My hair was blonder then, and I was big on tanning. I looked like a beach girl, and I was desperate for stardom. In stepped Griffin Maxwell, who was sexy and persuasive and promised me the world.'

Nate's eyes narrowed. His dislike for the guy was increasing, if that were at all possible, and he didn't like to hear him spoken of in flattering terms.

'How old were you when you signed up?' Adam asked, sitting beside Nate on a two-seater cream leather couch opposite Tania, who sat in a single leather seat.

'I was all of nineteen and surprisingly naive in retrospect. I had been living with three girlfriends, trying to make enough money from working at the supermarket to pay for a modelling portfolio photoshoot. My parents refused to help because they thought chasing that dream was short-lived and I should get serious and go to college. I had once thought about nursing, which I'm studying now. But then, I was bummed out by Mum and Dad's lack of support, hence the reason I moved out in the first place.'

'How did you come across Griffin and the Wellness Studio?' Adam asked.

'It was at one of those beauty expos at the Exhibition Grounds where you went along, and there were stalls for a range of products, workshops, catwalk events and so on. I went with two of my flatmates, and the Wellness Studio didn't have a stand, but I picked up the flyer somewhere there. It offered affordable photo modelling comp cards… you know where they put three or four shots of you on a card with your details that you shop around to agents or clients directly.'

'Is that all it offered?' Nate asked.

'No, there were acting and modelling courses as well. But I started with the comp card, and then they talked me into a portfolio,' Tania said, stopping to sip her coffee. She placed it back on the table and continued, 'Then they selected several of us with potential.'

'I bet they did,' Nate said drily. 'Not saying you didn't have potential, but they were keen to tap into it.'

'Yes, as I found out,' Tania agreed. 'But at the time, I was flattered, and I felt my decision to model had been justified.' She gave a self-deprecating shrug.

'Understandable,' Adam said. 'Then I'm guessing they offered you income, modelling work, training and a chance to show your parents you could make it?'

Tania nodded. 'Precisely. I thought I had made it. I signed for three years with no hesitation whatsoever. For the first few months, it was acting classes, photographs, building my profile online with fairly tame acting parts and being on call to Griffin, which was completely consensual because I was in awe of him and thought it was the love story of the ages.' She laughed again, 'I was an idiot.'

'Don't beat yourself up,' Nate said. 'His power is his charisma. You weren't the first and won't be the last to fall for him.'

'You sound like you know him or have had a bad experience with him,' she said, her dark brown eyes questioning Nate.

Nate gave a sharp nod. 'We knew him when he was starting. He was a troubled teenager.'

Adam cut in. 'Would you still have the contract?'

'Sure,' she said and rose, leaving to grab it.

'Fantastic,' Adam said in a low voice.

Tania returned moments later with a small black compendium, opened it and found it under "C".

'C for contracts,' she explained and handed it to Adam, who gratefully took it and started reading through the document.

'So, you're a private investigator investigating Griffin?' she asked Nate.

Nate nodded, sitting forward and putting his finished coffee cup down. 'Adam is a psychologist, and I'm the P.I. My client has a daughter at the wellness camp and is not convinced she wants to be there. Can you leave if you want to, anytime?'

Tania made a small groaning sound. 'Mm, this is where it gets complex. Yes and no, it is not that simple to go, but you can. Some girls resigned before finishing their time, and others stayed on afterwards with a year-to-year contract. Some even live off-site and go there for work.'

'Really?' Nate asked, surprised. 'Doing what?'

'The same thing as the rest of us did. But there are only a few, and only because they are big earners. But I wanted to leave early, and when I broached the subject, I was told I would have to repay the debt for my board, beauty fees, tutoring and so on.' She put a strand of her hair back behind her ear and looked from one to the other. 'You know what's coming next?'

'The balance sheet didn't balance?' Adam asked, looking up from the contract.

'Yep, that's it. I asked why it couldn't come out of my earnings because I had good earnings after the first year, especially as the content got, well, racier,' she flushed as she said it.

'And what was the answer to that request?'

'That I owe a lot more than I've earned, but if I see the contract out, nothing will be owing, and I will get the money in full.'

'How unsurprising,' Nate muttered.

Adam moved the discussion along. 'I am sorry to hear you lost a child,' he said softly.

'Thank you. It seems like a lifetime ago and is so surreal. But you want to know if it was Griffins or Zachs?'

'No, that's none of our concern,' Adam said, and Tania looked surprised. She answered anyway.

'It was their child... one of them was the father. It didn't matter which one in the end.'

Adam nodded. 'I'm interested to know how you got to leave afterwards?'

'Ah, well, that took me by surprise, I have to say. Zach visited me in the hospital. I said I was too traumatised; I couldn't go back and act and model like nothing had happened. Surprisingly, before I left the hospital, I got a letter from Zach saying Griffin had released me from the contract and wished me a speedy recovery. I never saw Griffin again or returned for my clothing. Most of it was supplied by them anyway.'

'Did you get your money?' Nate asked.

'I got half. I guess that was generous. I spoke with my cousin, who is a solicitor, and he said to take the money and let it go. That I didn't have a leg to stand on with the contract I signed.'

Adam put the contract down and agreed. 'Yep, I'm not a lawyer, but it's fairly black and white and no wriggle room by the looks of it. Can I scan it?'

Tania nodded, and Adam snapped the pages with his phone.

'What do you think about the accusations that the studio is a smokescreen for a cult?' Nate asked.

'I think it is exactly that,' Tania said, surprising them both. 'When I first entered their world, I was swept away by this sophisticated, handsome man taking an interest in me. I was his woman for a few months until I was replaced, or he started spreading himself around again, and that was hellishly painful. The older girls treated me well because they knew what was coming, but the newbies like me and the one I replaced in Griffin's bed hated me. I felt the same way about the one that replaced me, and on it goes.'

'What was her name?' Nate asked, wondering if it was Skye but guessing she came a few years after Tania.

'Freedom. I can still see her. She was particularly nasty to me,' her jaw tensed as she said the words, remembering the feeling of being on the outer. She took a deep breath and let her body relax. 'She eventually came around when I fell out of favour. It's probably hard for you guys to understand what it was like.'

'Not at all,' Adam said. 'Griffin Maxwell was the same when I knew him. He made you feel like you were the most important person on the earth – he selected you when he could have chosen anyone to be his friend.'

Nate studied Adam. It was the most he had spoken of Griffin in his presence, and he was amazed by the ridiculous streak of jealousy he felt – like he was second best. He looked away as Adam turned to look at him.

'That is the feeling exactly,' Tania looked at Adam gratefully. 'And when he ignores you, I imagine it is like coming down from a high for a druggy. We all craved his attention and the prestige of being chosen for the night.'

'Could you say no to having sex with him?' Nate asked.

'You could, but we didn't want to. I didn't want to; I craved him. And we were also encouraged to be available to his business partner. We paid for it if we weren't available to both of them. We were treated like pariahs. We got the worst gigs and tips and were last with make-up and clothes, totally ignored by both of them. It was worse than being a leper, and I saw it happen to a few girls.'

'What's his name? The business partner,' Adam asked.

'Zach...' she struggled to remember his last name.

'Zachary Crowder?' Adam asked, surprised.

'Yes! You know him too?'

Adam's lips narrowed, and he turned to Nate. 'One of Griffin's close friends at school. I can't believe he's stuck by him.' He turned to Tania. 'Did you meet a guy named Ben Solomon?'

Tania shook her head in the negative. She finished the last mouthful of her coffee, offered them both another one and sat back when there were no takers.

'Who is Ben?' Nate asked Adam.

'Another one of Griffin's flock at school, but he mustn't have followed him into the business. He was tight with Zach.'

Nate nodded. 'Can we ask you just a few more questions? feel free not to answer if they are too personal.'

'Sure, go ahead. I'm happy to help if it means someone can get away without a drama,' Tania said as if she had no inhibitions talking about her history.

'Did you know the content you had to produce would go online and might get more intimate?'

'Not initially. But we all agreed to it because we were told it was not seen by the public. It was paid content only to a select audience. We were also told, which was true, that it would be a significant part of our earnings and build up a subscriber base who were willing to pay for our talents.'

'Could you keep that subscriber base when you left?' Adam asked.

'Yes, but we had to feature the logo for Griffin's business for the first few years of going alone.'

'Ah yeah, I did see that in the contract,' Adam said, tapping the document.

'If we could make considerable money from the work, that would let us be financially independent when our contract was done, even if half went to the studio, and as I said, we didn't want to displease Griffin or Zach.'

Nate stepped in. 'One last question from me?'

Tania gave him a nod and a smile that made her look every bit the model.

'What was the worst punishment for those who didn't play the game, so to speak? Were you ever in any real danger?'

'It depends on how you define danger – emotional or physical.' For the first time in the interview, she hesitated. 'There were reality moments that I don't think anyone ever got used to during the first year. You were always kept a little on edge.'

'How do you mean?' Adam asked and leaned forward with interest.

'They would terrify you – a possible attack, drowning, snake in your room, public punishment – stuff that they recorded for an audience who wanted real adrenaline viewing.'

'That's sick,' Nate said, and Tania nodded her agreement.

'There was something worse than that – a place called "The VIP House". It's another area where some of the girls moved to and stayed until their contract was up. I haven't seen inside, but rumours ran rife throughout the camp. Supposedly, they have these rooms, bondage rooms, you know the sort of thing?'

'Did girls go there consensually?' Nate asked, his voice laced with dread. He glanced at Adam, wondering if the childhood photos might inspire what went on there.

'Yes, because it was where the big bucks got made. External client visit, and I believe there were a few online voyeur rooms, but it was big on privacy and security. Leaf told me anything the client wants, the client gets.'

'Leaf? I wonder if she's still there,' Nate mused.

'One last question from me, and we really appreciate you giving us your time,' Adam said. 'Did you know anyone who left?'

'Not in my time there. Maybe never.'

Chapter 17

T hen...

The boys pedalled into the driveway of Adam's home and stopped while he keyed in a number to open the gate. Nate laughed.

'What?' Adam looked at him and grinned.

'It's just weird. You can ride right up to my front door and go straight in.'

Adam shrugged. He'd never known any different. As the gate slid open, he issued a challenge. 'Race you to the steps' and took off.

Nate whooped and hurried to catch up. They skidded to a stop, neck-to-neck, and both declared themselves the winner. They were wet from the creek, and Adam knew his mother didn't like him coming into the house dirty, but she was away, so it didn't matter; Audrey never minded.

'Starving,' Adam declared.

'Me too.'

They dropped their bikes in front of the stairs and raced through the long hallway into the kitchen. The house was enormous; no one was around, and their voices and footsteps echoed like they were in a hollow vault. Adam reached the fridge and pulled out whatever he could. They slapped butter on bread, ham and cheese and sat on stools at the bench.

'Want a drink?' Adam asked.

'Yeah, thanks.'

Adam pulled out a soft drink, and Nate laughed again.

'What?'

'I'm not allowed to have soft drinks at home.'

'Why not?'

Nate shrugged. 'Sugar and stuff.'

'You don't have to have any.'

'I want some, thanks.'

Adam filled the glasses with the orange bubbly drink.

'I know what we can do next,' Adam started. 'I got remote racing cars from Dad for my birthday. We could race them on the tennis court.'

'Yeah!' Nate's eyes widened with enthusiasm.

The boys looked up as they heard footsteps approaching; it could only be Audrey. Nate glanced at the mess; Adam wasn't worried.

'Ah, here you are, boys. I could have made you lunch if I'd known you were going to be home.' She smelled of expensive perfume.

'That's okay, Audrey, we didn't know we were going to be either,' Adam said, polishing off his sandwich.

'How are you, Nathanial?' Audrey turned her attention to Nate.

'Very well, thank you, Mrs Murphy.'

'You are welcome to call me Audrey, dear.'

'Thank you, Mrs Murphy, but Mum won't let me.'

Audrey nodded. 'A very sensible woman indeed. I am meeting Sylvia for lunch, Adam, but Charlie will be here in the house if you need anything. I will come back and say goodbye just before I leave.' She began to depart and stopped. 'Oh, Adam darling, Mr Maxwell called this morning on behalf of his son to invite you to a sleep-over. I accepted on your behalf, dear. He seems a nice boy that Griffin.'

Adam's thoughts rushed in several directions. Audrey had no idea of the photos that were in an envelope under his bed, and now Nate would be angry.

'I don't want to go, Audrey.'

'Nonsense, we can never have enough friends. I'm sure Nathanial could go as well. I will call Mr Maxwell back and ask.'

'No, Mrs Murphy,' Nate spoke up quickly, 'thanks, but I can't go.'

'As you wish then, but it is a friendship worth fostering, Adam darling,' she said and smiled at him. With a wave to the boys, Audrey departed to her wing of the building.

Nate climbed down from the stool. 'I've got to go.'

'Why? Aren't we going to race cars?'

'I got something on.' He headed to the front door without waiting. Adam raced behind him.

'I'm not going to the sleepover. I don't want to.'

'I don't care, go if you want to.' He picked up his bike and tore off down the driveway, hitting the green release button on the gate, and Adam was alone.

He stood staring after Nate for a while until he heard Audrey's voice.

'Was that Nathaniel I just saw leaving?'

Adam nodded.

'I see. He doesn't like the other boy.'

'How did you know?' Adam snapped to look at her.

'Because I'm old and sometimes perceptive, dear, but I fear I've made an error in judgement in this case,' she said, moving the hair off his head as she gently touched his face.

'I told him I wasn't going to go.'

'I shouldn't have insisted, and I'll know not to mention it in front of Nathanial again. I didn't think he'd be jealous.'

'He's not jealous. Is he? Why?'

'How would you feel if Nate found a new friend and didn't have time for you?' Audrey asked.

'Super mad.'

'Well, I'm sorry, dear boy, that I put you in that situation, but best you ride after him and tell him you are not going.'

'But I did.'

'He might need to hear it again, Adam. Remember,' Audrey said, ensuring she had Adam's attention, 'what are your father's lessons for succeeding in life.'

Adam gave a small sigh, not enough to get him in trouble, but it came from his chest involuntarily. He was out of sorts enough without a lecture or one of Audrey's tests.

'Have a goal.'

'Would you agree that is to keep Nate as your best friend?'

'Yes,' Adam nodded and continued saying the words as if he didn't understand them but had learnt them in rote fashion as expected. 'Identify the path to achieve it.'

'That's a good one... I believe the simplest path would be to get on your bike and visit Nate now, darling. What do you think?'

Adam agreed and tried to recall the third. 'Know when to walk away,' he blurted out as it came to him.

'Well, do you want to walk away, darling boy? How long do you want to be Nathanial's best friend?'

Adam's eyes widened as if he had never conceived that Nate wouldn't be in his life.

'Forever.'

'Then what are you going to do?'

'I'll go over now.'

'So much like your father,' she said, giving him an indulgent smile.

'So, I don't have to go to Griffin's for a sleepover?'

'Leave it with me. I'll make it go away,' Audrey said. 'Off you go.'

Adam grinned and kissed the proffered cheek before racing out the door in pursuit of the best friend he always followed.

Now...

Adam was getting the frosty treatment on the drive back to the office. He thought Nate would want to go through everything Tania had revealed, but he was wrong. His best friend sat tight-lipped, and he wasn't the type to be.

'What did you make of all that?' Adam prompted him, turning the car out of the street and joining in with the traffic.

'I'll have to process it.'

'She was a good source.'

'Yep.'

'At least we know that people do leave the camp, and he has some compassion,' Adam continued.

'No,' Nate said and looked straight ahead. 'We know one person left, and she lost his child, most likely. He probably didn't want a reminder of her in his face every day.'

'Right.'

They drove in silence, and Adam quietly sighed. He had pissed Nate off, and he knew exactly when he did it, but the description of Griffin Maxwell was fair, and he hadn't said what he did to hurt his best friend. They weren't eleven anymore, for the love of God. Griffin did make you feel like you were the most important person on the earth, that was his pull and his power. Until he turned his attention from you to someone else.

Adam was surprised Nate let it cut him. That can't be why he's pissed off, he mused. Seriously?

Nate grabbed his phone and spent the rest of the drive ignoring Adam, making calls to Burnsy and checking on Danielle. Arriving, Adam turned into the car park, and Nate was out of the car before he barely got his seatbelt off. He locked up and followed him upstairs. Jessica buzzed them in, and both men went to their offices. Adam could feel Jessica studying them.

After fifteen minutes or so, Adam received an email from Nate suggesting they find the other close school friend of Griffin's – Ben Solomon – and see if he was still in touch with Griffin and if he knew anything about the Wellness Studio. He was about to fire back a response but decided he'd deal with this head-on, and if he had put Nate off-side, he'd fix it. But seriously, there had to be more to it than that. Why had that touched a nerve? Did Tania say something too close to home? He rose and went to Nate's office, finding the door closed.

Jessica shrugged. 'He's alone.'

Adam knocked, walked in without waiting for an invitation, and walked up to Nate's desk. 'What's wrong, just spill it?'

'Nothing's wrong. Why would anything be wrong?' Nate snapped back.

'Because you are moody, avoiding eye contact, keeping your sentences short and—'

'Thanks, Dr Murphy. I'll give you a call if I need an appointment.'

Adam bit his tongue. He stood for a moment, gripping the back of Nate's visitor's chair and thinking.

'I've pissed you off.'

'No more than usual.'

'I know you don't like talking about—'

'It's nothing. I told you. I'm busy, and we'll talk later.' Nate picked up his phone, dismissing him.

Adam studied him for a moment, his jaw locked with frustration, his knuckles white where he clenched the visitor's chair, and then he decided the best thing he could do was remove himself from the situation before he said something to make the situation worse. He gave Nate a nod to say he accepted nothing was wrong and strode out of the office, biting back his anger at Nate's attitude. He felt Jessica studying him as he walked past.

He now knew exactly what was wrong; Nate was in an insecure period of his life, and Adam had added fuel to the fire. Sure, they weren't kids anymore, and he knew their bond was unbreakable, but maybe Nate needed to hear that or be reminded of it, especially since his wife had left him and the relationship with Jessica was up in the air. Nate would not want to hear it said out loud, though, because both men would deny that it was necessary, and that's putting way too much emotion out there. He just had to think how to do it.

Adam left his office again and stopped in Rob's ajar doorway.

'Come in,' Rob said, seeing him hovering.

'Got a minute?'

'Always,' Rob assured him, pointing to a chair and sitting back. 'What's up?'

'Nothing, I need your take on something.' Adam closed the door behind him and sat. 'It's about Nate.'

'Is he alright?' Rob leaned forward slightly.

'Yeah, it's about Nate and Griffin Maxwell and something old that's brewing.' Adam explained as best he could. He finished, 'For all his bluff and humour, Nate has his insecurities. Why?' Adam splayed his hands in front of him in a show of confusion. He felt Rob studying him as if he had missed the obvious.

'I don't have to tell you that feeling poorer than your friends in early adolescence is associated with loss of self-esteem, do I? You remember that class at university?' Rob teased Adam.

'Vaguely,' Adam gave his mentor a smirk.

'We judge ourselves by making social comparisons. You probably looked at Nate's family and wished you could have what he had... parents who were home at night, normal meals together, a father who came to your sports matches.'

Adam nodded. 'Hell yeah.'

'Like it or not, I perceive that is what you are trying for now with your modest home and your stable life. As kids, Nate looked at you and compared himself – your economic status was far above his, and it probably didn't bother him until—'

'I don't think it did,' Adam cut in. 'That's not what's going on here. His upbringing was so stable, his parents so solid, and as the only kid, Nate was adored. We shared everything. He had so much more than me.'

'Emotionally, yes, but both of you only know the life you were born into. You were and are his best friend in the world, and he's watched while whatever you wanted, you got. You've said yourself you only had to ask your mother, and she gave you anything. But then you made a friend – Griffin – who made it clear to Nate that he wasn't good enough for you, that he wasn't in the same class or moved in the same circles. Griffin's back and all those feelings have been triggered for Nate.'

Adam's jaw locked. 'Yeah, okay. I get that, but we're not eleven, for God's sake.'

'Look at how you act around Tom. Hardly rational, and that is because of a childhood slight.'

Adam took a deep breath. 'Yeah, damn it, good point,' he conceded, making Rob laugh.

'I probably fuelled it too by remembering Griffin in more flattering terms than he deserved.' He looked out the window as he thought and then, thanking Rob, rose, saying, 'I'll put an end to this now.'

Chapter 18

D anielle Walters had been on surveillance for close to three hours when she got lucky. There had been no movement at the site, not even people coming and going between buildings, although she did see a man on a ride-on-lawnmower in the far distance of the grounds, but she couldn't be sure that was still part of the Wellness campgrounds. Now, a car was coming out of the gate, and she had her camera at the ready and zoomed in. Danielle snapped a few shots of a young male at the wheel and his car number plates. It was a Lexus 4WD, and she didn't have to look it up to know you couldn't buy that car unless you had over $85,000 in your bank account.

'Company car, or are you a really well-paid employee?' Danielle muttered. Burnsy could find out who he was, if need be, she mused, and after waiting a few minutes until he was out of sight, Danielle packed it in and headed to the nearby village on the pretence of getting a coffee and to ask a few questions. She really did want the coffee. It was a pleasant village with several gift stores, an art gallery of sorts, and two coffee shops – one with a bohemian feel to it, the other was more intimate and seemed to be big on sprucing their coffee brand. Parking, Dan studied the area.

Where would Griffin Maxwell go if he went anywhere at all?

From what the boys had told her, she opted for the one that didn't look touristy. Departing the car, she stopped for a moment to look above at the towering heights of the rainforest trees and smell the clear air. It was so different from her home – cooler, less humid – but it was so nice to be back in nature. She headed to the intimate coffee shop, *Deco Coffee*.

Inside, Danielle discovered how it got its name. It had a striking art deco theme – blue, cream, gold, angular geometry shapes – very tasteful. The counter was all glass, and the two staff members looked like they had stepped out of the 1920s with their severe and stylish haircuts and large aprons.

'Good morning, staying or take away?' a guy about Dan's age asked, and she played into his hand.

'Does the coffee taste better if I have it here or in a takeaway cup?'

'Here, hands down,' he said with a grin.

'Then a large latte, please, double shot.'

'Ah, a woman after my own heart.' He rang up the sale. 'Can I have a name for the order?'

Danielle looked around. 'Are you worried you'll get it confused with another?' she said in jest and didn't wait for an answer before saying, 'Dan'.

'It's my subtle way of remembering customers for next time. Makes for good business,' he said with a wink. 'I'm a Dan too, Dan, but I'm guessing you're a Danielle?'

'That I am. I don't get up to Tamborine often, but I might become a regular and test you on my name,' she said, seeing an opportunity to discuss the Wellness Studio. She paid with her phone and lingered while he made the coffee. A couple of customers were sitting by the window, but no one was in earshot.

'Are you doing the touristy thing, or here on business, or looking to buy in Tamborine? Prices have blown out something chronic.' He looked like a man who regretted not getting into the market earlier.

'Not buying or working, but I was interested in doing a course or two at the Wellness Studio. I went to enquire, but it looks fairly locked up. Would you have a brochure for them or know anything about them?' she asked with a glance at the rack of cards and brochures near a table of newspapers and magazines.

'Griffin's place,' Dan, the barista, nodded. 'You look like you could model, or are you an actor?'

'I'm an amateur, but thanks,' she said. 'I'm not expecting to light up anyone's television screen any time soon, but these days, people are looking for diversity apparently, that's me.'

Dan agreed that she had a unique look as he finished heating the milk and concentrated on making her coffee. When he finished, he resumed the conversation. 'We don't get much business from the students of the Wellness Studio, but Griffin is in here every morning at 10am for his fix. He works out, then has a ristretto here, then back to it, I guess,' Dan said with a shrug.

'What's a ristretto?'

'Think of a smaller shot of espresso but using a finer grind of the beans. It's like a power punch for the day.'

'Hmm, a ristretto man, huh? Perhaps I should come back and talk with him in person then. Thanks, Dan.'

'Sure, Dan,' he teased and invited Danielle to sit, following her to the table carrying the latte. She wished she had a takeaway now so she could get back to tell Nate since it was nearly an hour's drive back, and she preferred to tell him in person rather than over the phone. But she played the game and, after a sip or two, conceded it was a damn good coffee and worth the stop.

Adam had been stewing in his office, trying to think how he would clear the air between himself and Nate without having to say much, at least nothing soppy. He made a living from listening, not from espousing drama, he groaned. This was ridiculous. He could see Nate was still in his office. His phone light came on and off with regularity. Adam checked Jessica's online diary, and seeing that he was free for a few hours to do his paperwork and reports, he grabbed his phone, intending to go for a walk.

He stopped in his tracks, returned to the window in his office and looked downstairs. He couldn't see any reporters down there, although Jessica had taken an interview request call this morning. *Crazy*. Before he could make his exit, Jessica tapped on his half-opened door and entered.

'What's going on? Is everything alright?' she asked, seeing Adam standing near the window. 'Did you and Nate have a fight? He's acting weirder than usual.'

Then Adam brightened; he would use the peacemaker between them – Jessica. *Why didn't he think of that earlier*? He gave a small shake of his head. 'It's this guy from school derailing us – Griffin Maxwell. It's okay, and it'll sort itself out.'

He walked back to his desk and sat; Jessica followed as he hoped.

'What does that mean? Is Nate okay?' she asked, leaning on the back of his visitor's chair.

'Yeah, he just has a pathological hatred of him,' he stopped. 'That might be a little strong, but we're about to encounter Griffin, and neither of us is looking forward to it.'

'How do you feel about him?'

'I don't like him, never have. He's always made my skin crawl... he's too intense and stifling. That's the best way I can explain it. But he's connected to Nate's clients, so there's no avoiding it,' Adam said, pleased he had his message across. 'Nate might have a different take on it.'

'Sure,' she said and wandered off. He heard her knock on Nate's door and enter. Problem solved, maybe. That should get back to him and remind him we're on the same team. He rose, grabbed his keys and phone and decided he would do something he hadn't done for a long while: take a drive by the old neighbourhood – his school, where Griffin's place used to be, Nate's old family home. This weekend, he'd be moving back to his old home with all its baggage.

Then...

James Murphy grimaced, drew a deep breath, and studied his mother, Audrey. She was a constant in his life and his son, Adam's life, and he respected her above all others.

'The boy's eleven,' he said. 'Isn't he too young for the talk?'

'I don't know, James. I can't profess to be an expert on that subject,' she said with a small sigh. 'But these are different times than when you were eleven, dear, and Charlotte senses something is amiss with him in her company.'

'Does he like her?'

'They get on very well. She's an asset, and I don't wish to dismiss her hunch.'

He nodded and pursed his lips. 'Do you think he's in love with her?'

Audrey smiled. 'I asked the same, but she said no, and that Nate was holding a flame for her.'

James laughed. 'I'd be in love with her if I were their age.'

'It can't hurt to have the father and son talk. Your own father was long gone before you needed your enlightenment.' She put her hand to her heart every time she spoke of her dearly departed husband, who died within a decade of their marriage, leaving her a very wealthy young widow – his fortune made in steel. James was sure that his mother's backbone was made of the very same thing – she was a woman of strength with a no-nonsense attitude.

'Why did you never remarry, Mum?' he asked out of the blue, surprising her.

'He was my one true love, darling,' she said as if that was obvious. 'I never met anyone like him. We did have five years together before we married – my parents insisted on a long engagement as we were very young.'

'I wish I had known him.'

'He knew you; you were one when he died, the apple of his eye,' she smiled. 'At least you had your grandfather for a male influence and to give you the birds and bees talk.' She looked startled, 'he did give you the talk, didn't he?'

James laughed. 'Well, whether he did or didn't, I worked it out as evident by Adam being born.'

His mother shook her head at him, her lips twitching in a smile at his irreverence.

'Yes, rest assured, he gave me some awkward speech about copulation,' James said and laughed. 'Right then, I'll chat to Adam if you think he needs it.'

'Don't shock the boy.'

'I'll do my best,' he said, smiling at his mother to reassure her that he had everything under control. 'Will you send him up?'

Audrey left to fetch Adam; James walked to the window, looking out across their river-fronting mansion and thinking how best to broach the discussion. Best to do it immediately, or he would forget and get caught up in business, and the boy would be 21 before he knew it. The last thing he needed was some girl's parents on the doorstep demanding they do the right thing by their daughter.

Adam appeared stricken. He looked up at his grandmother, his blue eyes wide with alarm.

'You are not in trouble, darling boy,' his grandmother said. 'Your father is waiting for you upstairs in his office.'

Adam nodded and swallowed. He looked to the staircase and the front door as if deciding whether he should run or see his father.

He's found out. He has to know about the photos. How does he know?

'I will in a minute, Audrey. I just have to check something.'

He turned and raced down the hallway to his bedroom, running in and closing the door behind him. He dropped to his knees, looked under the bed and pulled out a box which contained all his favourite and secret things. Flipping the lid, he dug to the bottom and touched the envelope. The photos were still there. Phew! *So how did he know?*

Adam pushed the box back under the bed, straightened, opened the bedroom door, and ran back down the hallway, taking the stairs to his father's office. The door was ajar, and he saw his dad near the window.

'Dad?'

'Ah, Adam, come in, close the door.'

Adam did so as if he were being sentenced and about to receive his punishment. His father moved from the window and sat in a wing-backed chair nearby, indicating the seat opposite for Adam.

'You wanted to speak with me, Dad?' Adam asked, dropping into the offered chair and sitting right on the edge, bracing for the fallout he expected.

'Son, I think it is time we talked about what happens when a boy and a girl, or rather a man and a woman, get together.'

Adam's eyes widened, and he knew his father had seen the pictures. 'Why?' he blurted out, surprising his father.

'Well, every father has this discussion with their son and every mother with their daughter. One day, you will do the same. You need to be very careful, Adam. There will be young girls who will want to have sex with you in the hope of having a baby and trapping you into marriage or alimony.'

'Sex?' Adam said, picking up one word in the conversation. He saw his father's look of confusion as he ran a hand over his jaw and sat back. He didn't seem to be angry.

'Maybe you are too young for this talk,' James said. 'But anyway, we've started now, so let's keep going. The basics... one day you'll like a girl and want to kiss her.'

Adam said nothing but thought of Nate being in love with Charlie. He was pretty sure Nate wanted to kiss her. He nodded, so his father continued.

'Then you both might feel that was really good and want to go further. You might want to take your clothes off together and make love. Do you know how that happens?'

Adam shook his head.

'I think you might be too young for this conversation,' James said again. 'Let's back up. Have you ever wanted to kiss a girl?'

Adam thought about Kelsey. He loved her and was pretty sure of it, even if he only met her once. But he hadn't thought about kissing her, just saving her first.

'Maybe,' he answered.

'Good, right then,' James persisted. 'There are books and photos that might explain this better.'

'Did you see the photos?' Adam blurted out. He couldn't stand it any longer. If he was going to be punished, he wanted it over with. He didn't want his dad testing him, waiting for him to reveal it.

'What photos?'

Adam grimaced.

He doesn't know about them. Now what?

His mind raced ahead, trying to escape the situation he had just put himself in.

'What photos, Son?'

Adam shrugged. 'Nothing.'

James leaned forward, clasping his hands between his legs. 'Adam, if you have something you would like to tell me or something you would like to show me, now is the time.'

Adam nodded. 'It's nothing, Dad.'

'Have you been looking at photos? Do you have some magazines?'

'No!'

'Did someone show you some photographs? Nate, maybe?'

'No, he knows nothing about them.'

'About them? Where are they?'

Adam knew his dad was really smart, and he looked down at his father's clasped hands as he thought. Would he get the strap for this? It had been a while since he'd been strapped, a couple of years ago when he tried to run away on the day of a photoshoot.

'Adam,' his father's voice cut into his thoughts. 'Look at me.'

Adam looked up into his father's eyes, blue like his own. 'I haven't got all day, so you are going to answer me now. What photos are you talking about, and what have you seen?'

Adam swallowed, then stuttered, 'I got them... they were a present... for my birthday.'

His father nodded. 'You were given some photos for your birthday?'

Adam nodded.

'What are the photos of?'

'I think it is sex and other stuff.'

'I see.' His father spoke in a calm voice like Adam had heard him do with his mother when she was having what Audrey called a "Winsome Wobbly". 'Who gave you these photos?'

'It was a present, with a camera. One of those instant cameras where you press the button, and the photo appears right away.'

James frowned. 'So, did you take these photos?'

'No!' Adam all but yelled, and his father held up his hands in a pacifying gesture. 'They were in the box, in an envelope marked "Top Secret" for me.'

'I see,' James said and continued to dig with patience. 'And who gave you this gift?'

'Griffin.'

'Griffin who? Is this boy in your class?'

'Yes, Griffin Maxwell.'

James sat upright. 'The politician's son?'

Adam nodded.

'Where are the photos now, Son?' James asked, and Adam relaxed a little. His father would call him Adam if he were truly angry.

'In my room.'

'Have you shown them to anyone else? Nate, maybe?'

'No.'

Adam's father studied him.

'I haven't, honest.'

'Good. Let's get them then, and we'll have a look.' James stood, and Adam rose, walking in front of him. He took the stairs down and led the way to his bedroom. As he pulled the box from under his bed, he heard his dad go to the door and call out to his grandmother.

'Mum, can you come here?'

Moments later, Audrey appeared looking surprised at his summons. Adam handed the envelope to his father, who sat on the bed and patted the bed next to him for Adam to sit down.

'What's going on?' Audrey asked.

'Adam received a very inappropriate birthday present from Griffin Maxwell. Did you go through the presents?'

'Of course not. The guest list was approved, and I am sure the parents purchased the gifts.'

'Yes, that's what I would have thought too, but that might not be the case,' James said.

Audrey moved closer to the bed and stood beside Adam. He felt her hand alternating between his shoulder and touching his head lovingly. He looked up at her, and she gave him a small smile.

James read the envelope and opened it, pulling out the instant photos, at least ten of them. His expression told Adam the shots were bad, really bad. He swore, and Audrey reprimanded him. James handed them one at a time over Adam's head to Audrey, who gasped.

'Adam darling, did you see these?' she asked, looking down at him.

He nodded. 'Yes, Audrey.' He knew he'd probably be grounded forever, but then she did something that surprised him. Audrey apologised.

'I am so sorry, my darling.'

Adam looked up at her. Then, his father said the same thing, and he turned equally surprised to look at his dad.

'I am sorry too, my boy, that you had to see this filth. This is not love. This is not what a husband and wife share or a boyfriend and girlfriend who love each other. This is bad. Do you understand?'

Adam nodded. 'They are awful.'

'They certainly are disgraceful,' Audrey shook her head and gave the photos back to her son.

'I'm going to take these, and you are not to speak to anyone about them. Is that clear, Adam?' his father asked.

'I have to tell Nate.'

'No, you don't,' his father said. 'This is a Murphy family secret, Son, and I will deal with this.'

'Are you going to tell Griffin's father?' Adam asked, alarmed.

'You need not worry or think about this again, Adam darling. Your father will deal with it,' Audrey said. 'Like he always does.' She said the last words with pride in her voice.

'Exactly,' James agreed. 'Pretend you never received this filth,' he said, putting the photos back in the envelope. 'Don't be worried about Griffin. I will handle this, and you won't be in any trouble, but I don't want you hanging around him. Understand?'

Adam nodded, not looking convinced but relieved that he would no longer be encouraged to foster the friendship.

'And you will tell no one, Adam. Loyalty to the family first and foremost. Yes?'

'Yes, Dad.'

But he was going to tell Nate because Nate was his family. They were like brothers and best friends, and Nate would not tell anyone either.

Then, to Adam's surprise, his father and grandmother both left, and he realised he hadn't been punished. He was so pleased he didn't care that he still didn't know anything about sex.

Chapter 19

Now...

At his request, Tom Hartigan – security guard to Adam and his family, whether Adam liked it or not – arrived to collect Jack Bernham at the airport after midday on Thursday. The famous singer was due to fly in with his fiancé, Winsome, tomorrow, but Jack's band wanted to arrive a day earlier and get a few practices in. Well, that would be the story he'd tell people; the truth was different. The band stayed with the equipment; Tom attempted to whisk Jack away, but he would have none of it. He happily signed autographs, posed for selfies with fans, and signed parts of body flesh presented to him by attractive women. After much stopping, they arrived at Tom's car and departed to Stones Corner so that Jack could see his godson, soon to be his stepson.

'Hopefully, he won't have a client,' Jack said. 'How is he?'

'Alive and kicking. I'm not sure he likes surprises as much as you do,' Tom forewarned him.

'I heard about the patient with the knife. I bet he wasn't expecting that. But he's always attracted his share of women falling in love with him,' Jack said with pride in his voice, as if Adam was his own. There was already enough speculation about whose son Adam was without adding a third to the lineage.

Tom didn't feel the need to make small talk. He preferred to focus on his surroundings while driving and do what he was paid to do. He suspected a few media cars were following them; there were a lot of sites with a lot of entertainment content to be made. He'd try and lose them at the lights, but it wouldn't be easy. Jack hummed next to him as he messaged people on his phone – a free performance for Tom.

Taking the tunnel had them in Stones Corner in good time, and Tom turned into the building that housed the offices of *Delaney and Murphy*. He used one of the visitor parks allocated to the business and was pleased no one had attempted to follow them in. The men alighted and took the stairs. Tom was alert and used the codes he had installed to buzz them through.

At the door, Tom smiled, and Jessica's eyes widened with excitement. She jumped up on seeing Jack. It was easy to like Jack; he was easy-going and down to earth. Jack grabbed Jessica in a bear hug, which she would boast about for the next week to anyone who would listen.

'He's not here,' she said on release, 'but he'll return soon. I'll call him and hustle him along.' She returned to her desk and hit Adam's automatic dial number; the engaged single came up.

'Where is he?' Tom asked.

'He didn't say. He's supposed to be doing reports, but he took off in his car. Rob's gone for the day, Nate's on the phone... no, he's off,' she said as Nate's door swung open, and he grinned on seeing Jack.

'You're here!'

'In the flesh.'

The men hugged with some enthusiastic back slapping. 'Where's your bag? Are you staying with the band or with us?'

'Bags are in the car, and I'm staying with you guys if that's cool?'

'Hell yeah,' Nate said, pleased for the company. 'Where's Winsome?'

'Flying up tomorrow. She had a dress fitting and other girl stuff to do,' he said, not revealing the truth that he and Tom knew and waving his hand as if the vagaries of what women do before marriage were too exhausting to fathom.

'Yeah, best to leave that alone,' Nate agreed, Jack laughed, and Jessica rolled her eyes.

'I'll try Adam again,' Tom said, calling the number and knowing he'd most likely be the last person Adam would pick up the phone for, and he was right, it went to message bank.

Jack reached inside his jacket and handed Jessica an envelope. 'Tickets to my concert, if you still want to go?'

She gave a small scream of delight and clapped her hands together. 'Thank you! How exciting, I've got to call Mum and tell her. Nate, can you try Adam again and hurry him along, please,' she ordered him, returning to her desk.

Nate rolled his eyes. 'You wouldn't believe I'm the boss,' he said drily, and the men laughed.

'Actually, Mum can wait, I'll make coffee.' Jessica jumped up again.

'I'm interrupting everyone, sorry,' Jack said. 'I was just going to visit on the quiet.'

'Impossible,' Jessica smiled at him.

Tom moved to the window and looked down at the street. 'We might have had a bit of media follow us.'

Nate and Jessica exchanged looks.

'So, Adam is still dodging them, then?' Jack asked, joining Tom at the window and seeing a couple of photographers loitering.

'He gets a few reporters here a week at the moment,' Tom answered. 'He's refused to do the family shot for your magazine deal.'

Jack shrugged. 'No big deal.'

The response angered Tom, who couldn't believe how everyone pandered to Adam when he wanted to grab him by the shoulders, give him a good shake, and tell him to wake up to himself. Recollections of protecting the kid who wouldn't speak to him or dragging Adam kicking and yelling to photoshoots were fresh in his memory. The kid was a brat, and the adult was entitled.

Nate hung up. 'He's almost here; he was on his way back.'

'Well, I can't surprise him now, but I'll happily have that coffee,' he said, following Jessica into the kitchen.

Adam almost sighed with relief when he saw Nate's number come up on his phone. The plan had worked – Jessica must have spilled what Adam thought of Griffin, and Nate was back on deck.

'Hey,' he answered.

'Hi, where are you?' Nate asked as if nothing had ever happened between them; his voice sounded normal.

'Cruising around. I drove past your old place.'

'Yeah?'

Adam heard the smile in Nate's voice.

'How'd it look these days? Mum couldn't believe the new owners cut down her tree in the front corner.'

'Yeah, it's still gone,' Adam joked, and Nate laughed.

'Jack's here. Get your ass back here.'

'Is he? Great. I'm two streets away. Mum?'

'Nope.'

'Right. See you soon.' Adam hung up and felt like a load had fallen off his shoulders. He could count on one hand the number of times in his life he had fallen out with Nate, and it never sat well with either of them. All was right in the world again.

Then...

Audrey wasn't dropping Adam to school today; it was one of her bridge days. But Adam knew something was up, even before he and Charlie left for school – the adults were acting strange. Audrey, Charlie and his dad were talking in low voices. They thought he was still in his room, but he heard some of it. There had been a fire... a resignation... leaving the country. He heard the rumble of his father's low voice.

'The choice was to resign or be exposed.'

'Did the fire get rid of all the evidence?' Audrey asked.

'If he were smart, it would have. But no.'

'You haven't kept the photos in your possession, Mr Murphy?' That was Charlie's voice.

'No. I gave them back to Maxwell on the proviso he got out of town but not before I showed several of the top brass, and they created a file.'

'Good thinking, James. You don't want him coming back on you and framing you for having them,' Audrey said.

'The inspector was intending to organise a raid, the fire is convenient,' his dad said. 'I've agreed not to run the story if Maxwell clears out fast, and only for his family's sake. I wouldn't care if he got buried.'

'How is he going to explain the hasty resignation?' Audrey asked.

'The old line – wanting to spend time with his family, the fire was a wakeup call of what was important, etc.'

He heard Audrey scoff and ask, 'What of the boy?' But Adam couldn't hear the answer. Then Charlie asked, 'When will the move be?'

'The sooner, the better,' James Murphy said.

Adam's heart was beating a million miles an hour. He didn't want to move. He had his best friend Nate and his friends at school like Stuart, and he was on the cricket.

Adam would never ask his father, and Audrey might have told him had she been taking him to school, but he kept his questions for the drive with Charlie, and as soon as the Jaguar left his family home, he turned in the front seat to face her.

'Charlie, I don't want to leave.'

She glanced at him, surprised. 'Why are you leaving?'

He breathed a small sigh of relief. 'I'm not?'

'No. Are you?'

'No, not if you say so.'

Charlie frowned as she studied the traffic around her and tried to focus on Adam as well. 'Did someone say you were leaving?'

'No.'

'Okay.' Charlie said and, arriving at the corner, asked, 'Are we picking up Nate?'

'Yes, please.'

She indicated left to take the slight detour past Nate's house as she usually did every Wednesday and Friday. Within moments, they arrived at his neat timber home with the timber fence, and Nate was standing out the front. He leapt in with a grin, which everyone in the car reciprocated.

'Hi Charlie, Murph,' he said, slamming the door of Audrey's Jag.

'Hello Nate, are you well?' Charlie asked with a glance in the mirror to him.

'Very well, thank you,' he answered politely and buckled up quickly because Charlie refused to drive on until he did.

The three of them enjoyed the journey in the prestige Jaguar with its leather seats, timber steering wheel, and clean scent. Given that Audrey was not with them, there was no talkback radio or quiz.

Adam turned side on to look at Nate and Charlie.

'Something has happened.'

'What?' Nate asked.

'I don't know, but Audrey, Dad and Charlie were talking about it. Someone's leaving. I heard it.'

Charlie's lips thinned as she pressed them together.

'Are you leaving Charlie?' Nate asked, worried.

'No!' Adam exclaimed, his eyes huge, his distress evident.

'I'm not leaving,' she assured them, 'no one in this car is leaving.'

Adam relaxed a little, but he knew something wasn't right. 'Tell me, Charlie, please,' he begged. 'What were you all talking about? Was it about the photos?'

'What photos?' Nate asked from the back. No one answered that question.

Charlie gave a small nod as if conceding that she would tell him everything. 'You'll hear about it at school today anyway.'

The boys waited, Adam not taking his eyes from her.

'There was a fire last night at the Maxwell household.'

Adam gasped. 'Griffin's place?'

'Yes. A large part of the house was burnt down, and this morning, Griffin's father resigned from his government position and announced he and the family were moving overseas. Griffin will be going, too.'

Adam turned to look at Nate, and then he grinned. Nate returned his smile.

'That's great, he's gone,' Adam said.

'I thought he was your friend,' Charlie looked confused.

Adam shook his head. 'Nate's my best friend. Griffin's like a bit creepy.' He turned to look at Nate as they neared Nate's school.

'Want to go to the creek after school?' Nate asked.

'Sure.'

Charlie pulled over, and the boys said goodbye; she watched until Nate entered the school grounds and then departed.

When Adam got to school, the buzz was the same. He thanked Charlie at the school gate because Audrey said he should always remember that Charlie was protecting him when she could choose to protect anyone she liked – so he was special. Audrey was the only one who said that to him; he was pretty sure his parents didn't realise he was special.

He ran up to Stuart, his backpack thumping on his back, and joined his group's huddle.

'Murph, you won't believe it. Griffin's gone,' Stuart said, and everyone added their version of events.

'There was a fire.'

'He got expelled.'

'His gangs going to break up now.'

'Do you think he started the fire?'

Adam breathed a sigh of relief. All was good in his world again.

Chapter 20

Now...

Adam's radio kicked back in when Nate disconnected his call; Adam listened to talkback and news, a habit he learned from Audrey and couldn't shake. He liked to know what was going on. An interview wound up with some guy who had written a book on throwing in his job and living off the land – he survived. Then he caught the news piece: 'Fans of *The Voice of the Nation*, Jack Bernham were quick to get on social media this morning when he was spotted with his band at Sydney airport heading to Brisbane. If he was trying to slip into town unnoticed, it failed. Hundreds of fans were on hand to greet him on arrival, and no, the *It Girl*, Winsome Keeley, was not with him. Jack told our on-the-ground reporter that Winsome was flying up after some last-minute wedding dress fittings. So, don't rush out there now. Jack has left the building, and good luck trying to get a ticket to one of his two concerts.'

'Surprise!' Adam mumbled and wondered where his mother was and when she was arriving. Then the talkback host added more to the story, 'It's been 14 years since James Murphy died, a long time for a beautiful widow to be alone. I can imagine the family and her fans must be very excited for Winsome.'

Alone! Adam scoffed. He felt like ringing in and offering his own talkback – his mother might not have been married the past fourteen years, but she never spent a day alone. She was always in some relationship. It always pained him when he heard his life spoken about by strangers. And as he came down the street to his office, he saw the media outside and sighed. If only he could detour into the office another way, but instead, he inhaled and faced it head-on. It only took a few minutes for them to realise it was him going in since they were waiting for Jack to come out, but it was enough time to buy him entry into the car park but not escape. Three ducked under the grill as it came down, including a young woman and two guys, one being a photographer.

He parked, got out of the car, and flashes went off. One of the young reporters held his phone up to video him.

'Hi Adam, are you here to see Jack?' he asked.

'I work here,' he said, then regretted saying that and making it public knowledge. 'But yeah, it's great Jack is in town.'

'When is Winsome arriving?'

'Before the wedding,' he answered, choosing his words carefully. He had learnt quickly that everything could be twisted. The last time he had responded that he didn't know or hadn't heard, the story ran off on a tangent that he was warring with his mother and of a family rift. Adam knew to stick to short, sharp facts.

He paced to the stairs and flipped open the exit door to let them out. 'You guys will need to go that way,' he indicated as he started up the stairs, but they followed him, asking the usual questions.

'Are you looking forward to the wedding?'

'Did you ever expect Jack would become more than your godfather?'

'Will your stepsiblings be coming?'

He almost bit at that one. He was an only child, but if he was the prime minister's son, he'd have stepbrothers and stepsisters. His jaw locked, and his expression stiffened until he saw Jessica and Nate at the door, ready to let him in without pinning in the code and behind them, the office blinds closed.

'Nothing to see here, thanks for coming,' Nate said to the media, and they closed the door behind Adam.

'Thanks,' he said and exhaled, then saw Jack near the window and grinned.

'I'm sorry to cause all this drama,' Jack approached him, arms wide and embraced Adam before pulling away and studying him, keeping a grip on Adam's shoulders.

'It's all good. Welcome back. Are you staying at the house?'

'If you'll have me?'

'Isn't it your house now?' Jessica said and scoffed. 'Well, legally, once you are married.'

'Yeah, as Jessica said, it's your house too,' Adam said. He and Jack grinned, but neither corrected her. Only Nate knew that Adam inherited the large river mansion and kept it for Audrey to live there for as long as she wanted to and to house his mother and soon-to-be stepfather anytime they visited. Currently, Nate was living in one of the wings, too. Adam would never move back; as soon as Audrey was gone, it would be on the market.

'So can we do a catch-up barbeque tonight, or have you busy people all got plans?' Jack asked, looking around the group.

'I have no life,' Nate joked, 'count me in. Jessica?'

'I'd love to!'

'I'll hustle up Audrey and Kelsey,' Adam said. He looked at Tom. 'Are you free?'

Tom's eyes narrowed. 'I know you would prefer I wasn't there. I'll have the security team ramped up on the boundaries since you all will be.'

'Come,' Jack insisted, 'you and Adam can surely bury your differences for one night.'

Neither man said anything.

'Or maybe not,' Jack answered, and Jessica stifled a laugh.

They sat around on the visitors' chairs in reception, and Jessica grabbed Adam a coffee and topped up everyone else, then followed with the biscuit tin.

'We only get the good shortbread biscuits when there are visitors,' Nate joked, taking two and making Jack laugh.

'I feel very special,' he said, winking at Jessica as he took a couple.

'So, what's the deal with Mum?' Adam asked.

He saw Tom look at Jack as if they both knew something more.

'She's arriving tomorrow. She just had to do a final dress fitting.' Jack didn't look at Adam as he spoke, so he knew there was more to it.

'The jig's up. Spill it,' Adam said.

Jack winced and then sighed, looking at Adam. 'She's arriving tomorrow with Stephanie...'

Adam felt all eyes turn to him at the mention of his ex-wife, his mother's publicist whom she deemed far too important to dispense with despite her son divorcing Stephanie. His feelings didn't play into it. He schooled his face not to react. He was well versed in that.

'Where's Stephanie staying?' Nate asked cautiously.

'At a hotel, a make-up artist is also travelling with them. The ladies have booked rooms near the wedding venue,' Jack said. He swallowed.

'And?' Adam asked with trepidation, and Jack grimaced.

'Your mum would like you to meet her at the airport and collect her from her flight with Tom, of course,' he added hurriedly.

'That's so nice,' Jessica said, and everyone turned to her. 'Isn't it?'

'So, this is how Mum will get her photo opportunity?' Adam asked. 'Did she not come with you today just for that reason?'

Jack gave a small casual shrug. 'You know your mum; she likes to give the press what they want.' Adopting an apologetic look, Jack added, 'She asked if you could wear a dark suit. Don't kill the messenger.'

Adam sat back, tapping on his leg as frustration raged through him. Then he realised why his mother wanted the dark suit, put his head back, looked at the ceiling, and muttered, 'Oh, wow, Stephanie's good.'

'What's going on?' Nate asked.

Adam looked at him, then Jack. 'I know what is going on here. Mum will put her arm through mine, look like mother of the year with the son who she claims ruined her figure and then...' he stopped and shook his head slightly.

'What?' Jessica asked, fascinated.

'You know what Mum and Stephanie are doing with this photo, don't you? I won't shoot the messenger, I promise,' Adam assured Jack.

'Nope, you're one up on me. I'm not privy to anything Winsome organises with her publicist.' Jack did Adam the courtesy of not mentioning Stephanie's name. 'Except if I'm required to be front and centre. What do you think is going on? Why the dark suit?'

Adam winced, suddenly uncomfortable sharing his thoughts. 'I'm probably wrong. Nothing.'

'Say it, you're amongst friends,' Nate said, and Adam would have dismissed him, but with their recent tension, he felt the need to reinforce they were the best of friends.

'It's been 14 years last week since Dad died. Stephanie's recreating the photo that ran when I was sixteen... at the funeral. I could be wrong,' he added again hurriedly.

'Ooh, I saw that,' Jessica said unashamedly that she had been checking out Winsome's life online. 'You were there in your dark suit, and your mum looked so gorgeous and petite clinging to your arm like you were the man of the family now. It was very glamourous.'

Nate nodded and tried to shut her down. 'It was a funeral.'

'Oh, of course,' she said, and Adam saw her look of embarrassment.

'Don't worry about it,' he said casually, 'it's history.'

'Let's hope you're wrong,' Nate said.

'Yeah,' Adam flipped it off, not wanting to be the centre of any more attention or overly dramatic. 'It's fine, I'll just do it, and she might give up on the family portrait at the wedding then, so Kelsey doesn't have to deal with that.'

'I'll collect you from here an hour before,' Tom said.

'My excitement knows no bounds,' Adam said drily, and Jack laughed a hearty laugh. Jessica and Nate did their best not to for Tom's sake, as the security guard rolled his eyes and stormed off, muttering under his breath.

Chapter 21

Griffin Maxwell knew the moment he had Rain under his control, and it started when he entered her room that evening after he had shared a few drinks with Zach and Ben. She was expecting him. At his request, Zach told Rain that Griffin wanted to spend one last night with her before she returned to care for her mother. For old-time's sake. Zach reported Rain was thrilled; it had been eight months or so since Griffin had last made his way to her bed. He admitted he was sorely tempted after watching one of her private content sessions for a client but restrained himself. He wanted to go several rounds with the new girl, and the release from the heightened frustration would be all the better for it.

He entered, closed Rain's bedroom door, and admired her as she stood in the window of the large room she was allocated. Griffin moved closer to observe her, and she invited his admiration. He wanted to strip off her silk garments, run his hands over her beautiful olive skin and through her long chestnut hair. Her dark eyes watched him so longingly; her full figure was in admirable shape, as he expected, and the red silk underwear she had chosen with the see-through wrap showed her to her best advantage.

Griffin knew how to play the game and did not say a word. He moved closer, cupped her face in his hands, and kissed her long, hard and intimately. Rain was putty in his hands. He broke off, saw her glazed look and led Rain to the bed. Griffin slipped off her wrap, letting it fall to the ground, and gently steered her to lie down in front of him. He looked at her as he hardened with longing and then left her waiting while he moved back to the window and undressed slowly. The girls knew not to undress him unless he requested it. The control was completely in his hands.

Rain watched as he removed every manly piece of expensive clothing: his dark linen shirt and white pants, polished shoes, and expensive watch. He turned to her in fitted white boxers that highlighted the impressive torso of a man who worked out to be admired. The discipline of mind and body would let him present nothing less.

It wasn't going to be gentle lovemaking, though, nor gentle sex for that matter, he had decided. He was seething with anger at her trickery. Griffin had almost released her with her funds intact and the contract voided so she could care for a dying mother, and she had played him. He was about to amend the contracts if she had just waited, but now, her deception ruled her out. His own mother had been the greatest love of his young life before their father took them overseas, and she deserted him. Left them both. He understood the love for a mother and hated his father for her departure.

Griffin pulled Rain back up from the bed, and she gasped slightly at his roughness. He pressed on her shoulders, dropping Rain to her knees, and she knew what to do, what was expected. She had hoped her lips would touch his again and that there would be some more kissing and passion, but he was putting her lips to work and was rough about it, holding the back of her head, twisting his hand in her chestnut hair streaked with gold which he had paid for, and forcing the speed he wanted. Before she could finish the job, he pulled her off him, turned her to face the bed and stripped her red underpants, entering her roughly.

Rain muffled a cry of pain as best she could; Griffin ignored her. He unclasped her bra, throwing it the way the wrap went, and grasped her breasts while he thrust in from behind. When he was sated, he lay her back on the bed and lowered himself on her. She expected he would reciprocate and deliver her pleasure, but he had no intention of giving her one more thing.

Griffin smiled as he moved side-on, leaned on his elbow, and looked down at her. Gently, he moved a strand of her hair from her face and ran his hand over her, watching as her skin goose-bumped and her breathing quickened in anticipation. Regardless of how rough he was, she still looked at him expectingly and with desire. *Stupid bitch.*

'I'll miss you,' she said, the first words she had uttered.

'Then don't go. You don't have to, do you?'

'My mum really needs me.'

'Given she's been dead for years, I doubt that.' He delivered the line without emotion and saw her flinch like she had been hit. 'Did you think I would not investigate?'

He knew how vulnerable she would feel now, completely naked, with him leering over her, having just taken what he wanted.

She opened her mouth, and Griffin hissed, 'Not a word. You have two options.' He waited, and she nodded, understanding. 'You can depart, and that suits me fine. Zach will give you an invoice and detailed account of what you owe us.'

'But I've earned six figures, Zach told me!'

'Oh, you have. You have been a great earner, Rain. Beautiful, desirable, every man's fantasy. But your costs are very, very high. Board, food, makeup, grooming, gym, clothing, beauty treatments...' he waved his hand around. 'We extend generous credit, so you have a few years to pay me back.'

Tears were now running down her face as the reality of the situation struck. She was so close to leaving, or so she thought, but now she would leave as she arrived, broke with nothing to fall back on.

'Or you can take your six-figure income, fully intact, when you finish your contract with us. But you will serve out your remaining contract at the VIP House.'

Her mouth fell open, and her eyes widened in shock.

'I don't want to be a prostitute.' She reached for the sheet to cover herself, but he battered it away. Griffin loved this part. There had only been three or four of his women over the years that fell by the wayside, but seeing how they still loved and needed him, how they doubted in the last moments that they should leave him, and then when he had them completely at his mercy, it was as good as any sex, maybe better.

'Can I stay working here, in the studio, for the rest of my contract?' she asked and bit her lips, her eyes begging for mercy from him.

He shook his head. 'I believe you have breached that contract. You'll find in your fine print the bit about the choice of roles, which is at my discretion. I've always been fair to you; you can't claim the same in return. I think bondage and fetishes will become you. So, are you leaving or staying, or do you need some time to think about it?'

Griffin particularly loved when the gleam in their eyes became one of hate. That boded well for the VIP House.

'I am staying,' she said so low he could barely catch the words.

'Excellent. You will earn even more at the VIP House. By the time you finish your contract, you will be a very wealthy, self-made woman.' He pushed himself off the bed, went to the window and dressed, putting all his clothes on with the same precision and speed at which he took them off. Turning to her, he wished her a good night, but then she did something unexpected.

Rain ran at him, beating him with her fists. At first, he thought it was amusing. She was not a threat to him until her fingernail scratched his face and drew blood.

His eyes flared with pain and anger, and his hands found her throat. Rain's eyes bulged, and she hit him harder, gasping, but Griffin did not let go. This was how it ended for another, and he was prepared to go all the way if provoked. She had provoked him, after all.

'I gave you everything,' he said through clenched teeth as his hands tightened around her throat. 'Even love.'

The more she fought, the harder he gripped. And then she was lifeless, the fight in her gone. He picked her up and threw her on the bed, done with Rain for good. Zach would clean it up later.

He touched his cheek, consulted a mirror and dabbed it with a tissue from her dressing table. *Stupid bitch.*

He headed to the spa. If Zach or any of the girls were there, that would be a bonus. He felt like company.

Skye could see a small light radiating through the curtains of Rain's room, but she wasn't sure if Griffin was still there, intended to stay the night – that was a rarity – or had left. He was due just after 9pm, and she knew from experience he would be gone by 10.30pm at the latest. It was nearing that now, and Rain had promised to come to see her the moment Griffin left, and they could have their last night together before Rain departed the next day. She knew Rain's secret, but she hoped the lie that would see Rain leave might work for her in time.

Sadly, Skye could understand how excited Rain was about Griffin's visit, pathetically, she wished he would desire her again too. He was a powerful lover and ruined her for an ordinary man. Although an ordinary life had a great deal of appeal to her at the moment. Zach, on the other hand, was an arrogant lover, only interested in his own pleasure and demanded his ego, along with other things, was stroked.

She moved out onto her balcony and looked over the estate. It was quiet, even with over a dozen people living on site, but absent of the noises of the suburbs that she was used to and missed. A walk, she decided, and then a subtle check-in on Rain on her way back, that would buy Rain a little more time. There was no need to grab her room key, no one locked their rooms – everything was supplied by the management, and there was nothing to steal that couldn't be asked for, even if she was in a more prestigious room due to her success and longevity.

Skye could hear voices and laughter coming from the pool area as she walked along the timber paths lit by solar lamps. Edging closer enough so she was not seen and invited to join them – she had promised Rain she would join her – she saw Griffin was in the spa with several younger girls, including the new girl, Dawn. Zach was there too, but he was drying himself as if to leave.

I hope he is not going to Rain as well for her last night.

The thought made her shudder, but it would not surprise her. So, Griffin was finished with Rain, at least. Two thoughts charged at her – a slight annoyance that Rain had not yet dropped in and then concern that Rain was heartbroken or too emotional after the encounter to visit her just yet. She turned and hurried back, arriving at Rain's door and knocking softly.

'Just me,' she announced and waited.

Maybe she's in the shower.

She knocked again a little louder and then opened the door slightly. Rain was lying on the bed, her eyes open, looking at the ceiling.

'Oh, Rain,' she said, her voice full of empathy as she closed the door behind her and entered.

Skye stopped in her tracks, and her hands flew to cover her mouth before a terrified guttural scream escaped. Rain's eyes were glazed, her neck was red and bruised, and her chest wasn't moving.

The terror froze her in her tracks. Then, unable to take her eyes off Rain, she stepped back and back again, bumping into the door. She went to leave and then thought better of exiting the way she came in. What if anyone saw her? Could this be pinned on her? Jealousy at Rain leaving? A fight over Griffin?

Skye ran to the balcony doors where she could go out unseen, climb over the railing and race back to her own cabin. But Skye heard a noise at Rain's door before she could do so. She wrapped the curtain around her, staying behind a chair to hide her feet and did not move. Her heart was thundering, and Skye was sure her fast breathing would give her away in the silent room. She had never seen a dead person or a murder scene. The horror of it nearly made her scream aloud.

They will kill me, too, if they find me here.

I'm dead. I'm dead. I'm dead.

Frozen, she listened and heard a man's voice. He was swearing under his breath. It was Zach, and he had either come to claim Rain for himself or been sent to do Griffin's dirty work and clean up. How could she ever act normally again around them?

I'm dead.

She heard him move away from the bed and head out again, slamming the door behind him, and Skye did not need a prompt. She raced out through the balcony doors, jumped over the small timber railing, and returned to her own room, grateful for the cloak of darkness, convinced now of the need to obey until her contract was up.

Chapter 22

Adam was always on time for the 9am Friday morning team meeting at *Delaney and Murphy*. He would actually prefer it to start at 8am, but that, according to Nate, would never happen unless they didn't want Nate in attendance.

'You're the Delaney of *Delaney and Murphy*,' Adam had reminded him. 'I think you are meant to be present.'

While many businesses started the week with a team meeting to plot what was ahead, not *Delaney and Murphy* – it was more of a week that was meeting on a Friday, and Jessica had the routine down. No appointments were made for the men until after 10.15am, the coffee order was booked the night before, and she picked it up on the way in. Adam had been trained to pick up a box of pre-ordered pastries from the baker three doors up after he parked – but Danielle had taken over that duty while Adam was being harassed by media loitering on the street. Adam was not likely to resume the duty given how capably Danielle handled it, or so he told her with a grin. Nate was given no jobs in the hope he could just manage to arrive on time. His excuse of dropping Matilda to school did not work on days when he didn't have her sleeping over, but that did not stop him from trying it on. Today, the entire team, including Danielle and Rob, were present, and Tom was due to pick up Adam for the airport trip at 10am.

The meeting was Jessica's idea to keep everyone connected and supported. While they waited for Nate and the girls talked about the wedding again, Adam texted his ex-wife, Stephanie.

'I know what you are trying to do with this photo opportunity today. Bit tacky, don't you think?'

It only took a minute, and she shot back a reply.

'Hi Adam, I have no idea what you are talking about. Stephanie xx'

Adam messaged back. *'Oh good. Well, safer then if I'm not there, and Tom can do his thing just protecting one person, Mum.'*

She fired back: *'Fine then. It will be a lovely photo. You were there supporting your mum at your dad's funeral, and now you are here welcoming your mum home to give her away. It's no biggie.'*

Nate rushed in, and Jessica called out to Rob that they were ready. Just then, Adam's phone rang, and he frowned at the caller, rising from the table to take the call.

'Hi, Mum.' He glanced at the clock. 'Okay... uh huh... bye.' He returned to the table, and Nate dropped down opposite him and said, 'Well, that was warm and fuzzy.'

Adam scoffed. 'Her flight's on time. They are departing now. She's looking forward to seeing me at the airport... in a dark suit.'

'Lucky you are wearing one then,' Rob added, sitting and accepting a coffee. Nate, Adam and Jessica didn't discuss the barbeque last night since Rob and Danielle weren't in attendance, but Nate asked, 'So when are you officially moving back into the River Mansion?' He reached for a croissant.

'That's not next on the agenda,' Jessica protested.

'What? Are you moving out of Adam's mansion, Nate?' Danielle asked, alarmed. Adam grimaced at the term mansion as Danielle continued, 'Although I guess we could flat together unless you want me out of your place, you know, if you got a girlfriend.' She looked at Jessica with no subtly. Jessica ignored her, hellbent on pushing her agenda.

'No, I wasn't planning on moving out,' Nate said and looked at Adam. 'Am I?'

Adam huffed. 'No. Stay, look after the place, manage the lawn mowing guy and cleaner, and look after Audrey.'

Danielle rolled her eyes. 'No wonder you don't want to move out.'

'I never see Audrey unless she needs a lightbulb changed in her wing. She goes out more than I do,' Nate said and added, 'which is a little unsettling given she's nearing eighty. My social life is sad.' He sighed and got a chuckle from the rest of the group.

'Is she planning on having a big bash to mark the occasion?' Rob asked, stirring sugar into his cappuccino.

Jessica tapped the table. 'We've deviated from the agenda!'

'I don't know,' Adam said. 'I think the wedding will be enough excitement for all of us. She might take a trip somewhere, but not like last time when she walked the Camino. Not enough wine bars, apparently.'

Rob laughed out loud. 'Yeah, it is a spiritual quest. I think it is meant to be short on wine bars.'

'Maybe she thought a spiritual quest would be the search for the best spirits – Vodka, Gin, Scotch,' Danielle suggested.

'Now that would be a great holiday,' Nate added.

Jessica ignored them all and called for order. She kicked off with an overview of the weekly admin, outstanding client payments for Nate, client bookings and media requests for Adam, and client updates for Rob. Then, each person around the table had their moment in the sun to give a brief update on their workload. 'Dan, it's your turn,' Jessica said.

'Oh good,' Danielle brightened and put down her jam roll. 'Two really interesting things on my surveillance duty... I did come back to tell you yesterday, Nate, but you were out seeing a client, and then you didn't answer my call last night.'

'Yeah, last night I actually was social,' he said. 'So, how did you go?'

'Only one person came and went the whole three hours I sat studying the Wellness Camp,' Dan said as she wiped her hands on the serviette and tapped the iPad to bring it to life. Here's some pics of the surroundings.' She up-righted it so they could watch the slide show.

'What's that at the back?' Rob asked, wincing at the screen.

Danielle paused the shot. 'It's like a separate premise, a large building with dark glazed windows, and a separate road that goes up to it.'

Nate and Adam exchanged looks.

'That'd be the VIP House, I bet,' Nate said, and Adam agreed. He filled them in on Tania's description of the house for external clients.

'It's still not illegal,' Danielle said with a shrug, 'if everyone is consenting.'

'True,' Adam agreed. 'Who was the one person you saw?'

'Ah yeah, a young guy departing. Here is the pic of his car and rego. It's an expensive car, so he's either a high-roller, on staff and paid very well – like hush money — or it's a company car. I also saw a guy on a ride-on-mower. That was about it for movement at the camp.' She started the slide show again and let it run so the men could watch at leisure.

'Anything else?' Nate asked.

'You bet,' Danielle grinned.

'That's my girl. What?' he teased.

'I found out where Griffin Maxwell goes to get a coffee every day at 10am on the mountain – his daily ristretto.'

'Trust him to drink something pretentious,' Nate said, and Adam chuckled.

'You really don't like the guy, do you?' Jessica asked, and Nate grunted.

'What's a ristretto?' Rob asked.

'I asked the same question, and the barista said it's a smaller shot of espresso using finer beans or something like that,' Danielle said with disinterest. 'It's like a power hit, apparently. He has it after his workout.'

'That'd be right,' Nate added.

'So, I could be there getting a coffee at the same time,' Adam said, bringing them back on topic, and all eyes turned to him. 'He might invite me to visit, have a sleepover,' he joked.

'You could check on the situation firsthand, maybe even meet Skye,' Danielle said.

Nate and Rob both spoke at once.

'—we need to think about this,' Nate grimaced.

'—not sure about that idea,' Rob added.

'It's only a coffee meeting,' Adam said with a shrug. 'He's not going to drug me and drag me back and make a porn star of me.'

Jessica laughed.

'I'd pay to see that,' Danielle said.

'Me too,' Jessica agreed, and Adam gave them a fake shocked look.

'I would as well,' Nate stirred his best friend, 'just so you earned some money that week.'

Adam gave him a smirk. 'Thanks. So, are we doing this?'

'We need to tell Tom at least,' Rob said.

Adam shook his head. 'Not yet. This would just be a first encounter. Let's see what falls out of it first. If I go to the Wellness Studio, we'll tell Tom if it is before the wedding. Afterwards, he's gone, so it doesn't matter.'

Rob gave a soft grunt. 'I don't like it, and I think you need to run through some scenarios of what this Griffin person might say and how you'll react before you even contemplate going there. Have a good backstory, too.'

'That's Nate's speciality,' Adam said.

'Totally agree with Rob,' Nate added. 'But I'll get onto Burnsy first and see if he can get me the car's driver's name and address. Let's find out what he is doing there.'

'Right. Are we done?' Adam asked.

'You and Nate haven't had your five minutes,' Jessica said, looking at the agenda.

'I've got nothing,' Nate said.

'Me either, and I've got a few appointments to change before Tom gets here,' Adam said, rising abruptly. 'Thanks, Jess.'

'You didn't answer the question,' Jessica reminded him. 'When are you moving home?'

'It's not my home,' Adam retorted. 'But Kelsey and I will be back from tomorrow. That okay?' he asked Nate.

'Sure, I'll be on hand to welcome you like I'm lord of the manor.'

'Which you are at the moment. We'll be leaving straight after the wedding buzz dies down,' Adam assured him.

'It's so exciting,' Jessica said. 'Do you think your mum will come in and see where you work so we can meet her?'

'No, I can guarantee you that won't interest her at all,' Adam said with a smile that indicated he was happy about that. Jessica thought it was rather sad.

Adam thanked the ladies again for the breakfast and went to the printer. He heard Jessica sigh and added, 'I was really hoping she would.'

'It wouldn't be good for business,' Nate reminded her.

'No, you are right,' she said.

Returning to his office, he saw Jessica glance at the door. Fame came at a price, and they didn't need any more stalkers or crazy fans trying to get into their secure sanctuary. She left the city for a safer environment, and he didn't want her to leave here because of his family circus.

Chapter 23

S tephanie Murphy had a win, and she couldn't wipe the smile off her
face.

Damm, I am good, she gloated.

She knew her ex-husband, Adam, would see right through her with the
photo and the request to wear a dark suit. His mother, Winsome, travelled
back and forth from Sydney to Brisbane regularly and never asked Adam
to pick her up or meet her at the airport. But if they couldn't get the
family shot for the magazine at the wedding, Stephanie was going to get
a mother-and-son shot one way or another, and thanks to Tom and Jack
working with her, she had a win!

They travelled through the airport with two of Tom's people assigned
to them from Sydney. Stephanie walked beside Winsome, and the make-up
artist travelling with them walked slightly behind, like staff. Stephanie
looked glamorous – tall, thin, blonde, dressed in a red suit with very
high nude heels. Beside her, Winsome looked petite and beautiful. As
recommended by her stylist, Winsome's look was sophisticated, not the
Avant Garde look of her youth. She wore a black dress with a high white
collar and white wrist cuffs. It was cut to highlight her slim figure, and her
short blonde hair was parted neatly at the side and worn in a pixie cut to
show off her pointy chin. Dark black tights and ankle boots finished the
picture.

The affection between the two ladies was evident despite no longer being legally related. Stephanie loved Winsome and was grateful she was not let go when she divorced Winsome's son. To her surprise, Winsome never even considered the idea; she blamed Adam for being inflexible and too conservative, and she blamed the influence of Audrey. Both she and James never shied from publicity and enjoyed all it had to offer.

Stephanie was the first to admit she and Adam were unsuited, but he could still make her heart stop on appearance, and she still wanted to bed him. But once the gloss wore off their relationship, the sex began to wane, and the fights began. He never wanted to take advantage of being in the in-set, and she wanted to be seen at all the best events. It was good for business, and Stephanie was a top-order social climber. Soon, her constant trips away put enough distance between them that separation became easier.

At work, Stephanie fielded plenty of requests for her services and accepted some jobs that she could assign to her small staff team. However, as for being hands-on, Stephanie only represented very elite clients, and Winsome Keeley was one of them. Winsome paid well and was easily promoted – the media lapped up her stories. Even though Winsome had moved into a more mature-aged model group, she was great magazine fodder. The column centimetres Stephanie had already achieved from the wedding was nothing short of sensational, and the media deal she secured was ground-breaking for an Australian model. After all, Winsome was marrying Jack Bernham, and there was that elusive, handsome son who might be the prime minister's child – a publicist's dream.

The flight was quick, and Stephanie had "leaked" to select fans and media what time Winsome was departing Sydney and arriving in Brisbane. She had given her favourite reporters and photographers the scoop about Adam being on hand to meet his mother at the Brisbane airport. The news sources in attendance would circulate the shot to all the media outlets who weren't there at a price. Her adrenaline was pumping and the thought of seeing Adam hadn't even occurred to her until they were in the air.

'What do you need me to do for this photo, darling?' Winsome said, moving closer in her seat to Stephanie, 'Or will it just be a "walking through the airport" shot?'

'Oh no, more than that, which is why I requested Adam meet you. If we can't get him to do the magazine shots at the wedding, then this will be perfect and get an enormous run, I'm sure of it.'

Winsome smiled delightedly, and Stephanie continued, 'I am trying to recreate one of your most iconic photos. I hope it won't upset you.'

Winsome looked surprised. 'I can't think of any shot that would.'

Stephanie opened her laptop and the file with the brief she had set up for the image. She opened full screen to the shot at the funeral.

'Oh my. I had forgotten how young I was when James died,' Winsome said, studying herself and Adam in the photo.

'Thirty-six.' Stephanie knew all the facts if asked – a good publicist always did. Studying the image over Winsome's shoulder, she added, 'Nearly the same age I am now.'

Winsome scoffed. 'You've just turned 30, darling. Don't rush to the next milestone birthday.'

Stephanie laughed, and the two ladies sobered as they looked at the striking photo with all its vulnerability.

'Yes, 36,' Winsome continued to study the image. 'James was 46, and Adam was 16, strikingly handsome for a young boy. It is a beautiful photo.'

'He is the best of you both,' Stephanie agreed.

'That's why you wanted the dark suit.'

Stephanie nodded. 'I thought it would be sentimental to remember him supporting you on his arm then and doing so again now when you are marrying his godfather.'

Winsome nodded and looked at Stephanie. 'What a beautiful idea, darling, how clever you are. Does Adam know?'

'Yes.'

'And he's agreed to it?' Winsome asked, her eyebrows raised in shock.

'He tried to back out.'

Winsome shook her head slightly, not surprised.

'But I suspect he figures if he does this, it keeps him and his girlfriend out of my clutches for future family shots,' Stephanie said and made a face.

Winsome laughed. 'Well, this will be most interesting.'

'There's a lot of media interest. We'll get your make-up touched up just before we land,' Stephanie said, and both ladies accepted a glass of champagne despite the early hour of the morning.

Perhaps the champagne made Winsome melancholy, Stephanie thought as she watched her scroll through the photos of that day.

'I barely remember the funeral at all,' Winsome said. 'It was like we were just going through the motions, getting through the day. I can't remember who attended, and seeing the coffin was such a shock. I remember that much. Audrey was distraught, her only son.' She continued to look at each photo in great detail. 'I don't believe I've even seen some of these.'

Stephanie left Winsome with the laptop and her memories and grabbed her iPad to continue working. Before landing, she motioned for the makeup artist and swapped business seats with her so the beautician could touch up Winsome, ready for the photographers.

Exiting the plane, Stephanie's adrenaline spiked. This was the moment she loved – the energy of the media scrum, hoping they would be there in big numbers and not a scattering of a few. And hoping the fans arrived in mass and called out for Winsome. She was not disappointed, and Tom's on-ground security stepped up, surrounding them.

It was then Stephanie saw Adam approaching with Tom and another security officer on either side of him, and she smiled. He gave her a return smile that did not meet his eyes; he could still make her heart leap. She swelled with importance; her office team would be sure to promote these photos on their social media feed. It was very good for business. The fan crowd was huge and swelling. Multiple cameras and people were calling out to Winsome.

Love you, Winsome.

Show us your engagement ring.

Are you excited to be marrying Jack?

Will you be going to his concerts?

Who is making your wedding dress?

Can we get a photo with you, Winsome?

Winsome, over here!

And on it went. Adam was jostled by several photographers stepping in front of him and around him to get the best angle and flinched when grabbed. Tom took care of it. His name was called by several journalists and just as many fans. Stephanie knew him well enough to recognise the steely look in his eyes, and the lock of his jaw reflected how much he hated this. She would win no popularity awards with him for this setup.

Tom instructed him to move through a different barrier, and he did as he was told, not making eye contact with either of his security guards or Stephanie again. Then he saw his mother. Reaching her side, she leaned up to kiss him on the cheek.

'Adam, thank you,' she said. She never called him dear or darling, which Stephanie found odd, but that was just the relationship they had.

Winsome weaved her hand through his crooked arm, and he began the battle to lead them out of the airport. The security team around them kept people back but, as Stephanie had instructed, left enough room to catch the shot she was trying to establish. She moved out of the shot and watched the intriguing, handsome pair walk through the crowds. Winsome glanced to her left to keep Stephanie close, and she gave Stephanie a warm smile, which Stephanie believed spoke her thanks for the shoot's success.

But then, something changed. Winsome looked up at Adam, and Stephanie could swear she blinked back tears. Adam saw it as well and leaned his head closer to his mother, alarmed.

'What's wrong, Mum?' he asked hurriedly.

In her breathless voice, she said, 'I miss James, and to see you, you are him.'

Adam's expression softened, and he put his hand on top of his mother's that was resting on his arm. And just for that brief moment in time, the look between mother and son was one of real affection; the cameras caught it.

It was the shot splashed all over the media sites for days.

It was the shot that Kelsey purchased and framed. She sat it on the dresser next to shots of the two of them, of Adam's dad, a boyhood shot of Adam with Nate, and another with young Adam, Audrey and her Jag.

It was the photo that Audrey studied with much curiosity and some relief, and that Jack loved and wished he was in as well, so they had a family portrait.

Behind Winsome, another first was unfolding. For the first time, Stephanie felt what Tom felt. Her love and devotion took a back seat to the son who did so little to earn the reward and affection of his mother. That look Winsome gave Adam at that moment dismissed all the criticism of Adam that the two outsiders fed on. Stephanie saw then that she and

Tom would never know that satisfaction despite their loyalty. That look, that love was for Adam and Adam alone.

Chapter 24

S kye usually hated workout day, but she was grateful for it today. The content was simple – stretch and workout as provocatively as she could while wearing the most revealing and skimpiest workout outfits. Several cameras captured her at various angles as she went through her poses. There was no acting or talent involved, and it was content purely for the viewer's pleasure. She blanched at the thought but called it for what it was, and it was not acting.

Sleep had eluded her, and for most of the night, she had stood in the darkness of her room, not taking her eyes from Rain's room. She saw Zach enter again carrying something folded – a sheet or sack, she surmised. After a time, he departed with a load over his shoulder wrapped in a dark covering. She wanted to follow him but was too scared.

Watching him for as long as she could, she saw Zach head to the house on the hill that she had heard of but had never been inside, not once in her two years at the camp – the VIP House. He was barely visible in the dark, and if she lost sight of him, it took her a few moments to find him again or to see the shape of something moving. Rain was gone, and would anyone miss her? If she was the one wrapped in a sheet thrown over Zach's shoulder, would her parents persist in trying to "save" her, or would she fade from memory and from the memories of the girls she knew and left behind at the *Fidelium Wellness Studio*?

The money meant nothing to Skye anymore. On that point, Skye was crystal clear. She had to leave and now. Pulling her wrap around her tighter, she knew there was no way she could ask for another audience with the boss. She was too frightened to tell Griffin or Zach that she had changed her mind and wanted to leave. What if Griffin finished her off as well? Maybe no one ever left before their contract was up.

Oh, God. I can't believe this is happening to me.

Sheer blind panic and desperation overwhelmed her, and her breathing quickened. Skye realised she only had one option left – to escape.

But first, she had to do something for Rain. She had stood by as new girls had their "reality" moment of terror, even collaborated as required, but Skye had to act now, and it would come at a cost to Alex – the technician who watched all her sessions as he recorded them and who let her use his phone. She felt a little bad about that, but Skye also knew that Alex would deny all knowledge of giving her phone access, and she was pretty confident he knew what was going on and was happy to turn a blind eye.

'Workout time,' he announced, sitting at the desk ready to record as Skye entered. 'You look good.'

'Thanks.' Alex was not an ogler, which she appreciated, and a compliment now and then made her feel better. She paused by his desk. 'Will you let me hear my mum's voice, please?' she asked.

Alex grimaced. He didn't like doing it, but all she ever did was call, breathe and hang up.

'I'll be quick; I just like to know she's alive and still living at home... she's been unwell. Griffin gave me a letter from her,' Skye said, and, realising she was overdoing it, she stopped talking.

Alex looked around at the security cameras and, ensuring no one was near their rooms, gave her his phone.

'Thank you, Alex,' she said in her best breathy voice as if he was her dearest friend in the world. He flushed slightly and gave a quick nod.

But she didn't dial her mum this time. She rang police emergency on triple zero, and when they answered, she hurriedly said, 'Murder, Fidelium Wellness Studio.'

'Are you insane?' Alex grabbed the phone from her hand. He cut the line. 'You'll get me sacked. I trusted you.'

'There's been a murder,' she exclaimed and then glanced around nervously, dropping her voice. 'Rain is dead.'

'Shut up, stop talking. I don't care.' He pointed to the studio, his expression a mixture of shock and anger. 'Get in there! Christ! I can't believe you did that!'

'I'm sorry, Alex, but she was a friend. It will be between us, and no one will ever know I made the call from your phone. I promise. Don't say anything.'

'Of course, I'm not going to say anything. Do you think I have a death wish?'

Skye nodded, and as he continued to ignore her, she moved away into the studio. Now she had to leave. The police would come asking questions, and if she could just see them arriving, she would leave with them and ask them to escort her out. She'd be free again.

It was a week before the wedding and possibly the first morning ever that Nate was in the office before Adam, and there was a reason for that – Adam intended to come into the office but not see clients in-house this week. As Nate arrived at the door, Jessica buzzed him in, saving him several attempts at the 'stupid' code word.

'Morning, ladies,' Nate said, greeting Jessica and Danielle, who were in; it was Rob's day off. Nate had no clients until later in the day, so he hadn't bothered with a tie but wore his customary suit; today's offering was pale grey.

'Goodness, right on time,' Jessica said, her hand going to her heart. 'Lucky I'm healthy, or the shock might have killed me.'

Nate gave her a smirk as Danielle laughed.

'Is Adam sneaking in behind you?' Jessica asked, expecting him to arrive at any moment in disguise.

'No, I'm picking him up in thirty minutes. We're going to the Deco Café at Mount Tamborine for a happy reunion.'

Danielle's eyes widened. 'Oh wow, have you prepared?'

'Have we prepared!' Nate scoffed. 'We spent a whole hour on Friday with Rob going through scenarios. But as Adam said, he's not returning to the camp with Griffin; it's just a shock meeting. Griffin may not even show up.'

'I hope Adam can perform well,' Jessica said. 'So, are you going to reacquaint yourself with Griffin too?'

'No, thank God. I'm just moral support and waiting in the car to drive the quick getaway vehicle if needed. Listen, while we're talking about Adam...' Nate got serious, which he rarely did. 'Don't mention the airport photo.'

'But it's gorgeous,' Jessica exclaimed. 'I just wish Jack was in it too.'

'They both look great, especially Adam,' Danielle agreed.

Nate shook his head. 'Just let it lie. He's had enough, and all weekend, it was all Jack, Winsome and Audrey were talking about. Then Stephanie arrived to go through stuff with Winsome and started on it. Adam and Kelsey almost moved out again.'

'I'd be wrapped if it was my pic. I never take a good photo.' Jessica sighed.

'Yeah, well, you know he's not one for putting it out there, so don't mention it. It's been done to death. Okay?'

The girls nodded.

'Have you told Tom about your visit to the coffee shop?' Jessica asked.

'No, and I'm not intending to tell him. I've got to go,' Nate said with a glance at the clock. He saw the girls exchange looks and shrugged. 'Tell Tom if you want to, but you will only raise his blood pressure. He doesn't need to be involved. If he wants to do something, tell him to move the bloody media away from the building.'

With that, he entered his office, grabbed his laptop and departed as quickly as he came.

Chapter 25

The photo had blown up his weekend. Adam wanted to crawl into a cave and not emerge. The three people who genuinely knew him – Audrey, Kelsey, and Nate – could guess how he felt about having his image displayed everywhere and his emotions displayed. His mother's delight was unfathomable, especially for what he thought was such a sad moment in context, but she and Stephanie thought it was the beginning of something big, like the door had been opened to more of the same now. Adam felt the complete opposite.

He was grateful that Kelsey truly understood – it was a classic introvert reaction and triggered enough bad childhood photoshoot memories to last him years. Rob would have a field day with him analysing that. But knowing and understanding his reaction did not make handling it any easier. The photo was huge on page three of the weekend paper, with the largest circulation of the week. The footage made the end of the nightly news on Friday night. He was not only in the limelight but expressing raw emotion.

Friday and Saturday night, he could not sleep for feeling emotionally overspent and mortified. Nate was supportive, but Adam could tell he didn't understand the depths of Adam's uneasiness. Kesley and Audrey had done their best to shy him from the rest of the family for the weekend – not an easy task when they were sharing a house, even if they were in a separate wing. The more he spent in everyone's company, the more irritable he became as they planned for more of the same. He was never happier to see Monday roll around and be in the car with Nate, heading up the mountain to the café where Griffin Maxwell had his 10am coffee hit. The isolation of the mountain was a welcomed balm.

Adam pulled out of the River Mansion driveway, noting Tom's security team nearby. They didn't follow; it wasn't their brief to track him.

'Are you sure you don't want me to drive,' Nate asked.

Adam shook his head. 'If Griffin sees me in your car, he'll be suspicious if I roll up later to the Wellness Studio in my Merc. The more authentic, the better.'

'As long as you're up to driving today.'

'Why wouldn't I be?' Adam asked, defensive, aggressive, edgy like he had been all weekend.

Nate didn't answer; Adam exhaled, told himself to chill the hell out and turned to their case.

'Are you going to tell your clients', Sarah's folks, about their daughter's fan site?'

Nate grimaced. 'I feel obliged to, but Skye or rather Sarah, is an adult, and she has her right to privacy. I wouldn't want you telling Mum I was making a fortune from my online porn site.'

Adam laughed. 'And the answer is no if you want me to join you as a partner in porn.'

Nate chuckled. 'The thought hadn't occurred to me, but it might have legs,' he joked. 'Speaking of fan sites, no bad flashbacks after seeing that stuff Jessica found for us from the Wellness Studio stars?'

'No. There were no surprises there, like father-like son as far as Griffin was concerned. Trust me, that stuff we saw yesterday was tame compared to what I saw in those photos Griffin gave me for my birthday.'

'Yeah?' Nate turned to look at him. 'Or maybe you were more innocent then, and it seemed worse than it was.'

Adam shook his head. 'Nope. Some of those images are burned in my memory. I'm not expecting to see that sort of depravity again too soon. The bondage stuff in the fan site was pretty formula.' He shrugged.

'Is that speaking from experience?' Nate ribbed him.

'Yeah,' Adam joked. 'I've got a special room for that.'

Nate scoffed. 'Yeah, can't imagine that, and not real keen to either. Were you ever going to show me?'

Adam looked momentarily confused and glanced from the road ahead to Nate and back.

'The photos,' Nate clarified, 'that Griffin gave you for your birthday?'

'Oh. I don't know. Dad told me it was a Murphy family secret, and I told him you were family. But if I told you, your folks might have stopped us hanging around together.' Adam shrugged. 'I was a deep thinker for a kid,' he joked, and Nate scoffed. 'It was too long ago. I can't remember,' Adam admitted.

They drove silently for a few moments while Nate looked at his notes.

'Were they his?' Nate asked.

'No. He said they were his dad's, and there were plenty more if I wanted some.'

'Sick,' Nate said and shook his head, gripping the dashboard as Adam took another sharp bend.

'I don't know why he gave them to me,' Adam said, thinking out loud. 'Was he boasting, or showing off, or freaked out and hoping his father would be exposed? Probably not the latter, given we were eleven.'

'You know what I'm going to say,' Nate said with barely disguised disdain.

'That he knew what he was doing and loved the shock value.'

'Something like that,' Nate agreed.

Nate put the window down, inhaled the smell of the rainforest as they started their climb up the hill, and put it back up when a bug flew in after he managed to get it out again. Adam felt his gaze, and he loosened his hands from the grip he had on the steering wheel of the Mercedes.

'I know you don't want to talk about it, but friend to friend, I was touched, truly moved by the pic,' Nate said out of the blue.

Adam rolled his eyes and glanced across to the passenger seat. 'So, you said several times on the weekend. Can we let it go now?'

'But it really was a beautiful photo. Like Jessica said this morning, you looked so handsome, and the pair of you looked like you actually liked each other.'

Adam groaned. 'Seriously, enough with the photo. It'd better not be bloody hanging up when we return to the office,' he said low and under his breath.

'Just admit it was a good shot.'

'Is that all you are after? Will you drop it then?'

'Deal,' Nate agreed.

'Okay then. Yeah, I looked model gorgeous like my mother, and we're the pin-up pair for mother-and-son relationships. Happy now? Is that what you want me to say? Can we move on?'

Nate chuckled. 'Touchy about this, aren't you.'

'Do I have to knock you out?'

'Really?' Nate grinned. 'You'd do that?'

'Of course not. That's what I have security people for,' Adam retorted.

'You're a wanker.'

'You're making me that way.'

'Yeah, fair point. Righto, consider it dropped. But trust me, the media will be looking for a repeat performance at the wedding.'

'For God's sake. What is wrong with people!' Adam's lips thinned as the anger welled inside him. 'I'm just over it.'

'Good.'

Adam looked at Nate confused and snapped, 'Good what?'

'That's where you need to be for this meeting. On edge, fed up, a little angry.'

His eyes narrowed. 'You've been stirring me to get me pissed off?'

'You're the psychologist, and I thought you would have caught onto that right away when I introduced the subject out of nowhere.'

'I just thought you were being an idiot.' Adam took a sharp corner and slowed down as he continued the wind up the hill.

'Forget about the photo,' Nate said. 'It's yesterday's news, and the girls in the office won't mention it. I've seen to that.'

Adam exhaled and gave a small nod of thanks.

'But I don't want you laid back and comfortable when you meet this guy. Be on edge, be sharp. He's a snake in the grass, always was, always will be.'

Adam took a quick look at Nate – all that he could afford with the winding road.

'I'm not just saying that because I don't like him,' Nate said, correctly interpreting Adam's look. 'I'm an ex-cop. I know the type. He'll play you.'

Trust me, I'm uncomfortable about this meeting and won't let my guard down. Griffin was a first-class manipulator when we were teens, and I expect he has honed his skills to perfection.'

'Right, good,' Nate said, and they drove in silence for a short while. 'Sorry about that.'

'It's okay.'

'I thought you and Kelsey might have moved out on the weekend.'

'We discussed it. It wasn't worth the drama. Besides, it's good to see Jack, and Audrey enjoys having us all there, maybe not Mum so much.'

'Are you going to his concert?' Nate asked.

'Nuh. He sings enough around the house. I've started putting in requests.'

Nate laughed. 'So yeah, back to porn. Did you get punished?'

Adam glanced at Nate and smiled. 'No, Dad and Audrey were shocked, though. I was just about to get a talk about the birds and bees, and Dad got side-tracked by the photos, and I never got it.'

'Did you want me to fill you in, or is it too late now?'

Adam grinned. 'Thanks, I'd appreciate that. How did your dad deliver the talk?'

Nate smiled, thinking about it. 'He waited until Mum went to lunch with my aunty and then said it was time to tell me about girls.'

'What? He never thought for a moment you might bat for the other side?' Adam teased his best friend. 'The dolls weren't a giveaway?'

'Give me a break,' Nate chuckled. 'Besides, I don't think it ever occurred to Dad I might,' Nate said honestly. 'Anyway, he told me it all started with kissing and cuddling a girl and to be very careful once that started.'

'Explains a lot,' Adam joked.

Nate gave him a smirk and told him to turn the next right.

'This car has navigation.'

'I know, you tell me every time, but I don't like the interrupting voice.'

'So, did that mean you gave up the thought of kissing and cuddling with Charlie?'

'I wanted to marry her. I never thought about kissing her; I was eleven!'

'That's so sweet. I feel like I'm seeing you in a whole new light now,' Adam said with a smile.

'Shut up,' Nate told him and smirked. 'So, you never got the sex talk?'

'Yeah, Charlie gave it to me. That's why I'm so good in bed, apparently,' he joked.

'You lucky bastard,' Nate said enviously. Moments later, he warned, 'Slow down. It's in this group of shops.'

They saw the sign for Deco Coffee above one of the smaller cafes.

The energy in the car shifted. Griffin Maxwell had that effect on people.

Then...

Charlie pulled the Jag over to the curb, wished Nate a good day, and watched as he exited the back seat and entered the school grounds. Once he was through the gate and into the schoolyard, she pulled the car out again into the traffic and slowed down, hoping to fit in her discussion with Adam before arriving at his school.

'You know, Adam, you can tell me about anything. I'm on your side, always.'

'Uh huh, thanks,' he said, nodding very seriously, his large blue eyes studying her with a mix of caution and curiosity. He was a beautiful boy; she could imagine Winsome's disappointment in being unable to parade him around, but Audrey had made it clear those days were over.

'You could have told me about the photos, and I would have helped you.'

Adam's eyes widened, and his mouth dropped open in surprise. 'But Dad said it was a Murphy family secret.'

'Well, because I have to look after your safety, I'm given special access to some information,' she said. 'Did Nate see them too?'

'No way. I just put them under the bed.'

'Good thinking,' Charlie said. 'Did you want to talk about them?'

Adam shrugged.

'Did you see them all or just a few?' She was not surprised he was not forthcoming. Getting answers from kids at the best of times was hard work, and eleven-year-olds were no exception.

'I saw them all, but not for long. I don't know what some of the people were doing.'

'Yeah. They were horrid.'

'Did you see them?' he asked, shocked.

Charlie nodded. 'Some, not all. I wouldn't want to see them again.'

'Me either.'

She could feel Adam studying her, so she waited in case he was working up to a question. Audrey had given her permission to answer his sex questions since she wasn't sure James got to the sex talk, and Charlie hoped it would strengthen their trust.

'Do adults do that stuff?'

Aagh, hard question. She thought for a moment before answering.

'Some adults like to do different stuff with their partners if they both agree it could be fun. But it should never be done if one of the adults doesn't want to do it or is scared. That's not lovemaking.'

He turned to look out the window.

'Do you want to know how adults make love and why it is so special?'

He shrugged. 'Would Nate know?'

'His Dad will tell him when he thinks the time is right, just like your Dad was going to tell you, but he wanted to protect you from the photos first. So, Audrey's okay with me telling you.'

Adam looked back at her, his frustration evident.

'Don't worry,' Charlie said. 'Everyone gets told about it at some time. My mum told me when I was about your age. It's important to know, especially if you get a girlfriend.'

He nodded his agreement.

'So, when you love someone...' and she began, keeping it brief since his school neared. When she finished, Charlie added, 'You can ask me questions next time if you come up with any more.'

'Okay.'

They got out of the car, and she walked him to the school gate. 'No wild parties today at school, Mister,' she teased, and Adam grinned.

'See you, Charlie. Thanks.'

'Sure.'

She watched until he joined his friend and then returned to the car. *Thank God that's over*, she mumbled to herself. She couldn't help but smile all the way home, thinking of his cute questions in particular, 'So have Dad and Mum only done it once since there's only me?' and, 'If you don't like the girl anymore, do you have to keep having sex?' and her favourite, 'Will I look different afterwards?' Let's hope so, young man. Let's hope you will be very satisfied.

Chapter 26

Now...

Adam did everything with slow deliberation. It took some work to look natural and not self-conscious, to appear as if you are right in the moment, thinking only of what you must do that day and not being conscious of anyone around you, like Griffin Maxwell. And that is how he strode into the coffee shop, like an unsuspecting man seeking a good coffee, just before 10am when Griffin Maxwell was due for his daily fix.

'I'll get it as a takeaway, thanks,' he said to the guy he presumed was named Dan.

'Your name for the order, please?'

'Adam.'

He turned, feeling someone nearby, and his eyes locked with Griffin Maxwell. The same height, the same colouring, dressed in the same way, the same power. Adam narrowed his eyes slightly as if recognising the face but played the game. He turned back to the barista, paid for his coffee and moved away from the counter.

The man behind him moved forward and studied him.

'Adam Murphy?' he asked.

Adam did his best-surprised expression and answered with a hint of suspicion. 'Yes.'

Then Griffin smiled. 'St Joseph's Catholic School for Boys.'

Adam attempted an even more surprised look and then slowly smiled.

'You're kidding? Griffin?'

Griffin Maxwell laughed and offered his hand. 'Well, it's been a while. Have a coffee with me.'

'Sure.'

Griffin turned to the barista. 'Dan, make them both to have here, thanks.'

'Will do, Griffin. Take a seat.'

Adam followed Griffin, who he assumed had a regular seat. They sat opposite each other at a small table, studying each other.

Adam smiled and shook his head as if he couldn't believe it. 'So, you're back in the country?' He studied the adult version of the boy he knew and looked for similar traits.

'The rumours are true,' Griffin joked, and Adam laughed.

They attracted glances as the pair looked powerful and intriguing. Adam could feel Dan, the barista, studying them from behind the counter, and a couple of ladies at another table eyed them off. Adam hoped they hadn't seen page three of the newspaper or the evening news.

'You live or work up here at Tamborine?' Adam asked.

Griffin nodded. 'I run a Wellness Studio just a few kilometres over,' he said, pointing north.

'Wellness, like yoga and finding yourself?'

Griffin smiled. 'All that and more. And you? What have you become now that we're all grown up?' Griffin thanked the female waiter as the coffees were placed in front of them.

'Not dissimilar to you, I guess. I'm a psychologist.'

'Ah, helping people get out of their head then?'

'Pretty much.'

The two men continued to study each other with curiosity. Adam had to admit – not that he would to Nate – that Griffin still emanated power.

Maybe it was the confidence that came off him in waves, the expensive cut and fabric of his clothes, the three-day growth so perfectly groomed for effect, or the way he had of looking at you as if he was reading you and he wanted you in his circle of friends.

Adam cleared his throat and broke his gaze, 'Are your parents back?'

'No. Dad remarried and stayed in Malaysia; Mum is doing her own thing.'

Adam nodded and did not pursue it. He didn't care what Griffin's parents were doing, and it was just small talk.

'We never knew what happened to you. We just got told at school that there was a fire and your family moved away. It was all anyone spoke about for days.'

Griffin smiled and looked at his coffee as if rating it before taking a sip. Adam wondered what fate Dan, the barista, might befall if the coffee wasn't up to scratch. Griffin returned his attention to Adam. 'You never got to stay over.'

Adam smiled. 'No.'

'Are you still friends with that guy from the state school? What was his name?'

'Nate. Yeah, we share an office. He does consultancy work.' Adam didn't let on that Nate was an ex-cop and still well-connected, but he saw the tightness around Griffin's eyes at the mention of Nate.

'Are you still friends with anyone from school?' Adam asked.

'No, not really. Though Zach works for me, remember him?'

'Zach? Not Zach Crowder?' Adam asked, knowing full well Zach Crowder was there.

'Yes. He does my legal work.'

'Right.' Adam said nothing more about that, knowing Griffin would read between the lines of his dislike for Crowder.

'So, is your business up this way? Funny we've never run into each other before,' Griffin said.

'No, my office is just outside the city, but I had a client I saw early this morning... an assessment. Sometimes, it is easier if I come to them, and to be honest. I was keen to get out for a few hours.'

'Ah yes, I saw the weekend press and all the hype about your mother getting married. Are you still running from the media? Looking for an escape?'

Adam smiled. 'Trust me, now more than ever. I'm not interested in a profile, and my business doesn't need that kind of exposure. My clients don't want to be photographed coming into the building,' he said with an exaggerated sigh.

'You never wanted to be in the limelight from what I remember,' Griffin said, sipping his coffee. 'You were too good looking for your own good.'

Adam scoffed and looked embarrassed.

'Come and stay with me at the studio for a while,' Griffin offered. 'A day, a week, whatever you like. You can work out, swim, meet the ladies who are there doing acting and modelling studies... just get out of the limelight for a while. It'll be a good break. You can even work from there for a while if you like.'

Adam knew it was a challenge. Give up working with Nate and work with Griffin. Still, after all these years, the competition was there. He reached for his coffee, desperate to yell, 'Let's go', but he acted restrained. Instead, he answered, 'It would be good to fall below the radar for a while. The wedding is next week.'

'Swap numbers,' Griffin said, and Adam recited his. Griffin put it in his phone and then messaged Adam. 'You've got mine now. Think about it. You could stay at the Wellness Studio for as long as you like, rock up for the wedding, and retreat here until it all dies down.' He gave a casual shrug. 'We can really catch up with Zach too. He'll remember you, I'm sure.'

Adam grimaced. 'Zach gave me a hard time often enough. I'm not sure if it will be a break with him anywhere near.'

'Don't worry about him,' Griffin assured Adam as he always did, keen to win him on his side. 'I have Zach on a very short leash.'

Nate studied Griffin Maxwell through his binoculars as he sat far enough away in the passenger seat of Adam's car not to be seen. He just wanted to see him close up, and it annoyed him seeing Adam and Griffin together. It annoyed him that he felt annoyed. But something about the two of them together bothered him more than he cared to admit, like they were in a class that Nate would never be in, even if he tried – and he had no intention of putting on airs and graces. But it didn't stop him from wanting to know what it was like to be born into money and power. To wear the latest watch and drive the latest car without giving the expense a second thought. To say that you want something, and it gets delivered. But most of all, to never wonder about fitting in. People fit around you. He lowered the binoculars.

His phone rang and startled him. Nate answered. 'Hi Dan, what's up?'

'Not much. What's wrong? You sound flat. Are you there?' Danielle asked.

'Nothing's wrong, and yeah, I'm watching Adam with Griffin Maxwell as we speak.'

'Ah, that's what's wrong. You guys are funny.'

'How so?' Nate asked, not taking his eyes off the men he could see sitting back comfortably, talking like old friends.

'Guys reckon girls are bitchy, but your hatred of Griffin and Adam's of Tom is bitch-extreme.'

Nate made a snorting sound and left it at that.

'Tom just rang and asked where you and Adam were going. He heard you left the house together.'

'Did you tell him?'

'Yep. He's on his way.'

'What's he think he's going to do? Storm in and stand next to Adam like a bodyguard? Doesn't matter,' he said, 'they're winding up, and we'll pass him on the way down the mountain.'

'I told him that it was only a coffee in a public café.'

'How's it going with you two? I thought you were hitting it off for a while there.'

'Me too,' Danielle said and sighed. 'But—'

'Don't tell me,' Nate cut her off, 'he slept around.'

'Yep. With Stephanie, Adam's ex.'

'Get out of here,' Nate said, sounding like one of Danielle's girlfriends and keen for the news. 'When? How did you find out? She just arrived in town. Bastard.'

'After they arrived at her hotel, Kelsey told me, he sure is.'

'Kelsey? I didn't know you two were friendly.'

'We are. She kind of surprised me. Kelsey said she was stepping up to ensure our party was safe at the wedding and asked what I needed her to do. So, we've been talking; she's a good chick. And she overheard Stephanie boasting about bedding Tom to Winsome.'

'Oh.'

Danielle laughed. 'Yeah, Winsome wasn't that excited. I don't think Stephanie knew about her and Tom's connection. He's a dickhead.'

'Yep. Adam could have told you that... oh, he did! Got to go, Adam's coming. Talk soon.' Nate hung up and moved down in the seat in case Griffin Maxwell headed the same way, but then he saw him slide into a black Porsche parked to the right of the Deco Café.

'That'd be right,' he mumbled.

Adam slipped into the driver's seat, belted up and started the car.

'I'll let him get a head start,' he said.

'Are you alright?' Nate asked.

'Yep. Got an invitation for a sleepover, just like old times.'

'Can I come?' Nate joked.

'Nope.'

'Just like old times,' he agreed.

Chapter 27

Jessica overhead Danielle's conversation with Nate, and when Danielle emerged from his office later, she sympathised. 'I overheard; I'm sorry about Tom. What an ass.'

Danielle gave a small shrug. 'It wasn't a stretch to imagine him doing that. He had a reputation for being a womanise when I was training with him in the Army Reserves.

'But with Adam's ex? Seriously, if he wanted to find ways to piss Adam off, he's doing a fine job – first his mother, then his ex-wife. Does Adam know?'

'No. Unless Kelsey told him. Maybe we shouldn't mention it,' Danielle suggested.

'Here they are now,' Jessica said, the security camera showing Adam's car turning into the car park. The buzzer went off, and Jessica looked at the screen. She buzzed in Sergeant Matt Burns. 'Burnsy is on his way up. Timing!'

Danielle moved to the door and let him in.

'Well, thanks,' he said, taking off his police hat. 'You two home alone?'

The ladies laughed.

'Yes, enjoying a short reprieve,' Jessica said and noticed how he looked at her with greater attention than Danielle. She either had to say she was not interested, or Nate had to step up after the wedding. She hoped the latter would happen first so she could avoid the former.

'Got some news?' Danielle asked.

'Yes. When are the boys back?'

'Now, you just beat them up the stairs,' Jessica said. 'Tom has just pulled in downstairs, too.'

'Oh, good, nothing like a bit of tension,' Burnsy said, rolling his eyes.

Adam and Nate came in noisily, greeted Burnsy and Dan, and Tom came in straight behind them.

'Nice stunt,' Tom said, glaring at Adam. He turned to Nate. 'I can understand him not cooperating, but I thought you'd have a bit of sense.'

'Only a bit?' Nate asked. 'Mate, it was just a coffee meeting in a public place in broad daylight, and I was outside in the car on patrol.'

'We're not doing this,' Adam said, turning to face Tom. 'Your job is security for the wedding. This is our work. End of story.'

'Unless you get knocked off or injured before the wedding,' Tom said.

'Should I be so lucky,' Adam muttered under his breath.

'I'll get the coffee on. Burnsy's got news,' Jessica said, and Nate indicated the boardroom.

'If you are putting yourself in any danger, expect to see me,' Tom said. 'Seven days... just do your best to stay out of trouble for the week, and then I don't care what you do.'

'Touching,' Adam said, putting a hand over his heart. 'I'll be in the office for the rest of the day.'

'Right, thanks,' Tom snapped, and both men glared at each other for a moment before Adam moved into the boardroom. Tom turned to Danielle, who gave him a less-than-impressed look.

Jessica heard her say in a low voice, 'I hope your night with the publicist was good. Will it be Audrey next, or have you finished working your way through the Murphy family?'

Tom's mouth dropped open.

'Adam warned me. Apparently, he was right,' she said and moved past him into the boardroom, giving Jessica a sly glance as she departed. Jessica saw Tom throw his hands up in the air, and he departed, slamming the door behind him.

'Any insights?' Burnsy asked after Nate and Adam met with the Wellness Studio owner, Griffin Maxwell.

Adam gave a small nod and said with a serious face. 'I'm a better actor than I thought. Perhaps I should consider a career on the stage and screen.'

The group laughed.

'And give up all this,' Nate said, waving a hand around.

'Yeah, you're right,' Adam said. 'As for Griffin Maxwell, he's still full of his own self-importance. He invited me to visit and have a break from reality, and most telling, he said he had Zach on a short leash.'

'We guessed he was manipulating the stars of the studio, but apparently, it extends wider,' Nate said.

Jessica came in with the coffee pot, cups, and biscuits on a tray and began to pour, listening to the discussion.

'It's interesting the kind of loyalty he engenders,' Adam said. 'Zach's a solicitor, so he could work anywhere, but I imagine his salary and the benefits are far greater than he would make in the real world. I imagine he is also a big man amongst the ladies.'

'Having Griffin's seconds?' Burnsy asked, and the girls grimaced. 'Sorry,' he mumbled, but Adam agreed.

'What have you got?' Adam asked.

'A very interesting call came in yesterday,' Burnsy said. 'Someone rang the emergency number and said there had been a murder.'

Both men's stillness betrayed their interest.

Burnsy opened the file in his possession and told them, 'A whispered female voice on an unidentified number called.' He read from a slip of paper. 'She said "Murder, *Fidelium Wellness Studio,*" and then you could hear a male voice saying, "Are you insane?" and the line went dead.'

'Did you trace it?' Adam asked.

'Well, that part is interesting. The phone is unregistered, so all we can do is trace the call to the area, and it was definitely in the Tamborine Mountain area.'

'That's pretty wide, though,' Nate said. 'Outside the camp, thousands of residents must live up and down the mountain.'

'At least,' Burnsy agreed.

'Over eight thousand,' Danielle said and gave a small shrug. 'I research the areas that I do surveillance on.'

'So professional,' Nate said and gave her a wink. 'But that's enough to give you grounds for access, Burnsy.'

'I bet Griffin Maxwell supplies those untraceable phones to his employees,' Danielle said, 'and one of them has fallen into the hands of the ladies on site.'

'There's more,' Burnsy held up his hand. 'We got a warrant immediately, and a team visited the premises last yesterday afternoon. It's a huge place, so they didn't search it, but there was nothing untoward, no one supposedly missing, and no one willing to say anything had happened – the team on duty spoke with about a dozen people living on site.'

'That's no surprise,' Nate said, frustrated. 'One step forward and one back.'

'Your friend, Griffin, suggested it was a hoax call, and they often get them. Sometimes from disgruntled clients or models who didn't make the cut,' Burnsy said, and Adam huffed.

'Sure, they do.'

'What about the number plate? Did you get a chance to check that out – you know, the car leaving the premises on Dan's surveillance shift?' Nate asked.

'Yes. There was a guy at the wheel,' Danielle said.

'I did. The car is registered to a video technician, Alex Narula, 27 years old.'

'Ah, maybe he is an employee of the Wellness Camp with access to the girls,' Adam mused, his eyes narrowing. 'Could this Alex guy be letting Skye use his phone to call home and hang up, but this time she didn't call home? She called the police.'

'That'd make sense. Explains the calls her parents are getting with just a breather on the line,' Nate agreed. 'When Skye said murder, he freaked out and cut her off.'

'Her parents might recognise her voice if they could hear the call,' Danielle suggested.

'Good thought,' Burnsy said. 'Alex has to be worried his job will be on the line if the call is traced back to him.'

'And I suspect the woman who made the call is laying pretty low, too. It was a brave thing to do,' Adam said. 'I think I should go and have a couple of day's break at the Wellness Studio, work from there and find myself.'

'You've been missing for a while,' Nate agreed, ribbing his friend.

'Not now that a murder has been reported there,' Burnsy said, looking at Adam as if he were out of his mind.

'It's the perfect time to be there,' Adam said.

Nate agreed. 'I hate to say it, but Adam could watch the internal goings-on. If anyone mentions the call or the police raid, he can gauge Griffin's reaction and be privy to anything being discussed. If we're lucky, he might even get the chance for a one-on-one with Skye.'

'Will Kelsey be okay with that?' Danielle asked.

'Probably not, but she'd understand why if there are women in danger. She'd want to charge in herself,' Adam said, thinking about her difficult background.

Burnsy shook his head. 'Okay, I'm going to remove myself from this discussion. However, if you intend to go up there, you must let Tom know.'

Adam thought for a moment and nodded. 'Yep, you're right.'

Burnsy looked surprised. 'Wow, didn't see that coming.'

Adam gave him a smirk. 'Tom might want to come and find himself too... I wonder if Griffin will let my bodyguard attend with me.'

Nate chuckled. 'I can just see you and Tom sharing a room.'

'Unless I go as your bodyguard,' Danielle suggested and shrugged. 'I'm trained.'

'And Dan is going to guard your table at the wedding, so there's truth in that story,' Jessica said.

Danielle continued, 'Tom should stay and look after Audrey, Kelsey and Nate. But a female with you would be less aggressive and, given the nature of that place, probably welcome. The ladies might be more inclined to talk with me than Tom.' All three men looked at her.

'He'd probably be checking out who he could bed,' Jessica said, not holding back.

'You know, I was only joking about taking Tom with me,' Adam said, 'but maybe it's not a bad idea if you did come, Dan. Griffin knows about the wedding; we spoke of it. So, he'll buy the story about me having full-time security.'

'You could couch it that you're stuck with Dan anyway, so she may as well enjoy the camp and have a few days off,' Nate said.

'He used to see me with Charlie every day,' Adam recalled, 'so my having security isn't a lot to swallow.'

'Charlie? Guy or girl?' Danielle asked.

'Girl, all women,' Nate said and smiled, then got serious. 'We should move if we are going to do this. The clock might be ticking for whoever called in the murder. That could be Skye or any of the women there.'

'True,' Adam said.

'I'm going to call on Griffin's other school friends, starting with Ben... what's his name?' Nate asked.

'Solomon, Ben Solomon,' Adam said.

'Yeah. See if he has any insights or was approached by Griffin to join the cult. The more information we have, the better.'

'Okay, I'll break the good news to Tom.' Adam grinned.

'Try not to look like you'll enjoy his angst,' Burnsy suggested.

'Spoilsport,' Adam said, rising to depart.

Chapter 28

Audrey enjoyed the opportunity to entertain when she could suffer the people in attendance, and tonight, she was most pleased with the small and intimate group, although she would have liked Jack to be there. She loved Jack, as her son had, and her grandson Adam did, but tonight he was away performing. Winsome had gone along with Stephanie in a VIP box to enjoy the show, and Jessica was also there with her mother using Jack's VIP tickets. The only unwelcomed guest at her gathering tonight was Tom, who betrayed her son's marriage. But she understood the necessity of him being there – Adam wanted to speak with them about a pending work commitment, and she imagined it had its risks.

Why Winsome continued to give Tom work, Audrey could not understand. Interestingly, she had noted some cooling between them. Something had changed, and it was coming from Winsome – Tom still seemed smitten. Audrey didn't care enough to ask. She smiled, watching from the kitchen window as Nate and Adam stood around the barbeque, laughing about something. Adam had shared in confidence that Nate knew he owned the property, and she imagined that knowledge had relaxed Nate and made him not feel beholden to her or Winsome for his stay. She enjoyed having the energetic young man around. He had a lovely energy, she mused.

'Thank you, ladies,' she said, engaging Kelsey and Danielle to help her carry the bread rolls and salads to the table.

Once seated with Nate's barbeque offerings served, drinks topped up, and Tom returned from his tour of the grounds to check on security, Adam broached why he had wanted the gathering.

'We have a situation; a client of Nate's might be in danger, and I'm going to be away a few days to check it out.'

'Uh oh,' Audrey said, knowing Adam and Nate only too well. 'A *situation* involving you two boys, how unique.'

The group laughed except for Tom, who managed to smirk; Nate explained what was going on.

'Griffin Maxwell!' Audrey exclaimed. 'Well, there's a name I haven't heard for nearly two decades. That young boy and his undesirable father... so that's what became of him.'

'But you are saying he is not doing anything illegal, except the girls feel trapped because their options are limited, is that right?' Kelsey clarified.

'That is how it appears except for the anonymous phone call to the police and the parents of Skye concerned that she can't leave without seeing her contract out, even if she wants to pack it in,' Nate said.

'You're not going into that place, not even for a night. Over my dead body,' Tom snapped at Adam.

'As much as I'd like that, Tom, I am going, especially now that Sarah, Skye, or whoever called the police might be in real trouble.'

'I am going with him as his bodyguard,' Danielle announced.

'That's an interesting idea, young lady,' Audrey said. 'I know you will do that at the wedding, but this is a bit different. What danger might you be in there?'

'I'm trained, Mrs Murphy... Audrey,' Danielle found it difficult to call the septuagenarian by her first name. Her mother would be mortified. 'I am confident I can manage myself and have Adam's back.'

'And you won't be outnumbered by men at least,' Kelsey added. 'If Griffin is your friend, Adam, or thinks he is, you should be safe to do a bit of undercover snooping and see what is truly going on in there. But only if you get access to some of the ladies.'

'Snooping?' Adam said and grinned.

'So that's how you regard my profession,' Nate teased Kelsey. 'Chief Snoop Dog.'

Kelsey laughed. 'Senior snoop more like it.'

'I'll do my best snooping,' Adam promised, 'and if I don't, Dan might be able to get a word with the girls.'

'Yeah, I might even make some content,' she joked. 'If they pay more than Nate, I won't come home.'

Everyone enjoyed the break in tension except Nate, who gave her a less-than-impressed look, concerned he might lose Danielle to the highest bidder.

'What do you remember about the fire and Griffin's father moving away, Audrey?' Adam asked.

'Ah yes, that was a good outcome,' she said and sat back, looking skyward as she thought before returning her attention to the group. 'William Maxwell, Griffin's father, was very ambitious, so he befriended your father, Adam. He dreamed of becoming prime minister and was on track to be the state's premier. He was the opposition leader, and an election was looming; the polls were very favourable. William networked with all the right people, but his impropriety brought that to a quick end.'

Adam quickly explained to Danielle, Kelsey and Tom about the photos Griffin gave him for his eleventh birthday.

'Wow, you pick some shady friends,' Tom said.

'We did try and weed them out,' Audrey retorted with a look that said she included Tom amongst that lot. It was a look that put him in his place.

Adam continued, 'Dad took the photos and said he would deal with it. That's the last I heard about it. A few days later, Griffin wasn't at school and never came back.'

Audrey nodded. 'Your father owned a significant portion of the media and was close friends with a few top men in the police service. He showed several people in high places the images and advised he was going to suggest William Maxwell leave town immediately.'

'But the police should have arrested him!' Danielle said.

'They should have indeed, Danielle,' Audrey agreed, never shortening names. She declined another sausage from Nate; Tom accepted it.

'It was a different time,' Tom explained. 'Things were often buried under the carpet, deals were done with a handshake, and justice delivered off the record.'

'That's very true,' Audrey agreed. 'James told me if a case was sticky and short on evidence, his reporters might be called into the police station for a briefing only to find a file sitting on a desk in a closed room. No one ever came in. They would get what they need, write the story, and justice would sort itself out. A win-win for everyone. Your dad even got tips from police friends he met socially.'

'Wow, bet that doesn't happen today,' Kelsey said.

Nate shook his head. 'When I was a cop, the relationship between the police and media had declined a lot, mainly because the media had started reporting on cop corruption, and the cops wised up and got their own publicity officers in-house to respond officially. The days of leaks are largely over.'

'So, what happened to William Maxwell?' Adam asked, bringing them back on track.

Audrey nodded. 'After your father, James, spoke with his contacts, and they copied the photos for evidence, he went to see William. James returned the photos, told him who knew about them, and suggested that he resign and move on quickly.'

'He burnt the photos then?' Nate asked.

'Yes, Nathanial dear, in a manner of speaking. There was a fire that night at his house. Everything was completely destroyed.' Audrey tapped her glass as she thought. 'From memory, William Maxwell told the press that it was arson and fearing for his family's safety, he was resigning, and they moved overseas to somewhere in Asia very quickly.'

Adam shook his head. 'Fear for his family? Hmm, good one. His son is a—' he hesitated.

'Go on,' Nate teased him. 'I love it when the psychologist calls someone a nutcase.'

Adam gave him a smirk. '—a troubled person.'

'I am not surprised, given his role model,' Audrey said and sighed. 'It was one of the few times I had seen your father truly enraged. He wasn't quick to temper.'

'Why?' Adam asked, surprised. 'I'm sure William Maxwell wasn't the only deviant to cross his path.'

Audrey frowned, studying him. 'Because you were exposed to the photos, darling boy. He was most upset and would not say, but I believe there was a fight. He came home with blood, well, never mind.'

She saw Adam's surprised look and knew that, sadly, moments of true affection between the boy and his father were rare.

Adam's phone pinged, and he looked at the message. 'Speak of the devil.'

'What's he want?' Nate asked.

'He says, "Hey, great to see you again today. Come stay".' Adam put the phone down.

'So how long are you going into this camp for and when?' Tom cut to the chase.

'The sooner, the better. It's not like I can see clients this week with all the wedding drama and media hanging around the office. I'll message Griffin back tonight, go tomorrow, and just stay for a few days. What do you think?' Adam said with a look at Danielle.

'That works for me,' she agreed.

'Okay. You'll be back by Wednesday or Thursday at the latest?' Tom asked.

Adam nodded. 'Plenty of time before Sunday's wedding for you to annoy me some more before you finish up.'

Tom made a snorting sound. 'Don't get bruised or break anything. I'd have a hard time explaining that.'

'It would be bad for photos,' Adam agreed and brightened at the thought.

'No!' Kelsey said, reading his mind, and he grinned.

'What if he makes you give up your phone like the girls have to do?' Nate asked.

'I'll just say no. I'm not under his control. I'm a guest. Besides, my patients need to contact me.'

'What if he offers you one of the girls for the night?' Audrey asked. 'From what you tell me, it sounds like the men on site are enjoying those pleasures. You will have to let him know you have a beloved girlfriend.' She patted Kelsey's hand.

'If he offers me that, I'll accept so I can talk with them, but nothing will happen. You know that,' he said to Kelsey, and she nodded.

'I trust you,' Kelsey said.

'For the record, I'm strictly against this,' Tom said.

'But only this week,' Adam said, showing Tom's hypocrisy.

He hesitated in responding, knowing Audrey was present, and it reflected on how little he cared for Adam then and now. Tom was spared from answering by Kelsey.

'There's an interesting irony here,' she said.

'What's that, dear?' Audrey asked.

'Your mum, Adam, is accused of bringing down a prime minister and his government, and by taking receipt of those photos and giving them to your dad, you innocently brought down a potential politician aiming for the top job as well.'

'If I were the opposition leader, I'd hire you right away,' Nate joked. 'Have you ever thought of running for leadership? You're photogenic enough.'

'Oh wow,' Danielle said, 'you would do so well. Like a young JFK!'

Kelsey laughed, knowing that would never happen.

'There's a career change for you, darling boy,' Audrey teased.

Adam rolled his eyes and ignored them. 'Any sausages left?' He rose and followed Nate to the barbeque.

Chapter 29

Nate wondered what Ben Solomon's motivations were in agreeing to see him. Nate had identified himself as a private investigator and requested a meeting due to a mutual connection. He was relieved but not surprised that Ben didn't recognise the name or his face. Nate had gone to a different school, and if Ben had ever encountered him, it was only when Griffin tried to befriend Adam a handful of times, and the boys were 11. He studied the man before him in a navy suit, white business shirt and no tie. He had an air of arrogance... no, that wasn't it, more like attitude. He was a big man – like Adam had said – fit and solid; Nate wouldn't want to meet him in a dark alley.

'Thanks for your time.' Nate entered alone as Danielle was playing bodyguard to Adam.

Ben offered Nate a coffee, which Nate thanked him for but declined. The men sat opposite each other across a table in a small meeting room.

'Nice offices, every mod con. You own this business?' Nate asked.

'Yeah, I went out on my own a year ago – I.T. and systems management.' Ben gave a casual shrug like it was no big deal. 'So, what have I done?' he joked.

Nate grinned. 'Nothing that I know of, but confess if you want to.'

Ben grinned. 'Thank God for that.'

'To cut to the chase, I hope you can give me some insights.'

Ben nodded and swallowed like he was nervous.

'I'm enquiring about an old school acquaintance of yours – Griffin Maxwell.'

'Wow, that's a blast from the past,' Ben said and chuckled. 'Why are you interested in him?'

'His name came up recently in my enquiries, and I'm trying to get a read on him. I'm contacting some of his former acquaintances.'

'Yeah? Like who, if you don't mind me asking?'

Nate did mind but thought he'd test the waters. 'I'm looking up Adam Murphy and—'

Ben snorted and cut him off. 'Murphy had nothing to do with our group. What's Griffin supposed to have done?'

'I have two clients who are concerned for their daughter's safety. They believe she has entered a cult masquerading as a wellness camp and can't leave of her own accord. The cult, or rather the wellness camp's owner, is Griffin Maxwell.'

Ben's eyes widened with surprise, and then Nate watched as he feigned nonchalance, but Nate had done his research. He knew Griffin was one of Ben's biggest clients, and he hoped Ben might be keen on self-preservation and throw Griffin under the bus.

'Griffin Maxwell was at my school for about a minute and then left. Don't know where he went after that.'

'Right,' Nate said. 'So, you didn't stay in touch or reconnect?'

'No.'

'Do you remember another of Griffin's friends,' Nate looked at his notes, 'Zachary Chowder.'

Ben almost gave himself away with a grin but pulled himself up. 'Zach, I remember because we went right through high school together. I haven't stayed in touch, though.' If he was lying, it was effortless. 'I saw him at a school reunion at the ten-year mark... he's a solicitor, I think.'

'That's him. Did Griffin go to that reunion?'

'No. This is the first time I've heard his name since school. His father was a big wig, wasn't he?' Ben said, putting on a worthy performance.

'Ex-politician,' Nate confirmed. 'So, do you know anything about the *Fidelium Wellness Studio* at Mount Tamborine?'

'Nope, can't help you with that one either.'

Nate nodded. 'Yet they are your clients, according to your website.'

Ben stilled outwardly and grimaced. Nate could almost hear Ben's mind racing a hundred miles an hour as he attempted to save the situation.

'They must go by another name when I do the accounts or have multiple businesses. I didn't recognise the Fidelium part.'

Nate shrugged. 'Maybe Griffin Maxwell and associates?'

Game on.

'I have several guys on staff, freelancers; it might be one of their clients.'

'Right,' Nate said, unconvinced. 'So, you are still in touch with Griffin Maxwell's people if not the man himself?'

Ben's lips thinned as he thought, and then he took a different tack.

'Okay, if I share some information with you, where is it going?' Ben asked, narrowing his eyes.

'Starts and stops with me,' Nate assured him. 'All I want is to find out if my clients' daughter is safe and if she wants to come home, she can freely.'

Ben nodded. 'Who is your client's daughter?'

'I can't say, privacy and all that.'

'I might know her.'

'How?'

Ben hesitated for effect. 'I was being honest when I said I had little to do with Griffin Maxwell, but I was hired to do some I.T. security work at his camp. I had some freelancers put in cameras and so forth. But I am a guest at the VIP House.'

'What's that?' Nate asked, knowing the answer,

'It's part of the business interests at the camp. A private club for those who like their sex with a bit of spice and heat,' Ben said and gave a smile that was supposed to be conspiratorial. It was not reciprocated.

'A brothel?'

'If you want to call Griffin Maxwell a brothel madame, you are probably right, but I like to think of it as a very private club.'

'What's the price of admission?'

Ben shrugged. 'Don't know. I gave them a discount on the work and was offered a free membership. That's why I asked who your girl was; I might know her from there.'

Nate hesitated, considering the consequences of mentioning Skye's name and determining that it wasn't worth the risk.

'Do the girls work there willingly?' Nate asked, not providing a name.

Ben laughed. 'You bet. They make an income there they wouldn't make anywhere else. Trust me, they are keen, I've been told by the ladies themselves.'

'Who are some of your favourites?'

Ben smiled, knowing Nate had outsmarted him. He mused and then said, 'Harmony, Leaf, Sunny...' he threw a few random names but saw no hint of recognition on Nate's face.

'Interesting names.'

'Yeah. Well, sorry I can't help you with anything else, but that's about the extent of my knowledge. My visits to the club don't go on your records, right?'

'Right,' Nate agreed.

'I hope your clients get their daughter home, but from my limited exposure to the girls there, they are not in a rush to leave. In fact, they are quite competitive when it comes to picking clients,' Ben said and rose.

'Is that so?' Nate asked, rising as well. 'Thanks for your time.'

Nate knew Ben Solomon would either be on the phone to Griffin in a heartbeat or head there in person to tell him of Nate's visit and enjoy the spoils that might follow. It was risky to interview Ben, and Nate knew it. But it might bring matters to a head, and the sooner, the better.

Griffin didn't seem to care about Danielle's presence or that one of his guests deemed a bodyguard was necessary – the Murphy family was no ordinary family, after all. Griffin's entire focus was on Adam Murphy. Danielle watched with fascination, like a patron at the cinema watching a film on screen with two leading men. Something about them both spoke of power and confidence, something Nate didn't have with his briskness. What was it? Was it innate or learnt with privilege?

Griffin wore white linen pants, a long black linen shirt, and tan deck shoes. His hair was about shoulder length and tied back with a black band. He was strikingly handsome and charismatic, and when he did deign to look at her, his dark eyes held her attention. Adam wore his customary dark suit, cut perfectly to size, with a white business shirt and no tie. You could see your reflection in his shiny black shoes. They were of similar height and quietness, and yes, that was it, she thought; they were self-aware. Adam was beautiful, and Griffin was mysterious.

'I'm glad you decided to come,' Griffin said in a low voice to Adam.

'Thanks for the offer. It's just what I needed; you have no idea.'

Griffin nodded and gave him a small smile. A woman appeared, blonde and curvy – everything Danielle wasn't, she mused. Griffin did the introductions.

'This is Leaf. She's in charge of our female guests.'

They both greeted her and then Leaf turned to Danielle. 'Come, and I'll show you to your room. I promise you Adam will be safe here. We have a good camera network set up on the exterior, and no one is currently at any of the gates around the perimeter.'

Danielle wondered if her car had been checked out when she stopped briefly on surveillance. It was a public road, so she doubted they would check every car that passed. She played along and gave Leaf a grateful smile like a relieved bodyguard would. Grabbing her bag, she followed Leaf with a glance at Adam.

'I'll be back as soon as I settle,' she said, and he nodded. She heard Griffin say, 'She's protective. I like that. Come this way, I've got a suite for you, and tonight, we'll catch up over dinner with Zach. I hear there was a reunion recently. Did you go?'

'No.'

'Me either. I should call and invite Ben too, remember him?'

Danielle heard the name and glanced back at Adam. *Ben!* Nate was seeing him today. As soon as Ben arrived and saw Adam was presented, surely, he'd suspect something. He was bound to mention that a private investigator, Adam's old friend, spoke with him today. Would Ben remember Nate? Would Griffin? This would stir the pot.

'Come and meet some of the other ladies,' Leaf was saying, and Danielle hurried to catch up. They needed a plan, and she needed time with Adam to make it.

Chapter 30

Then...

'Befriend him, Son, and be quick about it,' William Maxwell snapped in a no-nonsense tone. He had summoned his son, Griffin, into his home office to ask about progress with Adam Murphy, son of James and Winsome.

'I'm trying, Dad, but he's got friends and has turned down all my invitations.'

'You're not trying hard enough. Come here.'

Griffin's fists clenched. He moved closer to his father's desk, and the bamboo cane kept nearby for punishment, but this time, his father pointed to a chair in front of the desk, and 11-year-old Griffin Maxwell sat down, his body un-tensing, knowing he was not going to be struck.

'This conversation is not to be repeated to anyone, do you understand?'

'Yes, Dad.'

'If I find out you told Adam or anyone, you know the consequences.' His hand reached below the desk to the side where the cane rested, and Griffin nodded, understanding him perfectly. Sometimes, he hated his father.

'You are the son of this country's future premier and prime minister. People will be desperate to be in your circle of friends, and everyone will want something from you,' his father said, sitting back and webbing his fingers on the desk in front of him. 'Trust me, Son, you'll be invited to everything and anything, and when you come of age, you can rise through the ranks in my footsteps. Would you like that?'

Griffin knew there was only one answer.

'Yes, Dad,' he answered with as much enthusiasm as expected.

His father smiled and nodded. 'And I will be there to guide you all the way. You have something, my boy, like me. Not everyone has the gift of leadership.'

Griffin nodded. He had heard this part of the speech before.

'Consider Adam's father, James Murphy,' his dad continued, 'quiet, strong, powerful, and brilliant.' He tapped his temple. 'It is one thing to have charisma, but you must have the smarts to go with it, especially street smarts. I am spending a fortune sending you to that school—'

Griffin had heard this speech before but sat through it, tuning back in when his father mentioned Adam.

'You and Adam are the right fit, given you both have powerful fathers and good pedigrees. How we appear and whom we are seen with will make us. Get that boy across the line and make him your best friend. Do you hear me?' His father almost hissed the last words like they were a threat. But even at age 11, Griffin was becoming his own person. He would tolerate the cane while his father was bigger and stronger, but the day would come when that would end.

'Yes, Sir. I'm invited to his birthday party,' Griffin said smugly, and his father smiled.

'Excellent. I will drop you off in the limo. If James is not home, I'll catch up with Audrey.' His father leant forward. 'Lift your game, Son. I will tell Audrey that Adam is invited to a sleepover. Surely, if you have all night here, just the two of you, you can ingratiate yourself into his life.'

Griffin nodded. 'Easy,' he agreed. He was his father's son, after all.

His father cocked his head to the side. 'Do you know what that word means? Ingratiate?'

Griffin hated to admit his father got that one over him, so he guessed, given the conversation had only been about one topic. 'Get him to like me?'

'Near enough,' his father said. 'Look it up and give me the formal definition next time we meet. You'll be doing a lot of ingratiating in the years to come. Dismissed.'

Griffin rose and departed. *Dismissed*, he smarted. Still, he liked the word *Dismissed* and would use that on his group or someone who annoyed him. The thought brightened him.

Now...

Griffin could not believe Adam Murphy had come to stay willingly, almost twenty years since he had first invited Adam to stay over at his place. He inwardly laughed at the thought, given the inordinate amount of time he invested at school trying to get Adam across the line, into his group, to be his closest friend, even when it angered his group. He didn't care, they didn't get it, they were followers, and Adam was an equal. But that other kid from the state school had always been in the way.

But here he was, Adam Murphy. The media chased him and his mother all over the news, and now the son was staying at his wellness camp, enjoying his company and hospitality. He fully intended to ring his father overseas and tell him how he had succeeded where his father failed. Their relationship had become a game of barbs and one-upmanship. He reasoned his father had started it. Griffin flinched involuntarily, still to this day, when he thought about the beating he suffered when his father discovered the photographs he had given Adam for his birthday. The scars from the welts were visible across his back. Griffin mused bitterly on those years that followed until his father became a big man again in his Asian business world.

Ambition was raw and powerful; like his father, he wanted it all, too. If his father had just kept his nasty predilections to himself, William Maxwell might have been premier, then prime minister. Then, Griffin thought, the media would be chasing me now like they were chasing Adam. Imagine how their friendship would have hit the media. They'd be the golden boys. Still, they could have that if he scored an invitation to the wedding. People would remember his father's rise to fame, and hopefully, not many were still around who knew the reason for his departure.

A well-placed photo of him and Adam together and his rise in popularity would begin. He'd get rid of the studio and all its hangers-on, sell it or let Zach buy it, and he'd start his own political campaign. He had several agendas that he knew would tap into the psyche of a young voting audience, and with his proposed social media rise, he'd nail it. Griffin Maxwell felt the rise of excitement within him but calmed himself.

Stick to the plan. Win Adam Murphy over first, and that had begun.

Adam was no stranger to being uncomfortable; it described a good chunk of his life – being made to model when young, being forced into the limelight by his parents, and the constant questioning over his paternity. A few nights at Griffin's wellness camp was nothing by comparison. Except for the fact that he had to endure dinner and whatever followed with Ben and Zach tonight, and if there were two people he had less interest in catching up with, it was those two clowns. Tom would be the third. He almost smiled at his joke.

'This is excellent, thank you,' he said to Griffin, knowing how important gratification was to Griffin. It only took Adam a few minutes to recognise Griffin's need for control and approval, and it still ran strong. But he wanted to keep Griffin slightly on edge and needy to ensure incentives would be thrown his way... like the chance to meet the girls. It didn't take much. No effusing, no wild admiration or plan making. Just be present and slightly aloof. The insistence on keeping his phone was a round won easily.

Adam had a plan, and as soon as he recognised Griffin Maxwell had not changed, he knew how to get around tonight's drama if Ben rocked up; he just had to get a moment alone with Danielle and assure her it would work. Assuming Nate had met with Ben, he had yet to hear how that went.

'These are the best rooms,' Griffin said, calmly walking to the doors that lead out to the veranda with a view so impressive he could see the ocean and a little of the Gold Coast skyline in the distance. Griffin opened the glass doors and walked out.

'Have I unbedded anyone?' Adam asked, following him out to the veranda.

Griffin laughed. 'No. There are only a few large rooms in this wing. One is mine, and I keep the others empty for special guests. No one is allowed up here, so you will have complete privacy. I am on the other end, and there are two empty rooms of the same size between us. Unless, of course, you want someone to visit?' he asked with a raised eyebrow in Adam's direction. 'Some company and relief, maybe.'

Adam smiled and looked out at the view. *Here it is; play it carefully*, he told himself. 'Discreet?' he asked.

Griffin looked surprised and then a little insulted. 'Of course. There are no cameras in your room or outside, and no one has a phone here except you, me, and Zach. This is not a trap, Adam,' he said a little too sharply.

Adam studied him, saying nothing for a moment, and Griffin reined in his anger.

'I imagine you've heard that before,' Griffin conceded.

Adam nodded. 'Even from girlfriends, and then I find photos online or stories sold to magazines. Forgive my suspicion, it has become inherent.'

Griffin nodded and exhaled. 'I understand more than you know.'

'I'm sure you do,' Adam said, giving him a branch of friendship, establishing they did have something in common.

'I give you my word, on my honour, anything you do here will never leave here,' Griffin said, placing both hands on the veranda rail and looking out over the vista. 'I won't tolerate that.'

'It's happened to you before, here?' Adam feigned concern.

'Let's just say if it did, it never got further than the front gate,' Griffin said, turning side on to Adam and giving a small smile.

I bet, Adam thought. He cleared his throat. 'Then, I will take you up on your hospitality and enjoy some company, thanks.'

'Excellent. Tell me then what your preferences are. Female, male, colouring, size... I will prepare someone for you.'

Adam's eyebrows shot up. 'Prepare? What's that involve?' he laughed.

Griffin smiled. 'I'll pull them from their schedule, and they can be groomed.'

Wow, control to an art.

'What I like for fun is the opposite of what I want for life,' Adam said, knowing that would make Griffin feel like he was given another private insight.

'I understand,' Griffin nodded. 'I like vodka, but now and then, I want champagne.'

Adam laughed and lowered himself into a large, comfortable chair on the veranda, and Griffin took the seat opposite. Handsome bookends.

Looking out at the view, Adam said, 'Blonde, medium height, curves, sensuous, not young, innocent, or silly.'

'Nothing like your mother,' Griffin said and surprised Adam. If he compared Kelsey to his mother, he could not have chosen anyone more opposite physically or of nature. Griffin was right; the woman he just described was nothing like his elfin, whimsical mother.

'I never thought of that,' Adam said and gave a small shrug.

'And you, the psychologist,' Griffin teased him, and Adam shot him a grin.

'I must be off the clock.'

Griffin laughed. 'Good, that's the effect this place aims to achieve. I have several ladies who would fit the bill and love to meet you. Settle in while I talk with Zach, and then you can meet some of the ladies at lunch and select your favourite or favourites. Later, just give me a name, and I'll organise it.' Griffin rose and departed with Adam's thanks.

Adam waited until he saw him heading up the path and back to the office. He rose, re-entered the room, opened his bag, changed into jeans, runners and a blue linen shirt that would give Griffin a run for his money, and left to find Danielle.

Chapter 31

Nate hurried into the office, even managing to pin in the code without bouncing off the closed door as he often did.

'What's up?' Jessica asked, startled, rising from behind her reception desk.

'Nothing, maybe something. Where's Tom? I've just got to call Dan.' He entered his office, and Jessica, calling for Rob, followed. She was quite used to Nate in a state. Moments later, Rob appeared at Nate's office door.

'Have you heard from Adam and Dan?' Rob asked.

'Just calling Dan now,' Nate said with his phone to his ear. He moved it away and put it on a conference call. 'Stick around a minute if you will?'

Rob entered and sunk into a chair in front of Nate's desk. Jessica took the other chair nearest to the door so she could bolt if the phone rang.

Dan answered in a hushed voice. 'Sorry, I've got it on vibrate as phones are not encouraged, and it took me a minute to work out that it wasn't my vibrator.'

Nate chuckled. 'Good one. Is your room free of bugs and cameras?'

'So, I've been told. Apparently, Griffin likes to visit the girls and won't have any recording devices in the rooms.'

'Works for us,' Nate said. 'Okay. You're on an open call; Jessica and Rob are with me. We might have a problem.'

'Hi guys,' Danielle said. 'What's the problem?'

Nate told of his meeting with Ben and added, 'I could tell he was lying the moment he started to speak. I wouldn't be surprised if he were on the phone with Griffin right now.' He frowned. 'It was a mistake to see Ben before Adam's visit; I should have cancelled. But it will bring about action, which might be timely given that Adam is in the camp.'

'Ben's coming to dinner tonight,' Danielle said.

'Are you sure?'

'No, but Griffin told Adam he'd invite him, and they would all catch up like old times.'

'Damn.' Nate ran a hand through his hair as he often did when frustrated.

'Did Ben admit he was in contact with Griffin or worked for him?' Danielle asked.

'No.' Nate filled them in on his visit and how Ben bluffed about his connection with Griffin.

'Hmm, so Griffin, Zach and Ben are still friendly; maybe some more of the school gang are, too,' Danielle mused when he finished. 'Hold up. Adam's here.' She waited until he closed the door to her room behind him.

'Could you be any further away from my room?' Adam sighed with frustration.

'That's not good,' Nate said.

'Nate, Rob and Jess are on a conference call,' Nate heard Danielle explaining.

'Thank God, I thought I was hearing Nate in my head now.'

Nate laughed. 'You should be so lucky.'

'Hi, team. Nate, did you meet with Ben?' Adam asked, and Nate hurriedly updated him. 'We've got a problem.'

'It's not that big a deal. I've got a plan,' Adam said. 'I'm going to kill two birds with one stone. I'm going to tell Griffin I want to catch up with just the two of us. He loves that shit, and it will stroke his ego. He can see the other two anytime. Besides, he knows I don't get on with them, and if he is serious about bonding – Lord help me – then he'll come to the party. That buys me some time, hopefully before Ben can pull him aside and suggest something's not right.'

'It's risky. He might be calling him now,' Nate said. 'You won't make any friends banishing the other two.'

'That's nothing new,' Adam assured him. 'Zach will invite Ben tonight, so hopefully, Ben won't get a chance to talk with Griffin beforehand. Griffin doesn't deal with trivialities. He has Zach organising a lunch as we speak and inviting some ladies for me to meet.'

'Zach sounds like he's the lackey,' Nate said.

'He probably prefers the title right-hand-man,' Adam scoffed.

'Will Skye be at the lunch?' Jessica asked.

'We're hoping,' Adam informed them.

'Do you know where they all stay on the site?' Rob asked.

'Not yet. But not near Griffin and me. We're in a wing with just four large suits, and Griffin told me we're the only two occupants.'

'Dan, maybe you should stay in Adam's room tonight. Subtly if Griffin's room is nearby,' Jessica suggested.

'That could work,' Adam said, 'it's big enough, and his room is at the opposite end of the wing. But I doubt Zach or Ben would visit me overnight.'

'I don't,' Nate said.

'What's the other stone, bird-throwing thing since you were killing two?' Danielle asked.

Nate heard Adam chuckle. At least he was calm, he thought.

'Griffin asked if I would like some company later tonight. I told him what type I like – Skye's type – and he is going to introduce me to several women of that ilk over lunch. Then I just have to tell him which one. If Skye's there, I'll ask for her and talk to her tonight to find out what's happening.'

'It's all a bit risky for my liking,' Rob said.

'Yeah,' Nate said, 'I'll alert Tom.'

'No!' Adam said. 'He'll storm here and close everything down. Just hold tight, it's alright.' Adam's voice sounded calm as it came down the phone line. 'Dan and I know the risks, we can get out of here if needed, and seriously, Griffin is up to something, he has some use for me. He hasn't changed.'

Nate grunted. 'Okay. Keep us posted as much as you can.' They said their goodbyes, and hanging up, Nate turned to Rob and Jessica. 'I'm informing Tom on the basis he is ready to go but doesn't storm the fort.'

'I couldn't agree more,' Rob said.

'Me too. I'll call him and ask him to come in,' Jessica said, and the two left Nate's office.

He moved to the window and looked down on Stones Corner. He didn't like Adam being there and Danielle being separated in different quarters. He didn't like Adam being in Griffin's company, and he sure as hell didn't like the feeling of being second best to Griffin Maxwell again.

Skye finished her content session with Alex and left the small booth to rejoin him in his studio area. She stood looking out the studio window as he checked the feed before giving her the all-clear to leave. She saw Griffin walking around with a stranger – another one of Griffin's powerful friends with dark fetishes, no doubt. He was a beautiful-looking man, this new addition to the camp. Experience told her the more beautiful they were, the crueller they could be – Griffin was a case in point. She knew the new guy would be given the VIP House tour and full access to it. At least she wasn't working there yet.

'Who's that, do you know?'

Alex was barely talking to her anymore unless it was a work command; it was understandable. She took advantage of him and broke his trust when she called in the murder. He glanced her way, squinted to see the two men and gave a shrug, returning to his work.

'Have you seen Rain?' she persisted.

He exhaled, frustrated. 'According to you, I couldn't have since she was murdered.'

'I saw it, Alex. We can't just let that go.'

'*I* can. I'm here to do a job. I arrive, do it, and leave. That's it. And thanks to you, I'll probably be kicked out of here as soon as they trace the call to the cops from my phone.'

'You said yourself you've got an unidentified burner and no caller I.D. Besides, it was a female voice calling it in. You're safe.' She glanced outside again to see Griffin and his guest heading towards Griffin's quarters.

'Now you're a tech expert,' he muttered.

She turned and sat on the window ledge. 'I'm sorry, Alex, I really am.'

His jaw tightened, and he gave a barely discernible nod. 'What are you going to do now?'

Skye bit her bottom lip as she thought. 'I guess it is only a matter of time until Griffin and Zach investigate, but I'm guessing they won't start interviewing us girls until Griffin's guest leaves. And that buys me a small window of time to escape.'

Alex whirled around in his chair to look at her. 'You're kidding?'

'I did have a plan...' She closed her eyes and exhaled. There was no point getting emotional about it, and her first plan had failed. 'I had hoped to talk with the police when they came on site and ask to leave with them in their protection, but I was here in the studio, and the searches were done and over before we finished.'

Alex didn't look surprised.

'You knew they were here?'

He grimaced before admitting, 'We were paged by Zach. Told to ensure everyone was working and unavailable while the cops were here. He selected a few people who could be interviewed.'

'Of course, he did,' she said, crossing her arms over her chest, her head dropping. 'I miss Rain. I can't remember a time when I have felt more alone.' She blinked away tears and knew there was no value in getting emotional. Most men didn't handle that well. She cleared her throat and put her chin up.

'So, you've got another plan then, to escape?' Alex studied her, swinging his chair slightly from left to right, watching the reality drama unfold before him.

Skye wiped her hands over her face. 'Well, I don't feel like I have much choice.' She scoffed at her situation. 'If I ever considered telling Griffin I've changed my mind after our discussion, and I want to leave, I can't now.'

'Yeah,' Alex agreed. 'It might be kind of obvious.'

'I'd immediately be the number one suspect for the girl that called the police.'

'So, stay, finish your contract, take your money and get out.'

Skye looked at him as if he was soulless. 'Alex,' she hissed, 'my friend was murdered. She wanted to leave, and on her last night here, Griffin killed her. Zach came, wrapped her in a black sheet and got rid of her like garbage. How many more went the same way? If I stay, how do I know that won't happen to me?' Her voice finished on a slightly hysterical note. She covered her face with her hands, then dropped them suddenly and looked at him wide-eyed. 'You won't tell Griffin or Zach I'm leaving?'

'Of course not,' he assured her. 'That would mean you and I had been talking, and then I'd be the one who looked suspicious.'

She exhaled with relief and nodded in agreement. Skye knew if he did squeal on her, she'd return the favour, but she didn't want to go down that path. She would, though, if needed. His lack of compassion, total disregard for the girls, and, more interestingly, the fact he wasn't shocked by Rain's death told her he knew more and that this might not be the first death he had heard about. It made Alex as guilty as the other two as far as she was concerned. An accessory to abuse, murder, a cover-up.

They heard a beep from the desk, and Alex turned. 'Your content is good to go.'

The claim that it was live was not quite true; Griffin Maxwell was too much of a control freak to do that. It had a time delay, so Alex could pull it off the air if one of the girls went rogue. It hadn't happened yet, but Skye was a perfect contender in her current state.

'Thanks. I've got to change; I've been summoned for lunch.'

'Skye, be careful,' he said. 'I've enjoyed working with you.'

She softened and gave him a small smile. It didn't hurt to keep Alex on her side, and he was right; it would be easier to shut up and carry on. But for some reason, she felt like she was on borrowed time, and she had to do something for Rain and any other girls who might never have left the camp.

Departing and hurrying back to her room, Skye eyed the formal invitation card from Griffin to attend lunch and meet his guest.

'Nice touch,' she murmured. Griffin was all about show and tell. After lunch, she would use her afternoon off to disappear. Griffin would be distracted, Zach was working at the VIP House, and Skye calculated she had at least four hours before dinner before they realised she wasn't around. Plenty of time to get to the main road and hitch a ride. Plenty of time to leave this life for good.

'Sarah.' Skye tried her name on as she finished her grooming as if she had forgotten it. She donned a white dress; Griffin liked white on blondes, and this would be her last performance – sitting at his table and being charming to his guests. God, she hardly recognised the girl in the mirror. How far she had come in those two years from the naive, ambitious, star-struck girl that first arrived here believing all the crap she was told. She wanted to go home, sleep in her childhood bed under her parent's roof, and start again. Maybe she would go to teachers' college. How lovely to be in a classroom with bright minds and hopeful faces. That would please her folks, too.

A ripple of panic hit her as she saw it was ten minutes to the hour; Griffin didn't tolerate tardiness. She sprayed on a light touch of perfume and hurried out, up to the clubhouse and Griffin's private room within it, where he hosted guests. She was often paraded there; everyone liked to meet the blondes. Sometimes, she was invited to spend time with his guest; not accepting the invitation was frowned upon. It would be easier to accept if they all looked like the new guy that arrived, but that was rarely the case.

She entered and saw the grimace Zach gave her.

'Cutting it fine,' he said quietly through gritted teeth.

She nodded and entered, the last at the table of ten. The room was spectacular, the view was breathtaking, and the three men were there to enjoy lunch with seven women.

'And this is Skye,' Griffin said, and the handsome man sitting two seats from him rose from his seat to extend his hand. The blue linen shirt he wore really made his blue eyes pop. He had a jawline to die for and dark hair, fashionably cut.

'Adam Murphy.'

She took his hand and greeted him, noting he waited until she sat before he did so. A gentleman. Bet that doesn't last behind closed doors, she thought. There was one girl at the table she didn't know, a dark, beautiful woman.

'This is Danielle Walters. We work together,' Griffin's guest introduced Skye to the only non-blonde person at the table.

'A pleasure,' Skye said, wondering exactly what kind of work they did. Then, it was lights on, cameras rolling, and she played the role expected – sophisticated, beautiful, glamorous, and sexy. And she noticed it was working. Adam Murphy looked at her more than any other girl around the table.

That was a problem; she didn't want to be sought out. She wanted no one to notice she wasn't around for as long as possible.

Chapter 32

So, this was her – Skye or, rather, Sarah Lyons – alive, here in the flesh, and her parents were correct. Something was not quite right. Skye was performing, the smile never reached her eyes, and her mannerisms and behaviours were for maximum effect. Adam could read the trepidation coming from her. He tried not to glance too often at Skye; Danielle was studying her freely, and she could get away with that while he tried to watch the blonde woman subtly. There would be no opportunity to talk with her now, but tonight, maybe if he requested her, he could get the full story, and they could work out a plan.

Adam returned his attention to the group as one of the girls laughed at something Zach said, and Adam did his best not to scowl at him. He was still an idiot, and Adam had no desire to reminisce. He'd try the private catch-up line with Griffin later and wipe the smirk off Zach's face. Perversely, the thought gave him pleasure, even if it meant time alone with Griffin.

Adam didn't have to say much; no one expected it of him. The girls charmed him, Griffin held court, and Zach managed the whole affair. Danielle studied everyone, adding the occasional comment as required, and the whole event was painful and too long. He was pleased when it was over, and the group disbanded.

'Thank you for organising lunch on short notice,' Adam said to Griffin.

'The pleasure was mine.'

'You have some charming ladies learning their craft here,' Adam said. 'Speaking of work, I've got to make a couple of client calls and check in on a few patients who have gone off the rails.'

Griffin huffed. 'Everyone wants or needs something.'

'Don't I know it,' Adam played along. 'I'll just do so in my room if you have no objections?'

'Absolutely. You'll find the Wi-Fi is good, but there are some office rooms in another wing if you prefer. Just let Zach know, and he'll open them for you. So, did you find someone to your liking?' Griffin asked in a low voice, and Adam gave him a smile that he hoped fell somewhere between lecherous and hungry.

'Skye.'

Griffin grinned. 'You won't be disappointed.'

I'll make sure of it,' Adam thought to himself.

As expected, Tom Hartigan was not happy. The last time he had been in the office at the Murphy mansion on the river, James Murphy was alive, and Tom was there to advise of the abduction attempt on young Adam, then 10 years old. Tom had lapsed in his duty, and it was sheer bloody luck that he had managed to thwart the attempt by the man Adam called Uncle Allan. No one said it, but everyone knew it. The kid hated him then, but he did not always. James had been dead for 14 years now; Adam was 20 years older and still hated him – nothing much had changed.

Audrey, Nate, Kelsey, Winsome, and Jack were in attendance mid-afternoon with Tom. He couldn't understand the necessity of Winsome, Jack, or Kelsey being there, but Audrey reasoned that they would not be on the back foot with the wedding so near if anything should go pear-shaped.

'Couldn't he have gone there after the wedding,' Winsome said as if the world revolved around her, and it did. Tom saw Kelsey and Audrey's restrained reaction.

'A girl's life was in danger, and as Adam was an acquaintance of the Wellness Camp owner, we thought he could subtly find out if she could leave or was being trapped,' Nate explained.

'I spoke with Adam this morning, and he was fine. A lunch had been organised, and Danielle was with him,' Kelsey said, reassuring Winsome.

'I spoke with him thirty minutes ago after lunch,' Nate said. 'All is well.'

'I remember the boy's father, William Maxwell,' Winsome mused, 'James knew him. He was always inviting us to this or that, but we would never be home if we went to everything politicians invited us to.

'He was the leader tipped to win the election who cleared out of town, wasn't he?' Jack frowned, recalling.

'Yes,' Audrey said. 'Confidentially, James discovered, or rather Adam did, some very sordid photos pertaining to William Maxwell, and James suggested William move on, and the photos wouldn't surface. It was a very convenient fire that burned the Maxwell house to the ground that evening.'

'Why did I not know this?' Winsome asked, surprised.

Tom looked to Audrey to see if she would be honest – because Winsome didn't care to involve herself in day-to-day parenting, but Audrey chose a more diplomatic answer.

'You know how James liked to shield you from things.'

'We're not expecting any issues, but I just thought you'd like to know where Adam is,' Nate said, getting everyone back on track. 'He's aiming to stay no more than two nights enjoying Griffin's hospitality, and he's already seen the girl.'

Tom's eyes widened. 'She's there, alive and well? I'll go pick up Adam and whatever-her-name-is and game over.'

'But what about the next girl and the girl after that?' Kelsey asked. 'It's a good opportunity to find out if the girls can leave or if they are being held against their will.'

'Exactly,' Nate agreed. 'Adam said Dan would try to talk with Skye this afternoon, and we'd have a better picture then. He's also got dinner plans with Griffin and two of the old gang – Zach and Ben.'

'He never liked those boys,' Audrey piped in. 'That won't be pleasant at all unless they've grown up to be decent men.'

'Hmm, probably only their mothers would say that,' Nate said.

'Is he in danger, Nate, or not?' Tom cut to the chase.

'No. But he could be.'

'Then I'm going there and taking another guard with me.' He held his hand up to cut Nate off. 'We won't storm in. Just let him know we're on the perimeters and can act at any time. No one will know we are there.'

Nate's phone rang before he could protest, and seeing Danielle's name, he asked the group to wait. 'It's Dan. She'll have an update.' He spoke for a brief moment and then hung up. 'Skye's gone.'

Chapter 33

Skye's heart was racing. She hurried into her room and changed into her swimsuit, slipping over it a pair of dark shorts and a navy T-shirt. There was nothing green in her wardrobe that might work as camouflage, but by wearing dark clothing, she hoped to blend in with her surroundings. Her legs would be scratched going through the brush wearing shorts, but it was best to look like she was heading down to the creek for a swim. Skye had nothing to take with her; everything would remain behind; everything was the property of Griffin Maxwell, and the small bag of clothing she had arrived with was not worth taking or slowing down her escape. This was a fresh start, travelling light.

Skye took in the surroundings from her window, checking no one was coming towards her room. She had planned the route a long time ago, thought about this moment over many months, and wasn't sure when the day would come that she would enact it, but that day was here and taking the path towards the creek and through the brush to the road was the best way to go. It had crossed her mind to hide in the back of Alex's car and sneak out, but he parked near Zach's office, and it was too risky.

It was time to leave, and she felt sick. With one last look at her room, Skye exited, closed the door behind her and hurried down the few stairs, taking to the path and moving quickly. She didn't see the woman watching her – the woman from lunch who worked with Griffin's friend – and once Skye got off the path and could see the creek, she breathed a little easier.

The lunch had gone on longer than she hoped, and it was nearing three o'clock. It would be dark on the mountain just after seven; she had those hours before sundown to get a lift, and there were bound to be tourists and a few workers heading home for the day.

Arriving at the creek, relief swelled in her chest – no one was there; it was going well, all too well. She glanced back once or twice but preferred to keep her head down and hurry along. Quick, fast, not attracting any more attention than necessary. A sense of foreboding, a shadowy premonition, gripped her, telling her someone was watching, someone was always watching.

Another fifteen or twenty minutes and she would be on the road. Freedom was in sight. In her whole life, Skye could not recall ever being as frightened as she was now, except for her "reality" experience, but that was a different fear. It was unexpected, reactive and pure adrenaline. This was pre-mediated and came with the heightened dread of all that might come. Her heart was thudding in her chest, adrenaline was pushing her on, and breathing was painful – short, sharp, shallow.

Go, go!

Danielle was on her way to see Skye when she saw her heading away from her room in a hurry, a towel draped over her shoulder but dressed in a T-shirt and shorts… overdressed for a creek swim, or maybe she didn't want to invite male attention.

Good, we'll talk while we swim.

It never occurred to Danielle to bring her swimsuit; she wasn't planning on doing anything but security work. She wasn't shy about swimming in her underwear if necessary, so she followed behind.

Something's not right here.

Skye looked back often – short, sharp glances as if she didn't want to draw attention to herself or thought she was being followed. Danielle was good at stealth, and she was fairly confident no one was following Skye except herself. But the woman was uncomfortably quick in her step. It was not the body language of someone heading to the creek for a dip. Was she on the run or just in a hurry to go for a swim?

Why would she skip out now?

Did she think Adam's arrival was something sinister? Surely not when he was introduced as Griffin's old-school friend.

Danielle came to a sign pointing to the creek and a nature walk. She worked harder not to make a sound as the underbrush thickened. Skye was hot-footing it, making a reasonable amount of noise for someone who looked like they were on the run. Danielle was pleased she had on shoes for action, running or fighting. She hurried her steps to match Skye but stayed out of sight to see what the woman was up to; maybe she was meeting someone. Perhaps Zach, given there were only a couple of men on site unless a guy was sneaked in. A gardener, maybe?

But Skye walked around the length of the creek, not stopping at the logical place to strip off and head in. She was heading towards a tree line. Danielle couldn't stop to message Adam or risk calling him. This was a dilemma.

Did she leave Adam and chase Skye, or let Skye go and stay and watch over Adam?

Both Nate and Adam were her clients... if Skye disappeared while they were visiting when she had the chance to save her, that would be a tragedy.

But if Ben arrived and started talking about the P.I. that was snooping around, would Griffin remember Nate's name? Unlikely, she debated, it has been twenty years, but you never know, then shit would hit the fan, and they would be in a world of trouble.

Frustrated, she did what she did best, made a snap decision and met the drama head-on.

'Skye, stop!' Danielle yelled and continued at the same pace, waiting to see now if Skye would take off or wait.

Damn, Skye took off. Danielle sighed and ran after her.

'Wait.'

She could see Skye rushing towards the bush on the edge of the creek. As she made enough noise to disturb the environment, she felt the scratch of the underbrush and the silencing of the cicadas.

She was faster than Skye and closer enough to call out again. 'Your parents sent us.' That did the trick. Skye stopped and whirled around to face Danielle. The woman looked stricken, and Danielle felt better for declaring herself.

'What're their names?' Skye asked suspiciously as Danielle closed the distance between them. It was not too late for the two of them to return to the creek for a swim with no one being suspicious.

'John and Robin, and you are Sarah. Adam and I are here on their behalf.'

She watched Skye bend over slightly as if catching her breath, and when Skye put her head up, she could see the woman crying.

'What was your name again? Sorry, I'm a mess today,' Skye said.

'Danielle – Dan – you can leave with us. We can go now if you want to,' Danielle offered.

'It's not that simple.'

They heard a snap in the bush, and both women turned to look in that direction. They waited. No one was there that they could see. Danielle moved closer so they could lower their voices.

'You called in the murder, didn't you?'

Skye nodded. 'Rain. I don't even know her real name. Mum and Dad asked you to come?' she said as if the words had just hit her.

'They hired my boss, Nathanial Delaney – he's an ex-cop and a private investigator. They said they were getting strange phone messages, breathing and hanging up.'

Skye exhaled and looked to the heavens. 'It was me. I borrowed the tech guy's phone. They understood, thank God.'

'So, this now... what you are doing, running away? Are you saying that you can't leave of your own free will, no one can?'

Skye shook her head in the negative. 'You can leave anytime you like, but if your contract is not finished, you'll not get a cent of your earnings – and trust me, we've earned that. Plus, you have to pay back more than you owe. But now that I know about Rain, Griffin is bound to put it together.'

'So, if Rain could leave, what happened? How did she die?'

'She lied. She was getting out with her earnings because she was going to care for her sick mother. It wasn't true; I knew, and Griffin found out somehow. He visited her room that night pretending to want one last night with her, and I saw Zach carrying away her body.'

'Oh, my God.'

Skye nodded. 'I'll never forget that sight.' Her voice quivered, and she inhaled to get herself under control. 'Rain and I were going to meet after Griffin left and have one last drink together before she took off the next day. She was my dearest friend in here... anywhere, actually.'

'Griffin and Zach, both of them involved,' Danielle said under her breath. 'You can trust me, I promise, but I need to make a call to Adam.'

'Who is he? What's his connection to Griffin?' Skye asked, alarmed.

'He's a psychologist who shares cases with Nate, my boss. He also went to school with Griffin and knows a lot about him, I mean a lot. Don't worry; he's not a fan. I have to call him.'

Skye looked behind her at the route she was taking.

'We'll work this out. Just give me a moment.' Danielle rang Adam's number. 'Can you talk?' She asked when he answered and explained the situation. They spoke for a few minutes, and then Danielle gave a small gasp. 'Right, immediately.' She hung up.

'What's going on?'

'We're going to have a swim and head back, like that was what we were doing all along.'

'Why, what's happened? Tell me?' Skye insisted, looking stricken. 'They know, don't they?'

'I don't know that, but I do know Griffin is looking for you.'

'Why? He knows.' She gasped and looked around. 'I've got to go as I planned.'

'Wait.' Danielle shook her head and looked contrite. 'He's looking for you because Adam asked for your company tonight. Adam was going to talk with you about whether you wanted to stay or if your parents were right and you wanted to go. He had no intention of pushing you for anything more. He has a girlfriend.'

Skye placed her hand on her heart. 'Okay, and Griffin is looking for me to "invite" me to keep him company.' She began to breathe easier again.

Danielle nodded. 'So, this is the plan. We'll go back after our swim, then I'm to get you out and come back for Adam and bring the cops... they've got a witness now, so they can take action.'

'But you'll get me out first?'

Danielle nodded. 'You'll need to hide in my car until we're clear of here; I'll say I have an urgent job, and since Adam is obviously safe, I'll return as soon as I can... that will be later tonight with the cops.'

'Your plan makes sense,' Skye agreed. 'I hate the thought of going back. My headspace is out of here.'

'I noticed,' Danielle said, and Skye gave a small smile.

'But you are right. I need to see Griffin. Accept the invitation, and then we can get out of here. Where are you parked?'

'In the VIP House car park.'

'That will work.'

Danielle was pleased Skye was breathing easier now. It was all coming together. She explained, 'I'm not wearing swimmers, so I'll just remove my jeans and say I was exploring, met you here, and had an impromptu swim.'

The girls stripped off, dunked, and got out hurriedly. Skye shivered, and Danielle guessed it wasn't just from the cold.

'Thank you for this, Danielle.'

'Don't thank me until you are in the arms of your parents.'

'I can't believe I will be again. I've made so many mistakes.'

'Well, let's not make this plan one of them,' Danielle said, and they hurried back the way they had come.

Chapter 34

Then...

Nate rode his bike away from the Murphy mansion towards his own modest suburb. He didn't tell Adam why he was angry; he should just know. Go hang out with Griffin; he didn't care. He had his own school friends that he could start hanging out with after school, too. He rode his bike into the driveway of his home and wedged it against the garage wall. Entering the kitchen, he found his mother unpacking groceries.

'Natty, you're home early, darling,' his mother said and saw his face. 'What's happened.'

'Nothing... just wanted to come home.'

'I'll make you a sandwich.'

'I've eaten, thanks, at Adam's.'

'And where is Adam?'

Nate shrugged, and his mother sighed.

'Don't tell me you two have had a fight. You never fight.'

'Nuh, I've just got other things to do,' Nate said, taking the stairs to his room in the modest house in the economic section of the estate. He never cared that Adam was rich; it wasn't about that. They both had no brothers or sisters and liked the same thing – the creek, their bikes, cricket, and other stuff. They were like brothers.

Nate didn't understand it. Adam had slept over lots of time and didn't care about being in a rich house, so why did he want to stay with Griffin

Maxwell? He wished now he hadn't left Adam's house in a huff; he didn't want to be home, and his mum would find him a chore to do soon. He went to his window and looked out to the street. He could go to the oval and see if any cricket teams were playing or practising.

Then, he saw Adam riding his bike into his driveway and was super relieved and happy. Nate's driveway was really short and had no gate, unlike Adam's long drive with the big black security gate and the intercom.

He heard Adam knock and come in and greet his mother. Nate edged his way down the stairs to listen.

'He is home, Adam dear. He just arrived. Is everything okay? I hope you two have not had a fight.'

'No, Mrs Delaney. Nate is my best friend in the whole world. We're going to be friends forever.'

He heard his mum's delighted laugh and drank in his friend's reassurances.

'I think you will be, too, like brothers.'

Nate ran down the stairs. 'Hi, Murph. Wanna' go to the creek?'

'Yeah!'

'Not before you take a sandwich with you,' his mother said and started making a second for Adam. They departed with Nate's mum calling several warnings to them and a wave in her direction. All was well in the world again.

Now...

Nate paced around his office as he waited for Danielle's call. A glance at the clock told him it was nearing 4pm. A lot was hinged on this, and everything would need to play out at once.

Jessica entered. 'No,' she said on seeing him.

'No, what?'

'No, no one has called since you asked me a minute ago.'

Nate grimaced at her.

'How did Adam's family take it?' Jessica asked, handing him a mug of coffee.

'Thanks,' he said, appreciating that she wasn't one for making coffee but decided he must have needed it. 'The family reactions were fairly textbook. Winsome couldn't understand why Adam didn't wait until after the wedding to save a girl in trouble. Audrey was cool, calm, and ever-practical. Kelsey supported Adam, and Tom lost it as expected.'

Jessica rolled her eyes. 'I can't believe he did the dirty on Dan.'

'Tell me about it,' Nate said with a shake of his head.

'Dan said they were only casual, but she wasn't sleeping around.'

'The guy is a dick,' Nate said, his voice laced with disgust. 'Nothing changes. Is Dan okay? She brushed it off when we were talking about it.'

Jessica stood beside him at the window, sipping her coffee and looking down on the streets of Stones Corner. He tried to keep his gaze on the street, but he wanted Jessica, and working with her was becoming increasingly difficult. He was confident that Jessica felt the current running between them, too. The wedding could not come soon enough. But for now, she gave a small shrug and responded, 'Dan's been pretty relaxed about it, but you know her better than me... she doesn't wear her heart on her sleeve.'

'I wish she'd bloody ring,' he muttered, looking at his phone again. 'Tell me he didn't sleep with Winsome too?' Nate asked, alarmed, the thought suddenly occurring to him.

'No, of course not, she's about to marry Jack. And what woman on the planet would cheat on Jack.' Jessica sighed at the thought of the singer.

'Right, silly me.'

Jessica grinned.

'Forget Tom,' Nate said, 'he's gone from our lives in a few weeks, for good, hopefully. You know, for a while, I had some sympathy for him. But now I see Adam called it as it was.' A thought occurred to him. 'Don't tell Adam that Tom slept with his ex, will you?'

The buzzer interrupted her response, and Jessica headed to the door. 'That'll be Burnsy. He was swinging by to see if we had an update,' she said.

'He could have phoned me,' Nate said, raising an eyebrow in her direction. 'Visiting you more like it.'

Jessica ignored him but stopped at the doorway, asking, 'Do you think Adam would care about Stephanie and Tom hitching up?'

'No, but he'll care about Dan being done over, and it will only make things worse with Tom,' Nate pointed out. 'Let's just get through the wedding, and then after that, when Tom is gone, tell him whatever you like.'

'I'll leave that to Dan,' she said, exiting, 'it's her news to tell.'

Nate glanced at his phone again and muttered, 'Call, for God's sake.'

Striding up the path, the two ladies saw Griffin walking back along the route that led to Skye's wing.

'Give it your best; don't let on you know he's looking for you,' Danielle said with a nudge and a smile, and Skye stepped up to the job.

'Griffin!' she called out.

He turned and smiled on seeing her and walked back her way.

'I was just looking for you,' he said.

'I went for a dip at the creek,' Skye glanced at Danielle and laughed, 'and I persuaded Danielle to get in.'

'I should have come prepared,' Danielle grinned. 'Thank you for lunch, it was lovely.'

'My pleasure,' he said, and Danielle understood how he sucked in the girls with his powerful demeanour and strong gaze.

'Well, I'll leave you to talk, and I'll get changed.' Danielle departed and hurried to her room to change. She messaged Adam that she would be leaving within the hour to manage a client and would return tonight. She kept the message subtle in case anyone else should attempt to read his phone.

A glance out the window confirmed Skye was on the pathway back to her room. No doubt Griffin told her she was "invited" to entertain Adam tonight. She surmised that the term "actress" was used very loosely at the Wellness Studio.

Danielle changed into dry clothes and heard her phone ping with a return message from Adam. The next minute, he was walking up the path to her door. She opened it for him.

'I've only got a minute,' she said.

Adam nodded. 'Do you need me to distract Griffin or Zach? I can talk to Zach about using one of the offices.' He kept his voice low and glanced outside regularly.

'Skye seemed to think it wouldn't be an issue. She could easily get to the VIP House car park, and there were no cameras. Griffin keeps it dark and private – it's better that way for business, apparently.'

Adam scoffed. 'I imagine so.'

'Why don't you just come with us?' Danielle suggested.

Adam thought about it for a moment, then shook his head. 'If we both leave suddenly, then they find Skye has left, they will know we're onto them. He'll destroy any evidence – maybe a big fire like his father did – and we don't want him to get away with anything.'

'True. Skye saw Zach carrying the woman's body out of her room wrapped in a sheet or similar.'

Adam exhaled. 'We need to catch them unawares. Give the police time to shut down and case the joint.'

'You'll be careful?' Danielle frowned, still not sure if she was taking the right course of action.

'Sure. I'm just meeting the old boys for a drink.'

'Unless Ben starts talking about Nate's visit to his office and Griffin puts it together. If he looks up your business, it's going to be hard to deny you know Nate when the business is called Delaney and Murphy.'

Adam grinned. 'Hopefully, I'll banish the boys, and it will be just Griffin and me talking about the good old days when his family house burned down with all the porn in it.'

Danielle huffed and shook her head at him. 'Right, got to go.' With her hand on the door handle, she took a stabilising breath. 'I'll be back tonight with the calvary. Tread water until then.'

'Will do,' Adam promised. 'Be careful, drive safely down the mountain, don't speed just because you're breaking out – the light is fading and the roads are winding.'

'Thanks, Dad, I'll drive safely, promise.'

'It's not the car I'm worried about, Dan,' he added.

'Thanks.' She gave him an affectionate smile, and they departed her room, going their separate ways. Danielle adopted a calm, professional expression that said – hopefully – *nothing to see here*, and swinging her handbag over her shoulder, headed to the car park. She did not feel any eyes on her or any threat. The path to Skye's quarters was visible but not

Skye. No problem, she could already be at the car park or on another route there.

Walking through the grounds, Danielle greeted two women who passed her, both beautiful and young. She took the path to the VIP House and then the driveway ramp down to the underground car park rather than try to enter the building and take the lift. It took her eyes a minute to adjust to the dark. Obviously, clients didn't like to be spotlit or see each other; no fear of that here. There was only enough lighting to make your way.

The car park was completely silent, and most of the camp was the same way, given it was located on a mountain with no neighbours in calling distance. Danielle made her way to Adam's car, pressed the keys and heard the familiar beep of the car unlocking. She didn't look around but opened the door, lowered herself into the front seat and adjusted it, quickly turning off the interior car light before closing the door. Turning on the ignition, she waited, holding her breath. It was 4.15pm. She wanted to get back to the Wellness Camp with the cops before Ben landed Adam in any trouble if that eventuated.

And then the back door of the car opened and closed moments later. Skye was on the back seat floor; they had done it. Danielle locked the doors.

'Okay?' Danielle asked.

'Yes,' Skye exhaled with relief. 'Yes.'

They drove out of the car park and, moments later, out onto the back road, away from the Wellness Studio grounds.

'We're clear, but stay down until we get off the mountain,' Danielle said.

'That was terrifying,' Skye whispered.

'I can imagine. But you did it. You're free,' Danielle said, a smile in her voice. She hit Nate's number, and he answered immediately.

'What's happening?'

'We're clear. I'm just about at the foot of the mountain. You're on speakerphone, and I have Skye with me.'

'Thank God.' She heard him exhale as if the weight of the world had been on his shoulders.

'Hard to be waiting on someone in danger, isn't it?' she teased.

'I'm not usually the passenger,' Nate agreed. 'What about Adam?'

'He's fine. He'll have dinner with Griffin tonight if we're not back with the cops before then, but the sooner, the better. Skye is a witness to the murder.'

'Let me hear her voice,' Nate said.

'Hello,' Skye said from the back seat. 'Thank you for believing Mum and Dad and coming for me.'

'Hi Sarah, they'll be so relieved.'

Dan continued, 'I'm going to stop at the bottom of the mountain and Skye, Sarah, can get into the front seat. I'll stick with Skye if that's okay, or I'll confuse myself?'

'Sure,' the voice came from the back seat.

'Will you call her folks and Burnsy?' Danielle asked. 'We'll be at your office in about thirty minutes, depending on traffic.'

'Done. Burnsy is here now, and I'll call John and Robin and tell them their daughter is on her way. Dan, great job.'

Nate disconnected, and Danielle glanced back, only seeing the edge of Skye, but she smiled. 'If the cops raid the place and arrest Griffin and his cohorts, you should be able to get your earnings back, and hopefully, that place will close down.'

'Not everyone will be happy about that,' Skye said. 'There are girls there that want to work and are happy to be available to Zach or VIP clients. But it's not the acting content we're making. It's porn, that's all it is... the acting lessons and the modelling are a smokescreen.'

'Then Griffin Maxwell should promote it as a business for working girls and be upfront. It's a great environment for creating content and hosting clients. If everyone is consenting and happy, who cares?'

'Yeah, but he makes more money from selling innocence and freshness. Or rather naivety. Plus, he likes to welcome new girls personally. They don't get offered around until he is finished with them or there's another new girl in the camp.'

Danielle shook her head. 'Pulling over now.' She found a wide and safe verge and slowed the car to a stop, unlocking the doors. Skye jumped out of the back seat and slipped into the front passenger seat. Dan locked the doors again and, once Skye was belted up, pulled back out onto the road.

'Let's go see your folks.'

Skye closed her eyes and exhaled. 'Yes, please, and get justice for Rain.'

Chapter 35

Adam returned to his room, made a quick call to Kelsey, and hung up afterwards. Taking a deep breath, he set his mind to having drinks with Griffin and whoever the wellness guru was roping into the entourage tonight. His phone buzzed, and he looked down to see Nate calling.

'Are you okay?' Nate asked before Adam could say hello.

'Yep, and you?'

'Of course, I'm okay,' Nate said impatiently. 'I'm in the office. What do you think is going to happen to me here? A rogue pencil sharpener gets me?'

Adam chuckled. 'Bit tense?'

'Shut up,' Nate said and drew a deep breath. 'I bloody hate waiting, and that's all I'm doing. Waiting on Dan, waiting for Burnsy to give our raid the green light, waiting on you to get the hell out of there, and waiting to get Skye back with her folks. Why aren't I in the thick of the action?'

'You're in the control tower. Just don't let any of us crash, Captain,' Adam assured him.

'So, you're okay?' Nate snapped, still unhappy.

'Yes. Is Dan there yet?'

'No, but I've heard from her, and she's due here soon. Burnsy is in your office making calls to organise the raid. I hope you didn't leave anything confidential on the desk?'

'Just your psyche evaluation,' Adam joked.

'That'll make good reading,' Nate scoffed.

'How did the parents take it?'

'Ecstatic. I've called Tom in as well,' Nate informed him.

'Right. I'm just about to rock up for drinks, and Lord knows what,' Adam sighed.

'I'm hoping with Skye's statement – Sarah's statement, whatever – we can get to you and break up your party early, especially if Ben decides to arrive and win brownie points with Griffin by mentioning my visit. What will you say if Griffin makes the connection?'

'That you're worth a thousand of him.' There was silence on the line. Adam knew Nate wouldn't handle that level of emotion; he could barely say the words himself, and Nate didn't have a retort prepared. Adam continued saving Nate from responding. 'Don't worry. Hopefully, Griffin will put Ben off until later. I'll tell him we have so much to talk about and catch up on, and he can see those two clowns anytime... I can hardly wait to hear all his stories and make up some of my own.'

'Good, but don't call them clowns, for God's sake.'

'Thanks, coach, I'll try and remember that.' Adam said with a roll of his eyes that Nate could not see. 'I have dealt with plenty of off-balanced people before.'

'Yeah, and you've got the bandaged hand to prove it.'

Nate's comment riled Adam. He was not new to this and tired of his career being disregarded, the worst offenders being his mother and ex-wife.

'Just calm down,' Adam said in a controlled voice. There was a momentary silence.

'Right. Sorry. I'm not good being on the peripheral.' Nate became serious. 'Don't underestimate him.'

'I won't.'

'Don't go to the VIP House if you can avoid it.'

'Why?'

'Because if we raid the place, you don't want to be found there, especially if the media get word of our raid. You want to disappear into the background and get out of there fast. One of them is bound to recognise you. Actually, I'll get Dan to come back in her car, not yours, so your rego is not recorded.'

'Yeah, good point. Mum won't want those headlines – "*The It Girl's son's porn habit*".'

'Where did she go wrong?' Nate joked.

'I know, with all the opportunities I had,' Adam joked, but a stab of bitterness followed, and he pulled himself out of it. 'Message me if you can when you're on your way, or get Dan to message me, and I'll tell the guys it's just my security detail returning.'

'Will do. Seriously, be careful.'

'Why are you so worried about this?' Adam asked, hesitating at the door as he was just about to leave his room.

'You're potentially three against one until we get there.'

'Then move it and stop talking to me.'

He heard Nate chuckle as he said goodbye and hung up. Adam pocketed his phone and went to be social with a man whom he believed to be a narcissistic murderer.

Griffin Maxwell studied Adam Murphy as his old school acquaintance walked up the path towards the clubhouse, where they would have a drink and watch the sunset over the mountain. Adam looked comfortable in his own skin, glancing at his watch and looking at the sunset behind the mountain. Unlike Zach and Ben, who acted like big men – driving the best cars, wearing expensive suits and watches – on Adam, it fitted him naturally. Strong, dark, silent, unreadable. Adam's eyes were not seeking approval from him like Zach and Ben's were constantly and from the girls. Adam had the ability to calm him, and for a man who prided himself on his sense of calmness, that was telling – they were kindred spirits.

Here was the one kid he wanted to befriend who did not bend to his demands. Why? Griffin Maxwell always felt good enough, except when it came to Adam Murphy. The pressure his father put on him to befriend Adam still made him grit his teeth in anger, but this, now, was a huge breakthrough. They were friends.

As if sensing eyes upon him, Adam looked up and around, his eyes meeting Griffin's, and he smiled as if he were pleased to see him. Griffin raised a hand in a wave as Adam made his way up the path. They had wasted years when they could have been creating something together. He cut off that train of thought as it always led back to his father and was followed by more anger. But with their networks and pedigree, they could have been much further advanced.

Now, Griffin had money, an obscene amount – his father was right, there was always a market for porn, but he had found a more tasteful way to present it. It was all about the tease. His first girlfriend had taught him that – Brooke was a cheerleader, and her costume included a tiny swishing skirt which he was keen to dispense with as often as possible. Brooke taught him that was the most enticing part of the uniform. It wasn't all on display; it was the promise of what was hidden, the temptation, and his thousands of customers paid big to peak daily, both online and in the VIP House.

Now, like Adam, Griffin was rich, successful and charismatic, and with Adam now before him, it was a promising start for the next phase of his business.

'Vodka?'

'Beer if you've got it?' Adam said.

'Of course.'

Griffin grabbed two boutique beers from the small fridge near them and returned; Zach made his way up the path. He greeted Adam frostily and got the same sentiment back. Griffin didn't offer Zach a drink; he knew where to help himself. But he glared at Zach – this was business and important. Don't stuff it up.

Let the bonding begin, Adam thought, accepting the beer from Griffin.

'It's a great way to finish the day,' he said, looking at the sunset and clinking his bottle against Griffin in cheers.

'It's what we do every day,' Zach agreed, joining them. Adam recognised the territorial comment for what it was.

Not tonight, mate, he thought.

Adam took the offered deck chair, sat back and watched the show – the orange flame sinking behind the mountain. The grounds were quiet, which was surprising given that a dozen or more people lived nearby. He saw a car heading up the back road to the VIP House and wondered if it was an early client for the evening or Ben arriving. It was not one of his team, and he would have recognised the car.

'You've done well for yourself here,' Adam said to Griffin. He was playing the game now, a bit of praise, speaking only to Griffin.

'It's a piece of paradise. But I'm about ready to let it go,' he said, and Zach snapped to look at him.

Clearly, Zach was not in the loop, and Griffin had not voiced his plans before.

'Ready for a change?' Adam asked, giving Griffin his full attention.

'I'm thinking of following in my father's footsteps – not leaving the country,' he said and laughed, 'going into politics.'

'Really?' Adam said and smiled at him. 'Wow, as an independent?'

'Yes.'

Adam nodded. 'You would do well. What platforms?'

'Glad you asked,' Griffin said, but before he could continue – and he needed to win Adam's endorsement – Ben Solomon appeared on the path from the VIP House where he had parked undercover and was walking towards them. Ben's countenance changed after seeing Adam Murphy.

Zach rose, and Griffin said lowly, 'You didn't become friends after I left the school?'

'No,' Adam said flatly.

'I'll get rid of them.'

Adam said nothing. It was all going to plan.

Chapter 36

The team of cars that made their way up Tamborine Mountain looked like a fleet of tourists arriving. The headlights of five vehicles followed in close procession with Danielle in the first car, Nate and Tom in the car following – as Adam would leave straight away with Danielle in her car – then Burnsy with his policing partner, and an additional two police squad cars took up the rear with eight officers between them. Tom believed he should lead as Adam's security detail, but as Nate pointed out, the first car they would be expecting was Danielle returning, so the plan was for her to take the lead.

Danielle and Nate left the Lyons family to reunite – there were tears and grateful thanks offered. As Danielle drove, Nate spoke to her by phone, reviewing the plan again. There had been little time in the office to bed it down with the family reunion and Nate pushing to get on the road.

'So Burnsy will stick to this plan?' Danielle asked, talking hands-free as she negotiated the turns of the mountain.

'Within reason. I thought he might have gone straight there, but it looks like he is playing safe,' Nate informed her. 'So, when we near the Wellness Studio, we'll all stop out of sight and let you get ahead. How far is the car park from where Adam will be?'

'A brisk five-minute walk at best. I'll park in the undercover VIP House; Adam knows where the car will be because we parked there when we arrived, and I'll make my way to him. He messaged to say they were in the clubhouse having drinks.'

'How civilised,' Nate said. 'Righto, once you have eyes on him and Griffin, message us the all-clear, and we'll drive the last leg, park and raid. Ben might not be there but try to see Zach. We don't want to be ambushed.'

'Gotcha. I won't stick around with Adam. Griffin won't welcome that, so as soon as I see Adam and make a big deal of saying I'm back, I'll turn straight around and come back toward the car park. Then I can direct you guys to the clubhouse and wait for him in the car,' she said.

'Yeah, that will work,' Tom agreed, adding his comments.

'Be careful. You're dealing with dickheads,' Nate said.

Danielle laughed. 'What's new?' She hung up.

They stopped at the Tamborine Mountain turn-off to wait for Burnsy and his team to catch up, and moments later, the cop cars arrived. They all continued on with no sirens.

Looking back in the rear-view mirror, Danielle took comfort in seeing the parade of cars behind her. She drove the remaining distance, thinking about Adam and Griffin and their strange worlds. She had known Adam a few years now through Nate. She imagined how different he could have been had he brought into his pedigree – if he had modelled, acted, or just taken advantage of nepotism – born into a celebrity. She almost laughed at the thought, and it was so not him.

She came to the turn-off and saw the other cars slow down. Danielle knew Burnsy wouldn't like waiting and was surprised the cop cars didn't go around Nate and just follow her. But she guessed knowing the lay of the land and where everyone was before launching the raid had its advantages, especially when there was evidence to be destroyed.

Danielle drove on, arriving at the VIP House. She drove into the dark underground car park, her eyes adjusting to the green directional lighting, and she dimmed her headlights and parked as close as she could to the exit so Adam could get away quickly. She killed the lights and said to herself, 'Let the show begin.'

Grabbing her handbag, which she'd prefer not to carry, but unless she swung by her room first, it would be strange to arrive with nothing but her keys for a female, that is, so she swung it over her shoulder and exited.

As she turned, Danielle gasped.

'You're back.'

Adam knew he had Griffin Maxwell in the palm of his hand the moment Griffin declared an interest in politics. Now he had a subject and could feign that was the reason he wanted to speak with him alone, to talk about the future and what Griffin could achieve.

'Been a long time, Murphy,' Ben said, coming up on the veranda and offering his hand. The two men shook.

'It has been. What are you into these days?' Adam asked. He didn't give a toss.

'Information technology. I run my own business. But you knew that, I'm guessing.'

Adam gave him a small smile as if Ben would be of no interest to him whatsoever.

'Would I?' he asked.

Adam saw Griffin and Zach's bemused look. Clearly, Ben had kept Nate's visit to himself, intending to tell Griffin about it tonight and look like the hero who had his boss's best interest at heart.

'Can I have a private word?' Ben asked Griffin.

'I have a guest,' Griffin said as if it were obvious, 'talk with me tomorrow.'

'It's rather urgent.'

'Then talk to Zach. He's the manager,' Griffin dismissed him by looking away and back out at the last light of the day.

Adam took the opportunity. 'Speaking of private words, no offence, guys, but I haven't seen Griffin since my 11th birthday party, and I know that you see him regularly.' He turned to address Griffith only, 'I was hoping we could catch up alone.' He realised how intimate and even stupid it sounded, but Griffin, the narcissist, would lap it up, and Adam was not wrong.

'I was thinking the same,' he said. 'Why don't you guys enjoy some time at the VIP House tonight? We'll talk in the morning.'

Adam watched as Griffin made it final, turning his back on the two men. Zach's anger was quick to hit his features. His eyes narrowed at Adam, his jaw locked, and if looks could kill, Adam would be a chalk outline on the ground.

'Seems we've been dismissed, Ben,' Zach said curtly, which earned him an angry look from Griffin, who would not welcome being embarrassed in front of company.

'I thought you'd appreciate the night off,' Griffin said to him calmly, meeting Zach's expression with a haughty look of his own.

'Right. Perhaps tomorrow you can also tell me of your plans for this place since you're considering moving on,' Zach said through thinned lips. 'Since I've run this place for you 24 hours a day for four years.'

Griffin gave him a cool nod, but his eyes were narrowed in anger. Adam had never seen him worked up and was curious what that would look like. The other two men—Zach and Ben—he could guess how anger manifested itself with them – using their fists.

'I really need to speak with you. Just a minute of your time,' Ben tried again.

'Later.' Griffin said one word, and his tone brooked no argument.

Adam watched the dynamic interplay with interest. The look exchanged between Griffin and Zach was as if words were exchanged, but nothing was said.

Zach stormed off down the stairs, with Ben hurrying to catch him, no doubt wanting to share what he knew to make an ally of Zach. Adam glanced to the road; no headlights yet. He had a small window of time until those two returned and demanded Griffin's time; he just hoped the cavalry was coming sooner rather than later.

'I'm sorry about that,' Griffin said.

'They are loyal to you.'

'I wonder,' Griffin said and took a seat beside Adam. He took a large mouthful of his beer before adding, 'Everyone's loyal to you until you can't give them what they want.'

Adam studied him. 'You've been betrayed.'

Griffin gave a small nod.

'There must be at least one person here who would stick by you if everything went bad... Zach, one of the girls?' Adam prodded.

'Leaf, you met her at the lunch. She's the best manager I've ever had, and probably Zach. Although I feel I buy his loyalty most days – he gets paid well, and the benefits are on tap.'

Adam nodded. 'I noticed.'

Still no headlights.

'You are right, though. The last time I saw you was your 11th birthday party when I gave you the photos.'

Adam chuckled. 'My first sex education lesson.'

Griffin laughed, visibly relaxing more and more in Adam's company. 'Trust me, when I stumbled upon my father's collection, it was a hell of a shock to me too.'

'Did he know you had seen them or took some?'

'Hell no. I don't even know why I gave them to you,' Griffin said. 'Maybe I just wanted an ally, someone to talk with about them.'

'You didn't show your group?'

Griffin shook his head. 'They would have made it a big deal. These photos were different; even then, I knew they were shocking and had to be kept secret. Did you give them to your Dad?'

'Not at first,' Adam said. 'I can't really remember the order in which it happened now... I think I started asking about sex, and they all ran around trying to give me the talk... somehow the photos surfaced. Were you at home when the fire started?'

'I wasn't even in the country. I woke up, Mum was in the room packing my stuff, and we flew out of the country that day without explanation. I didn't know about the fire that night or understand Dad's resignation and what was behind it until years later. Most people still believe an over-zealous voter targeted him, and to protect us, he withdrew his bid for premier and took his family somewhere safe.' Griffin scoffed as he finished the sentence.

'We both got lost in the fallout,' Adam joked. 'I had to ask my security officer for the sex talk. Dad forgot in his rush to get to the source of the pics.'

'He found it. I got the thrashing of my life,' Griffin said, finishing his beer. 'So, you know how it's done then, the sex thing?'

Adam laughed. 'Yeah, I'm brilliant.'

Griffin grinned. 'Of course you are.' Then his eyes widened in realisation. 'Oh, your security guard at school... the hot one gave you the sex talk?'

Adam nodded and smiled.

'Wow, she was beautiful. We all watched her walk you to the gate every day. A bunch of 11-year-olds with our first crush.'

'Yeah, Charlie, gave me the female perspective.'

'No wonder you're good,' Griffin joked.

Still no headlights.

Chapter 37

Danielle didn't need this distraction; time was of the essence.

'It's Leaf, isn't it?'

'Yes. And you're Adam's security. It begs the question, then, why you would be giving Skye a lift somewhere.'

Danielle didn't shock easily and sized up the women opposite her. Leaf was taller – a lot of people were, but Danielle was fitter, stronger and didn't suffer fools.

'I didn't know you weren't allowed to leave the premises. She asked for a lift to the city. Are you saying you are trapped here?'

Leaf looked as if she was caught off guard – a loaded question – and she hesitated before answering.

'Of course, we can come and go as we want.'

'Right then, did you want a lift next?' Danielle asked and, with a smile, added, 'I need to check on Adam.'

Leaf laughed. 'I'm sure he's in good hands. Zach told me Griffin was obsessed with getting Adam into their group when they were school kids. Apparently, nothing changes.'

'Apparently so.'

The woman continued to stand in the way, so Danielle began walking, and Leaf moved in front of her again.

'What do you want?'

'I want to know who you really are.'

Danielle sighed dramatically. 'I work in security, and I've been assigned as Adam's security detail until after his mother's wedding. Surely Zach told you that Adam had a security guard even at school... Griffin probably did, too. Now either walk with me or move.'

Leaf laughed. 'So out of the blue, Griffin runs into his old school friend. You two arrive, and you've driven Skye somewhere. Out of here for good?'

Danielle was running out of time and patience. 'I met Skye at the creek and said I was going to the city to catch up with a client. She wanted a lift. I didn't know she needed your permission. What do you care anyway? Are you Griffin's guard bitch?'

The air changed around them. And then a police siren could be heard.

'What have you done?' Leaf hissed, and Danielle smiled.

'Just brought a few friends with me.'

Griffin leapt to his feet as he saw the red and blue flashing headlights coming up the road beside the Wellness Camp.

'What's going on?' Adam asked, rising to stand beside him and giving his best performance of ignorance of the situation.

'I have no idea, but it's not the first time they've raided us,' Griffin said through gritted teeth. 'Head back to your room if you want to be discreet.'

For just a moment, Adam felt a wave of guilt that Griffin would try to protect him, the man who was throwing his host under the bus.

'Danielle should be back,' Adam said, suddenly realising she hadn't appeared as planned.

'Don't worry. The security is good here. Ben has cameras around all the perimeter, and his people are monitoring it.'

The police cars stopped outside the gates, lights flashing until the gates opened. Adam didn't ask how but assumed Zach had let them in.

'I've got to see to this, excuse me.'

'Sure,' Adam said and took his cue to disappear. He took the path to the VIP car park where Danielle was supposed to meet him and hurried as fast as he could without looking like he was abandoning a sinking ship. Grabbing his phone, he rang Nate.

'Dan's not here.'

'I know. We didn't hear from her, and she's not answering her phone, so we just decided to barge in.'

'I'm on my way to the VIP car park.'

'No... okay, I guess that's probably the best option,' Nate said, remembering their plan.

Adam hung up but saw Nate in his car following the cop cars in; he pulled into a car park near the reception office. As Nate hurriedly alighted, they locked eyes, but Adam continued. It became quieter as Adam reached the outer boundaries and the private road that led to the VIP House. It also became darker.

'Where are you, Dan,' he muttered, looking at the building on arrival; he opted to take the ramp down to the car park. He couldn't tell if there were clients inside the building as the windows were darkened and he hadn't yet got the tour, so he wasn't sure of the lay of the land, but as he hurried down the ramp into the dark car park, he saw three or four cars – clients maybe. One of the vehicles was probably Ben's. Adam's car wasn't there as planned, but Danielle's vehicle waited for him.

Adam hurried to the vehicle and tried the door. It was locked. A glance inside told him she wasn't there; that was a relief, at least.

'Looking for your security detail, Murphy?'

Adam recognised the voice and turned. 'Ben. Yep, seen her?'

'I have, actually.' Ben crossed his arms over his chest and stared at Adam as if deciding whether to share the information or not.

'And?' Adam pushed.

Ben smirked. 'I had a visit today from an old friend of yours.'

'Lucky you. So, where's Danielle gone?'

'Not at all curious, hey? That tells me you knew all about it.' He did the chin-up thing that he used to do at school like it was a code amongst the brothers, and he was on the inside.

'What do you want, Ben?' Adam snapped. He needed to find Danielle, and he needed to get out of there. He didn't have time for the roadblock in front of him.

'Your friend was asking about this place and if the girls were being held against their will. Supposedly, he's got a client, parents of one of the women here who think this is a cult and their beloved daughter is chanting and eating sprouts.' Ben laughed.

Adam knew it was stupid to incite Ben to anger, but there was no love lost between them. Ben was a schoolyard bully, and Adam was over idiots.

'Well, that's all very interesting, and from your laugh, I'm guessing it is not a cult, even though you and Zach are still following Griffin around like he's the guru. Got to go. Where's Danielle?'

Ben's reaction was swift, and he grabbed Adam by the collar of his shirt, swinging him around and slamming him into the wall. A shot of pain ran up his back.

'I don't care what Griffin thinks of you and your famous family. You're nothing to me,' Ben hissed.

'Where's Danielle?' Adam said through gritted teeth.

Stay on track.

Ben released him, pushing him back against the wall again for good measure.

'Leaf is giving her a tour of the VIP House,' Ben said and gave a small laugh.

The way he said *"tour"* had Adam on edge.

'Want to join them?' Ben asked.

Before he could answer, the lift door behind Ben opened, and Zach stepped out, a smirk on his face. Adam knew he was in trouble. He might have held his own in a fight with Zach – they were similar in height and build, but Ben was a big kid at school, and nothing had changed. With two against one, it would be all over before it started.

Zach grinned. 'Sorry to crash the party, boys. Are you coming to enjoy the VIP House, Murphy? Let's go then and find your fetish.' He stood back and indicated Adam should enter the lift.

'Not interested, thanks, Zach. I need to find Danielle.'

'Right this way then,' Ben said with a smirk.

He began to think they had planned this, and it started with Danielle being led away. The two men moved closer. Adam had been here before, but this time, no Charlie was waiting at the school gate and watching, and there was no Danielle either.

'Why is Danielle in the VIP House?'

'Clearly, she's more curious than you,' Zach said, attempting to rile him.

'Perhaps she's looking for a new career instead of playing bodyguard to—'

'Let's go.' Zach cut off Ben, not for the first time, and Adam saw Ben's jaw lock with frustration. Zach nodded towards the lift.

Every fibre of Adam's being told him not to go in there. But he was standing alone in a garage with two guys he'd never gotten on with, and the fight refuelled. He had no choice. Adam entered the lift, flanked by both men. Zach put in a code, hit the second-floor button, and they travelled in silence in the dimly lit box until Ben decided to share.

'Murphy thinks we follow Griffin around like he's the guru.'

The punch to his stomach came fast and hard from Zach, and he doubled over in pain as Ben delivered another swift blow low and fast to his rib area.

'Don't touch his face,' Zach scoffed, 'we don't want Griffin thinking we're damaging the merchandise.' He reached into his jacket for something, and then a needle appeared.

'Get the hell away from me,' Adam struggled as Ben rammed him against the corner. Zach injected whatever was in the syringe into Adam's neck. He slumped as they moved away.

'What was that?' Adam asked, his unbandaged hand going to his neck and wiping away a droplet of blood.

'Just something to make the game more fun.'

The door opened, and Zach exited, striding along the narrow passageway. Ben shoved Adam out in front of him. Adam winced, straightened, and followed Zach down the moodily lit hallway, which had half a dozen closed doors alternating on the left and right. Towards the end of the passageway, Zach swung open a door and moved aside for Adam to enter.

'Danielle?' Adam called and heard her voice coming from the room he was about to enter.

'Adam!'

He hurried into the room, and the door slammed behind him. Adam heard it lock. They were alone.

'Christ! Where are you, Dan?'

'I'm here.' Danielle said, and Adam followed her voice. She was lying on the floor behind a couch in the corner of the room.

He swooped down and helped raise her, lowering her to the couch before kneeling before her. 'How did you get there?'

'I just tripped.'

'Okay...' he tried a less literal question. 'What's happened since you arrived?'

She rolled her eyes. 'Leaf, Fern, whatever her name is, had a knife. She saw me getting Skye out. I don't know how, but she made me follow her, and here I am. I'm locked in, I think.'

'Your trippy is what you are,' Adam said, worried and guessing from the injection he was going to be the same in a short amount of time.

'I tried to find an exit. Why are you here?' She cocked her head to the side. 'Why didn't you leave?'

'I was looking for you, and you have the car keys.'

'Oh, crap, right. Do you want them now?'

'No. But I wouldn't have left without you.'

'Thanks,' she smiled at him. 'Adam...'

'Yes?'

'I've been injected with something. I think we're in a world of trouble. Why are you wincing?'

'Me too. I've just had the same injection.'

Danielle shook her head. 'I'm feeling a little... whacked.'

Adam studied her. 'Yep, your pupils are dilated. We've got to call Nate and get help before we both can't think straight.'

'This room... there are no exits. I've looked, no exits.'

'Okay,' Adam said, realising Danielle was on the edge of panic. 'I'll call Nate.' He reached for his phone and repocketed it quickly as the door in front of them opened, and Leaf, Zach and Ben entered. He didn't want the phone to be confiscated if they realised he had it on him.

'We're out of here,' Adam said.

'You think?' Ben smirked. 'The fun hasn't started yet.'

Adam threw up his hands. 'What do you want, Ben? We're not eleven anymore. I'm sorry Griffin doesn't want to play with you but get out of our way. I'm taking Dan now, and we're going.'

He felt slightly nauseous and reached out his hand to steady himself.

'You know what shits me, Murphy? We've worked with Griffin from day one, and you rock up and—' Ben stopped mid-sentence as Zach held up his hand.

'Then buy the place from him. Run it yourselves,' Adam said and saw Leaf's expression of surprise as she turned to Zach for an explanation. She looked a lot like Skye, a lot like most of the girls at the camp.

'I just found out myself,' he hurriedly told her. 'Griffin's thinking of moving on.'

'We could do that,' she said, her eyes lit up with excitement. 'We could make a killing with this place and run it how we want. Forget the models, do online porn content and the VIP House services.'

Adam watched, his mind feeling a little slower and hazier, stunting his ability to read the situation as quickly. So, these two were in a relationship, and she had power in the place, too. Griffin said she was the only person he trusted. He might have misplaced that trust.

Did I say that out loud?

Zach smirked at her. 'Speaking of a killing, the cops are here, and someone's squealed.'

'Skye,' Leaf said, spitting out the name with disgust. She glared at Adam and Danielle. 'This bitch got her out.'

'Woah,' Danielle said, swaying slightly as she rose. Adam reached for her, and she dropped down onto the couch again. 'Perhaps we should all get out of here because this place is not looking too good. It's getting really crowded in here.' Danielle was looking at the walls as if they were closing in.

Zach gave her a cool smile, and Leaf laughed, saying, 'Good stuff that.'

'You've got about five minutes, Murphy,' Zach turned his attention to Adam. 'Then the game begins. Just a hint, play for real because trust me, we will be.'

'Does Griffin know about this?' Adam couldn't help but ask out of curiosity. 'Did he know you were planning this?' He felt a rising sense of distortion within him like his organs were moving, and he knew the drug was kicking in – a hallucinogen.

'We planned a special tour of the VIP House for you the moment Griffin told Zach you were coming,' Ben said.

'But no, Griffin would never approve of his precious guest playing the game. Lucky he isn't here,' Zach said. 'When a new girl starts, we always like to put her through a scenario, so as you are both new to the camp...' Zach grinned as he hinted at what was to come.

'You mean you scare the shit out of her and film it,' Adam said, regarding them. He heard a voice behind him and turned. Then it was in the hallway. Maybe it wasn't there at all.

Zach continued, 'The difference is we won't stop at the end to welcome you and congratulate you on a fine performance... we'll play until you drop.'

Ben whooped like it was the most exciting thing in his day, and Leaf looked hungry for blood.

'Tick tock,' Zach said, and the three departed the room.

Chapter 38

Nate watched as Burnsy handcuffed Griffin Maxwell and gave him the spiel about his rights. Griffin looked around, seeing the stricken look of some of his loyal girls and then hearing Burnsy call Nate by name, Griffin's gaze settled on Nate, and he smiled.

'Well, if it isn't.'

'It is,' Nate said coolly.

Griffin shook his head. 'I should have known Adam would still have you tagging along.'

'Yeah, I've always been a follower,' Nate agreed, playing into Griffin's hand. 'Like Zach and Ben. Surprising, I'm not here working for you when you think about it.'

Griffin sneered. 'I'll be back here in no time as soon as this bogus charge is dropped, and then Adam will know all about your pathetic attempt to derail me.'

'Good luck with that. I'm so firmly entrenched in his life now,' Nate continued, being churlish but weirdly enjoying it. 'I'm living at his place on the river, going to the wedding as his guest. I wouldn't know what to do with myself if I wasn't following Adam around.'

Burnsy heard Nate's last comment and smothered a laugh as he pushed Griffin into the car's back seat and closed the door.

Speaking of Adam, Nate grabbed his phone and called him. It rang a few times before he answered and said two words. 'VIP House.'

'Adam? You're in the VIP House? Is Dan with you?'

'Yep.'

'Are you okay?'

'Maybe.'

'Adam, what's going on?'

'You'd better find us. We're about to play.' The line went dead.

'What the hell,' Nate muttered. 'Adam's still here, and he sounded weird! For the love of God, how hard is it to leave the premises?' he swore under his breath.

'Where is he?'

'Up at the VIP House, and something is not right. His phone cut out. Dan's there too.'

Burnsy looked up the hill at the large, dark building. 'Tom went up there, and my men are heading that way to look for the body that Skye said was taken into the premises.' Burnsy started to walk towards it. 'Let's follow.'

Nate looked at Griffin in the back seat.

'He's cuffed. He's not going anywhere.'

'I wouldn't put it past him.'

Burnsy called out to one of the younger constables and assigned him to watch the prisoner. 'Let's go. It's a weird place, and God knows what could happen to those two in the VIP House.'

Despite his instincts to have a go at the three captors in front of them, Adam wasn't sure he was up to it. He wanted to save Danielle, and for a moment, he had a wild sense of bravado and felt like he could take on the world. The next, he could see lots of people in the room and couldn't pick out the three he wanted to get. And then they were all gone. He realised Danielle was standing beside him, ready to fight.

'Your eyes are huge,' she said wide-eyed and looking at him.

'There's something on me,' Adam said, touching his neck. He brushed his hand down his shirt. 'It's on me.'

'Nope, there's nothing, but the black part of your eyes is huge,' she said again.

A voice cut into their conversation, coming from a speaker on the wall.

'You may leave the room in thirty seconds. The room will be folding in; do not delay.'

'Did you hear that?' Adam asked, checking he wasn't hearing voices.

Danielle grabbed his arm. 'The room is folding in already.'

'We've got to stick together and find an exit.'

'The walls are closing in,' Danielle said, beginning to panic. 'Where is everybody?'

Adam nodded. 'Yeah! If we find everyone, we can mingle in, and no one will see us if they leave, and we follow.' He frowned, unsure if he was making sense.

The room went dark, and a voice said, 'You have ten seconds to evacuate the room.'

They moved to the door, distinguishable only by a weak beam of light beneath it. Adam expected it to be locked, but it swung open easily, and they entered a darkened hallway with a small glow at the other end.

'That's the exit,' Danielle said, running toward the light, stumbling into the wall and righting herself. Adam followed, and then the hallway went red, strobing red. A fire alarm began to wail.

'Fire!' Danielle yelled and tried several doors near her, but none of them opened.

His sense of panic was acute.

Smoke, he could smell smoke. *They could burn alive.*

He felt like his heart was going to pump out of his chest.

'This way,' Adam said, stopping momentarily as one of the doors he tried opened. 'Quick, the fire's coming.' He could see the red flames travelling fast towards them. He grabbed Danielle, pulled her into the room and slammed the door. It was dark and cool, with soft blue lighting. The wail of the fire extinguisher stopped, and he exhaled with relief.

'We're saved,' Danielle yelled, and Adam winced. 'The water. Can you hear it?'

The shadows were long in the room, and the blue light made them more elongated.

'I see you,' a voice whispered.

Adam snapped around. 'Who's there?'

'It's me, Adam,' a young female voice said, but there was no one there. 'It's me. I'm so cold.'

Now, he could hear the sound of water running fast, and the water level on the walls was rising.

'It's getting deeper,' Danielle said, panicked. 'I can swim. Can you swim? What if we're in a fishbowl and there's no way out!'

Her eyes were huge, and Adam said, 'There's no water.' He looked around and assured himself. 'There's no water. No water, no water.'

'I can hear it. We're going to drown.' She ran to the edge of the room, hitting the walls until she found the door again, and it opened. Danielle took off.

'No, Dan, wait,' Adam raced to the door, but it slammed before he reached it, separating them and locking him in.

'Dan!' he thudded on the door.

'I can't swim, Adam, the water... the water is getting higher.' That female voice again.

'Who are you? Mum? Is that you?'

He turned, and now he could see the water. The blue waves around the wall, the water rising higher and higher.

'Who are you? There's no water,' he yelled and looked around. 'There's no water.'

But he could see it rising. His heartbeat pounded.

'Go to the door, save yourself,' the female voice said.

'Dan!' Adam tried the door. This time it opened, and he stumbled out into the hallway, falling to a carpeted floor, and the door slammed behind him. It was pitch black.

He sat where he fell for a few moments and listened.

'Come out and play, Adam,' a voice whispered behind him, right near his ear, and he thrashed out – nothing. Rising, he felt a presence and lunged but hit nothing but air as he fell to his knees again.

Breathe, relax. He coached himself, fighting against the wave of hysteria building in him. He knew it was the drug but couldn't fight it. The fear inside him was threatening to take over.

Something touched him, crawled on him, and he swatted it away. He rose unsteadily.

'It's me, hurry up, find me,' a male voice said.

'Nate?'

Get out, got to get out.

Adam couldn't tell if he was thinking the words or saying them. He felt something crawling over him again and began brushing it away.

Down the end of the hallway, a shape emerged backlit.

'Dan?' he yelled out, not caring who heard him. He was shivering now, freezing.

'It's me,' the voice said again, only it was male. 'Come on, this way. Hurry.'

Got to get out. He stumbled in the dark down the hallway to the figure he could see, and as he neared, he saw the face. Her face.

'Danielle?'

'It's too late. I'm dead,' she said. 'I'm dead, Adam.'

'So am I,' another female voice said from behind him. Adam wheeled around to see a woman, but all that was visible was her white face.

'I'm dead too. You didn't save us.' A second woman appeared with a face frozen in death.

'Come and play with us.' He felt a sharp pain as if he had been stabbed, but the hall was dark again. A red light came on, and his hands were covered in blood. Or was it just the red light making them look that way?

'Did you hear that voice?' Danielle asked beside him, and he jumped.

'Dan? Where have you been?'

'With the voices.'

'Me too. Someone's watching us.'

'They're always watching,' she whispered. 'Can you hear them breathing?'

The hallway lights came on bright, blinding them and then flashed off just as quickly.

Danielle gasped. 'You're bleeding. Your organs are gone!'

Adam's hand went to his body, where he felt the sticky substance. 'I felt them moving around inside me.'

'Someone took them. You're dead.'

'We're coming to bury you, Adam,' a voice whispered. 'In the earth, dark and deep.'

'Run!' Danielle screamed.

They beat their hands along the walls, trying to find a door, a sliver of light.

No exit.

Dead. I'm dead.

Get out. Don't die here.

A door opened, letting in a blast of blue light, and Danielle ran inside. Adam followed. He looked down and saw the dark stain on his shirt. It looked purple in the blue light.

Another door opened onto the stairs.

'Stairs!' she yelled with relief as if that were the answer to their escape.

'Run, Dan,' Adam pushed her forward.

He turned to block the stairs from anyone following. No one was there. Turning back to follow Danielle, a dark figure blocked his way.

Chapter 39

Tom tried the front door of the VIP House, but it wouldn't budge. He cupped his hands to try and see in, but the dark tint on the windows and door made it impossible. He thumped his hand on the door.

'Police, open!' It wasn't quite the truth, but it usually worked, and the police were on site. This time, it didn't work. The doors stayed closed.

'Why does he always attract trouble,' he hissed through clenched teeth, thinking of his charge, Adam Murphy. Tom left the front of the building and ran down the ramp into the car park. He recognised Danielle's car, and after determining it was locked and that there was no one inside, he looked around and found an elevator.

Tom exhaled with relief when he pressed the button, and the door opened. Entering, his luck ran out; no amount of button-pushing helped. It was going nowhere without a code or entry pass. He thumped the lift for good measure and exited, running up the car park ramp and back down to the clubhouse where the girls were being held.

'I need the code to the VIP House from the girls,' he told one of the cops on duty.

'Who are you again?'

'Security for the whistle-blower. Don't ask for a name, but Sergeant Burns knows.'

'Right,' a look of recognition dawned on the young policeman's face. 'Go for your life.'

Tom gave him a quick nod of thanks and rushed past him, addressing the group of women sitting around the clubhouse table.

'I'm working with the police and need the VIP House code or an entry pass urgently.'

Only two girls knew it; another had her pass, which would give him entry. She removed it from around her neck.

'Do you know what's on each level?' He considered taking her along.

'No, only the level I'm allowed on.'

He snatched the pass from her with thanks. 'Does anyone know the layout of the entire building?' Tom persisted. The women all shook their heads in the negative.

'Only Leaf, but she's not here,' one of the younger blondes answered.

He gave them an exasperated look as if their ignorance was unbelievable and took off, exiting the building and sprinting back up the path. Tom didn't give a toss about what happened to the owners of the camp or the women. His mission was to keep Adam Murphy safe – the bane of his existence. Once the wedding was over, he'd be happy never to see him or hear the guy's name mentioned again. Ever. Arriving at the VIP House, he ran down the ramp to the car park again, preferring to enter from the lower floor and make his way up, clearing each floor as he went. As the door closed, he noted there were several other vehicles in the car park besides Danielle's car. No more than before, but were clients in attendance? Were girls working at the moment? They were about to get a rude awakening.

The lift opened on the first floor, and he found the reception desk empty. No surprise. A corridor ran off each side of it, and he went left, throwing doors open as he went. One door revealed what he expected to find. The man roared at him to 'Fuck off,' and the woman scowled.

'Cops are here raiding the place. You might want to get dressed.'

'Jesus Christ!' The man started to struggle out of the leathers he was wearing, and Tom slammed the door closed. He would have enjoyed the drama if he hadn't been trying to find bloody Adam Murphy. He just hoped he didn't find him in one of these rooms dressed in leather or less.

The next room was empty. The one after surprised him – a couple reclined in a bath of chocolate or mud or whatever. 'Cops are here,' he shouted and closed the door, leaving them scrambling to get out. He finished and hurried to get to the other end of the hallway to the right. When he returned, a guy was sitting at reception.

'Who are you?' Tom barked at him.

'More important, who are you?' the man dressed in a suit, wearing glasses and looking like a techy nerd regarded Tom with a look of cool disdain.

'I'm the new security detail. There's been a breach, and I'm here to deal with it, with you,' Tom played him. 'Griffin didn't tell you?'

'What the hell,' the guy lost his demeanour and jumped to his feet.

'You look like you're guilty of something.'

The tech guy sat down again quickly and ran a tongue over his lips. 'I just lent her my phone to hear her mother's voice,' he blurted out. 'How was I to know she was going to call the cops?'

Tom looked at him, confused. 'I don't give a toss what you do with your phone. I'm looking for Griffin's guests – Adam and Danielle. Where are they?'

The man slumped with relief. 'They're not on this floor.'

Tom leant over the desk and grabbed the guy by the front of his shirt, reading the fear on the tech's face.

'Your name?'

'Alex. I just do the content videos.'

'You've got the vision for every floor?' He asked, knowing the answer as he saw the large security screen to the right of Alex.

'Yes.'

Tom pushed him back in the seat. 'Show me the second floor now.'

Alex grimaced and hesitated. 'There's a game being played and filmed. It's paid content, and they're not finished.'

'Do I look like I give a fuck if they've finished or not? Show me!'

Alex clicked on a keyboard in front of him, and the vision changed to a split screen with four different areas. In one square, Danielle sat in a dark stairwell, hitting the walls to find the exit door within her arm's reach. Two others were empty rooms, and in the last, a hallway was lit in blue, and a figure was slumped at one end.

'Turn the lights on,' Tom ordered.

'I can't,' Alex stared at him as if the idea was preposterous.

'Turn them on, or I swear...'

Alex hit the lights, and Tom watched as the floor lit up with bright white light. Danielle jumped up, swayed, and grabbed the door handle. Pushing it open, she ran out. On another screen, the figure in black, who was just about at Adam's side, froze in the bright light, turned, looked up towards where the cameras were hidden and quickly ran into one of the rooms, closing the door behind him. On the ground, leaning against the wall, Tom guessed it was Adam from what he could make out, given his slumped form. He was alive and moving.

'Hallucinogenic drug,' Alex said and grinned, 'makes for great content.'

'You've got to be kidding me?'

Alex quickly sobered. 'I just film it.'

'What's the quickest route there?'

'The lift and turn right when it opens. The stairwells lock.'

'Delete the footage,' Tom demanded.

'What? I can't. I'll lose my job.'

'You'll lose more than your job if I have to ask again. Stop it, delete it, in front of me.' His voice was dangerously menacing. Tom watched as Alex stopped the recording and pressed delete. 'Show me the bin and backup folders,' he demanded. He hadn't spent the last twenty years in private security without knowing a bit about what goes on.

Alex grimaced, caught out, and clicked on the areas. Not waiting to be asked, the tech expert deleted the file completely because Tom was emitting a low growl. Satisfied, Tom said, 'I suggest, Alex, you turn on all the lights, including exterior lights, unlock the doors and stairwells, and get your ass out of here. The cops are here.'

Alex needed no further encouragement. He hit a few buttons, lights came on everywhere, and the tech boffin abandoned the desk and rushed out the front door. Tom muttered a few colourful words and hurried to the lift, only to see Nate, Sergeant Burns and several cops rushing up the front stairs; one of the cops bailed up Alex. Tom returned to the desk and, finding the button, opened the sliding door for them, seeing their surprised expression.

'I just sent the kid running,' Tom explained. 'Danielle broke out. Adam is on the second floor.' He pointed to the screen. 'I'll go to Adam.'

'We've got Dan, thanks,' Burnsy said.

'Is he alright?' Nate asked, panicked and watching the screen. 'He looks like he's in slow motion? What's wrong with him?'

'According to Alex, they've both been given a hallucinogenic.'

'He's bleeding,' Nate said, seeing Adam front on now as he stood upright. 'I'm going to him.'

Burnsy issued orders to his men, telling them to split up, not to let anyone enter or leave, and to remember they were searching for bodies or where bodies might be buried or stored.

'I've got Adam covered,' Tom snapped at Nate as he hurried to the lift. 'The stairwells lock, apparently, come this way.'

'Trust me, even whacked out of his head, he's not going with you,' Nate said, and Tom conceded the point. They piled into the lift to go to the second floor.

'I'll call an ambulance,' Burnsy said.

'No!' Tom said sharply.

'We can't call an ambulance; the victims will be reported,' Nate explained, 'and Adam can't be here.'

'Right,' Burnsy said.

'We'll get one of the girls to take us to where Adam was staying,' Tom thought on the run. 'Then we'll take him and Dan there and lock it down until we can get them out safely late tonight or tomorrow.'

'Good idea. We'll need a doctor,' Nate said.

'No. We can't call anyone in,' Tom shut it down. 'Unless Audrey knows someone... she always does.'

The lift doors opened, and Burnsy and his team stayed and went a level higher in the lift; Tom and Nate started down the hallway towards Adam.

Adam swayed and then decided it was the ground moving, not him. He collapsed to his knees and fell back against the wall, conscious of the figure at the end of the hallway.

I'm dead anyway.

Nate will find me soon. I'll wait here.

'What are you waiting for?' he yelled.

The elongated, dark figure didn't move.

'It's late,' Adam mumbled. He had no sense of time, but it felt like he'd been here forever, and now he was floating. He looked down at his body, but it didn't seem to be moving, but he was moving somehow, and cold, freezing cold.

'Where's Dan?' he asked the tall man.

The black figure began to move towards him. It was huge, taller than any man could possibly be. He couldn't believe how fast his heart was beating when it was no longer there. It was gone along with all his other organs.

Then the lights came on, blinding him. He was shivering, unable to see momentarily, but he knew the tall man was almost beside him. Squinting, he heard a door open, and the tall man was gone. Another door burst open, and two more men came in rushing towards him.

'Adam, it's Nate and Tom,' one of the men yelled.

It was a trick. They did that, the voices.

'No!' He began to scramble to his feet and stumble off in the other direction.

'It's us,' Tom said, reaching him and grabbing his arm. Adam struck out, belting him in the face.

'For fuck's sake,' Tom reeled back, swearing in surprise at Adam's strength fuelled by the drug.

'It's us. You're found,' Nate said, grabbing Adam by the shoulders and restraining him against the wall. 'Look at me. It's me.'

'Where are you bleeding from?' Tom asked, pushing up Adam's shirt.

'Where's Dan?' Adam mumbled, slipping down against the wall.

'She's fine. Burnsy has her. We're all going back to your room to meet there now.'

'It's superficial,' Tom said, relieved. 'We'll get it cleaned up,' he added for Adam's benefit.

'You're going to be okay. It's just a drug, making you hallucinate. You're okay,' the guy who sounded like Nate was saying.

'Where's the real Nate?' Adam mumbled.

'It's me, trust me,' Nate said.

'What's our secret code word then?'

Nate frowned.

'Tell him,' Tom demanded.

'Christ, I don't know. We haven't used a secret code word for nearly two decades.'

'You're not him. You're both imposters,' Adam said and shoved Nate away. He took off down the hallway at an impressive pace for a man bleeding and drugged up.

Tom raced after him, reaching him before Nate and tackled him to the ground.

'Get off him! Take it easy,' Nate said, pushing Tom off. 'Malvern star!'

Adam laughed. 'Malvern star!' he repeated.

'I just remembered,' Nate grinned and heaved Adam to his feet, sobering quickly. 'He's shivering something chronic. Hold him.' He pushed Adam onto Tom as he took off his jacket.

'My organs are all gone – they cut them out. You should just leave me here since I'm dead.'

'You're not dead. I've got your organs. I'll put them back in when we get to your room,' Nate assured him as he put his jacket on Adam.

'Nate.'

'Yes.'

'Are you talking?'

'No.'

'Someone is.'

'Ignore them. Come on. Tom and I are taking you home, and we'll put all your organs back in and clean you up. You can talk to Dan.'

The men steered Adam towards the lift, but his knees gave out on him.

Nate groaned. He slung Adam's arm around his shoulder, and they bundled him into the lift. Going down one floor, the lift opened at reception, where Burnsy was calling out orders. Two officers burst through the stairwell. 'Senior sergeant, you're going to want to see this... three bodies.'

'Holy crap,' Burnsy grimaced.

'Stay put,' Tom ordered Nate. 'I'll run to the clubhouse, get one of the girls to show us to Adam's room and get a golf buggy to transport him. I saw a few buggies up there.'

'Nate!' Adam yelled, scaring the hell out of him.

'I'm here! Right beside you!'

'The floor is gone. We won't be able to walk on it.''

'It's okay, I've got this,' Nate told him. 'I've got special powers.' He cocked his head to the front door to tell Tom to get a hurry on and sat beside Adam, keeping him calm.

'I'm cold.'

'I know. We'll go back to your room, rug up, make a coffee, put a fire on.'

'There was fire and a flood.'

'There over now, all done,' Nate assured him.

'Nate?'

'Yes?'

'The floor is back, but it's moving,' Adam said, shivering. 'Is something on me?'

Nate sighed. Two of them whacked out. It was going to be a long night.

Chapter 40

Jessica couldn't help but grin at Adam as he entered the office Friday morning for their usual meeting. It was his first day back since the Wellness Studio stay a couple of days ago. Rob arrived at the same time, and the two of them were talking as they entered.

'Morning, you two. Got all your organs back?' Jessica teased Adam.

He laughed. 'I've got a few extra, I think – one of Dan's – and I'm pretty sure Nate's put them in the wrong order.'

Nate came out of his office on hearing their voices. 'Hey, you're back.'

'I am, and you're early for our meeting. What the hell?' Adam feigned shock.

'Don't get used to it,' Nate said. 'Some idiot called me early, so I figured I'd get to it.'

'Did you organise that?' Adam looked at Jessica with a mix of admiration and suspicion.

'No, but I wish I had thought of it,' she teased. 'Next week...'

Nate gave her a *'don't-even-try-it'* look and asked, 'Is Dan coming?'

'She's just arrived,' Jessica said with a nod to the screen where Danielle could be seen coming up the internal stairs with their coffee order.

'Want an update?' Nate asked Adam.

'Hell yeah.'

'Three bodies, four arrests,' Nate said and added nothing more.

'That it? I was hoping for a little more detail,' Adam said, making Jessica laugh.

'Dan's got coffee, and I've got pastries,' she said. 'Let's sit. There are no appointments for another few hours for you, Nate, and you've got the day free from patients, Adam, to catch up on stuff.'

'Stuff?' Nate said with a raised eyebrow, opening the door for Danielle as she neared.

'A heap of emails, work offers for forensic jobs, clients wanting in, media requests, and so on,' Jessica waved her hand around like that happened every day, and most days it did.

'And I've booked an hour in your diary with you so I can see if your headspace is together,' Rob said.

Danielle laughed as she entered, hearing Rob's last words.

'Perhaps when we were under, we were at our sanest,' she said in a spooky voice, making them laugh.

'Or perhaps you were not insane at all,' Jessica joked.

'Very Rosenhan,' Rob said.

'What's that?' Danielle asked with interest as they removed themselves to the boardroom and sat down.

'An experiment by a psychologist whereby eight sane people were put in psychiatric institutions to see if mental health professionals could tell,' Rob said.

'That's freaking me out,' Danielle said. 'You might not get out!'

'Did you see that tall man?' Adam asked her.

'No. I saw the fire and flood, though. And the voices, telling me they had drowned, and we didn't save them.'

'I had that too, those women with the whitest faces telling me we were too late to save them.'

'That's just creepy,' Nate said.

'Wow, what a trip.' Jessica placed the pastries and serviettes down and took a seat.

'I've had better trips,' Adam said, 'like the recent beach getaway. I've got to confess; it was truly frightening. I could hear my heart thundering... even after it was stolen,' he added with a grin.

'Well, you were bleeding, so it's understandable that you'd think your organs were cut out,' Nate sympathised.

'Hell yeah,' Danielle agreed, the smile fading from her face. 'I don't think I've ever been so terrified in my life. Everything was heightened; I was sure everyone was out to kill me, and the fire and flood were so real I could smell smoke – I was burning and then drowning,' she shuddered, 'awful ways to go.'

'I'm sorry I was making light of it,' Jessica said sincerely.

'Don't worry, it's all good,' Adam assured her.

Danielle continued, 'I grew up by the water, and I'm a good swimmer, but you can't trust water. It freaks me out.'

'Mum's the same,' Adam said, giving a rare insight into his family.

'Afraid of water? Is that why she won't stay in the wing with the water views?' Nate asked.

Adam nodded. 'She's not just frightened; she has a deep-seated paranoia of it.'

'Thalassophobia,' Rob said with interest.

'Is that the term for fear of water?' Jessica asked.

'More or less, it means an intense phobia of any large bodies of water, like the ocean, sea, rivers and lakes.' Rob looked at Adam. 'Do you know why she feels that way?'

Adam nodded. 'Her mother and grandmother both drowned.'

'Wow,' Nate muttered.

'Understandable, she would fear it then. She doesn't want to be treated for it?' Rob asked, his professional curiosity taking over.

'She doesn't want to even talk about it because she fears if it becomes public knowledge, that will be how she dies.'

'Of course,' Jessica said. 'Her secret is safe with us.'

'Speaking of fates,' Nate said to Adam, 'you must have resigned yourself to yours. I heard you yelling to the tall man to get on with it.'

Adam looked surprised. 'I think I thought I was already dead and wanted it over.'

'At least you are both not regular users, so there'll be no long-term effects,' Rob said, 'but still, be wary that you may not be at your best and don't make any major decisions for the next few days.'

'Lucky I've worked out what I'm wearing to the wedding,' Danielle said.

'I'm surprised Tom doesn't want you in uniform.' Nate gave her a smug look.

'I'm to blend in on your table like one of the guests. Kelsey and I have come up with a backstory about me being one of her oldest friends.'

'Yeah?' Adam looked surprised and pleased. 'I didn't know you two were collaborating.'

'She's quite the lioness, your girlfriend,' Danielle said. 'I thought she'd be freaked out.'

'She was,' Adam said.

'Well, the mouse has roared. Apparently, she's quite determined to get you both through it unscathed.'

Adam looked pleased. 'She mentioned that. Is Audrey in on this plan?'

'Of course, there's no party without Audrey.'

Adam made a huffing sound of agreement before returning his attention to Nate. 'So, they found Rain's body?'

'And two others,' he said, prying the lid off his coffee and adding sugar.

'Do we know how they died yet?' Rob asked.

'Yep,' Nate confirmed. 'Burnsy said Rain died of asphyxiation. Allegedly, she tricked Griffin; he didn't like being made look a fool, so he arranged a rendezvous with her. Griffin said she flew at him, and he fought her off.'

'Resulting in the need to strangle her?' Danielle asked, shocked but not shocked enough to resist reaching for a croissant and taking a large bite.

'Griffin admitted it?' Adam was truly surprised.

'Short of blaming Zach or Ben or saying there was an intruder, he probably realised he was good for it. Besides, Zach threw him under the bus.'

'Get out!' Adam said. 'I didn't see that coming.'

'Didn't you?' Nate looked at him, surprised. 'And you, a psychologist.'

Adam gave him one of his best smirks that had Nate laughing.

'I suspect when you asked Griffin to catch up alone, it didn't go down well with Zach and Ben,' Rob suggested.

'Ah,' Adam said and nodded. 'I'd forgotten about that in my post-hallucination-haze. Yeah, Zach said words to the effect that he was dismissed, and he and Ben stomped off. Apparently, his loyalty did have boundaries – he wasn't prepared to cop for murder for Griffin.'

'But he did dispose of the body, or at least Rain's body, according to Skye,' Danielle said. 'Are you going to eat your croissant?' she asked Rob, who declined, pushing it towards her. 'Must be the drugs. First, I couldn't sleep, then I slept for a whole day, drank a tank of water, and now, I'm ravenous!'

'Me too,' Adam said. 'It makes it worse that I'm not back at my own place because every time I turn around, Tom is watching me and forcing water, food, and lectures in my face.'

'Good, he should be,' Rob added.

Nate continued, 'The second victim, a young girl, had only just arrived at the camp... they do these videos when they first arrive—'

Danielle nodded, interrupting. 'Skye told me. They act out a horrible drama, and the girls think they are in real danger. They call them the "Reality Moment" like it's a wakeup call.'

'Probably is,' Nate said. 'After that, you know what you are in for, and it's not just acting lessons.'

'Like snuff movies?' Jessica asked, offering an extra pastry to Adam, who happily accepted before Nate could have it; he usually did.

'Yeah, except no one is supposed to die,' Nate said. 'But, according to Skye, a VIP audience pays big to see those tapes. People are sick.'

'What happened to the newcomer having her reality moment then?' Adam asked, getting back on track. He had years of practice in bringing patients back to the core topic of their visit.

'The newbie was all of seventeen, and she had a heart attack. No one guessed she had a weak heart. They frightened her to death,' Nate said, his tone showing his disgust.

'That poor girl, her poor family,' Jessica said, voicing what everyone was thinking. 'How long has her body been buried there? Why weren't her parents looking for her all this time like Skye's folks were?'

'Because according to big-mouth Zach, Griffin told them she never arrived. She must have got cold feet and changed her mind. We found her on the state's missing persons' list.'

'Except now, she's not, which is good and bad,' Danielle said. 'And the third girl?'

'It was a death in the first year when they opened the place. She got pregnant to one of them, and I don't know how she died yet, not sure I want to know, but both mother and child didn't make it,' Nate said.

Adam shook his head. 'Well, that's Griffin done then. He'll be in there for years.'

'Think he'll get cleaned up inside?' Jessica asked. 'He's a pretty boy.'

'Nope,' Adam said and looked to Nate, who agreed. 'He'll have his own group of followers in prison so fast the wardens won't see it coming. He's just the type.'

'Good work, lads,' Rob said, finishing his coffee. 'Another case closed, Nate. Good analysis, Adam, and excellent backup, ladies. You certainly got more than you bargained for this time.'

'It's going to make the next cheating husband case so boring,' Danielle said and sighed.

'And I have one of those for you,' Nate added, grinning.

The meeting finished without discussing work, and as Adam rose, he said to Nate, 'Got a minute?'

'Sure. My office or yours?'

'Yours.'

Nate headed in; Adam followed. He usually followed, and Jessica sighed as she watched them depart, her agenda ignored.

'Still liking the job?' Rob teased.

'Loving it.'

Danielle laughed. 'How could she not? No day is the same, and we've got a wedding to go to!'

Chapter 41

Then...

Nate finished the project he and Adam had started a few days ago
– a jump over the creek on a special bike ramp they had made. He didn't
like doing it on his own, but Adam had to go to a launch event with his
parents and wasn't sure when he'd be back and allowed out to play. He
wondered if Adam would want to come back or if Griffin and his father
would be there getting their photo taken with all the stars as well. Maybe
they'd hang out together, and Adam would forget about the ramp. The
thought made him miserable.

It had been nearly two hours, and Nate was thinking about going home
for lunch when he saw Adam riding his bike towards him, a grin on his face
as if he'd escaped from detention.

'Hey, I escaped as soon as I could,' he said, jumping off his bike and
grabbing a plastic bag that was swinging off his handlebars containing
four patty cakes that he had smuggled out of the function. 'Wow, you've
finished it!' Adam admired the ramp in front of him.

'What do you think?' Nate asked.

'It's brilliant.' The boys knocked off the cakes as they sat looking at the
creek.

'Was the launch good?' Nate asked, swallowing his last mouthful.

'Nope. Boring.'

'Did you get your photo taken?'

'A few times. You go first,' Adam said. 'You finished it after all.'

'Thanks,' Nate said and grinned. Nate usually went first – he was two months older. Mounting his bike, he looked behind to make sure Adam was watching.

'Want me to give you the starter gun?' Adam asked.

'Yeah.' Nate turned to face the ramp

'On your mark, get set, GO!'

Nate gave a loud war cry and raced down the small hill, not putting on the brakes even though he was getting up a lot of speed. He took to the ramp, flew over the dam they had built, and skidded on the other side, sliding off his bike and coming to a dead stop in the mud. Nate stood, covered in mud, and whooped. Adam cheered.

'That was brilliant,' Adam called down to him.

'Thanks. I've got to not fall off at the end, though,' Nate yelled up the hill to Adam.

'We'll get better.'

'Your go.'

Adam nodded, took a deep breath and started down the hill. He was halfway down the hill when his bike began to slide, hitting mud, and it stuck fast. Nate couldn't believe it; it was like he was watching the whole thing in slow motion. Adam went up and over the handlebars, landing with a thud against a tree and rolling back down to the muddy ground.

Nate ran towards him. 'Holy crap, are you okay? That was amazing!'

'I think so. I might have broken something.' He went to rise and winced. 'Ouch.'

'Yeah, you're bleeding on your knees and hands,' Nate said like he was cataloguing wounds.

'I think I've broken a rib.'

Nate pushed on both sides of Adam's stomach, and he yelped in pain.

'Nuh, if you'd broken a rib, you'd be screaming in more pain than that. My coach did that test on me when Warren Turner tackled me to the ground, and I couldn't get up for a minute.' He spoke from an 11-year-old voice of experience.

'That was cool,' Adam grinned.

'Want to go again?'

Adam straightened, tested his limbs and decided he was okay. 'Yeah.'

'I knew you'd come,' Nate grinned, high on the adrenalin of their adventure.

'Of course, I'd come. We're blood brothers,' Adam said.

'And we put this together,' Nate said, looking at their work.

The boys grabbed their bikes and headed back to the top of the rise to do it all over again.

Now...

Adam dropped into a visitor seat in front of Nate's desk and leaned back as Nate settled behind the desk and put his feet up on the edge.

'What a shit show that was,' Adam said, needing the time with Nate to sit and debrief or not if they chose to.

'Hell yeah. The clients are happy, though. They did the right thing; it might have been their daughter next,' Nate said with a small shake of his head. 'Thanks for your help with the case,' he added sincerely.

'No problem. When we started it, I never thought for a moment that Griffin and his henchmen would be involved. Makes you wonder about nature and nurture,' Adam mused. 'Those guys were exactly like they were at school almost twenty years ago, which means we must be the same too.' He gave a small laugh.

'I thought the same thing about the guys and girls at my school reunion. Bunch of losers.' Nate said and chuckled. 'Just kidding, they were okay, and we turned out all right.'

'Most days. You said four arrests?' he just realised.

'Griffin, Zach, Alex and the girl called Leaf.'

'Who is Alex?'

'The tech guy. He and Leaf will probably get off with a slap on the wrist, but he knew what was going on, aided and abetted it, and filmed it. He was the one who gave Skye his phone so she could hear her mother breathing.'

'Right, that'll work in his favour.' Adam sighed. 'What a place.' He sat bolt upright. 'The footage! Dan and me high and—'

'Tom saw that it was deleted. No copy exists or backup,' Nate cut him off.

'Really deleted? Not in the cloud or whatever—'

'Nope, totally deleted. I got my tech guy in the next day just to be sure.'

Adam slumped. 'Thanks. Imagine that coming out... Mum and Jack would have me in rehab, and Stephanie would be telling stories about the poor, rich kid falling off the rails and my redemption afterwards. Nightmare.' He ran his hands over his face. 'Not to mention how embarrassing... yeah, let's not go there.'

'So, the wedding is this weekend at last,' Nate said. 'I thought it would never come, and you've got no visible bruises, so Tom did his job. It will be the last you see of Tom.'

'I've heard that before.' Adam studied Nate for a reaction as he said, 'And you and Jess will be partnered.'

'Yeah.'

Adam smiled and left the subject alone. 'Getting your hair cut beforehand?'

'Yes, Mum.'

'Good,' Adam chuckled.

'I'm sorry I threw you in the deep end on this case. So, you feel okay?' Nate asked.

'Sure, it's all good.'

'What was the scariest thing, you know, when you were hallucinating?' Nate asked, his curiosity getting the better of him.

Adam didn't have to think for too long. 'The tall guy. Probably because he was so menacing and seemed to take so long to reach me.'

'Yeah, creepy, I saw him,' Nate said.

Adam smiled. 'I told the tall man when he took my liver that you'd come.'

Nate huffed. 'Of course, I'd come. Where blood brothers. Who else is going to put you back together again?'

THE END

Next in the Delaney & Murphy series

H itched

    Twelve-year-old Adam Murphy didn't know anyone who had died, and nor did his best friend, Nate Delaney. While testing new speedometers on their Malvern Star bikes, that changed – the pair witnessed beautiful Holly Castle, 16, hitch a ride to Sydney seeking fame and was never seen again, presumed dead.

Twenty years later, Adam's model mother, the *IT Girl* Winsome Keeley, gets hitched to the nation's favourite singer, Jack Bernham, and the official photographer—Eric Castle—recognises Nate from their school years. The younger brother of the missing girl is still pursuing his sister's cold case.

Adam and Nate are invited to take a ride.

Also by Jack Adams

The Delaney & Murphy series:
Asylum
Ten-year-old best friends Nathan and Adam really liked Joe. He was their friend, an artist, the man they spoke to through the wire fence of the lunatic asylum.

But something happened behind those walls, in those rooms, on the grounds, at the river. The inmate sketched it all – fine lines, truth in the negative space, truth in the pencil strokes. Then, one day, Joe was gone.

Twenty years later Nathan and Adam receive a letter.

Stalker

Adam couldn't wait... his Uncle Allan was coming to watch his cricket game that afternoon; Adam's father was always too busy to get there. Uncle Allan believed Adam and his best friend, Nate, would one day be chosen for the Stateside if they kept practising... Adam's bowling was really improving.

Adam doesn't have an Uncle Allan.

Hitched

Twelve-year-old Adam Murphy didn't know anyone who had died, and nor did his best friend, Nate Delaney. While testing new speedometers on their Malvern Star bikes, that changed – the pair witnessed beautiful Holly Castle, 16, hitch a ride to Sydney seeking fame and was never seen again, presumed dead.

Twenty years later, Adam's model mother, the *IT Girl* Winsome Keeley, gets hitched to the nation's favourite singer, Jack Bernham, and the official photographer—Eric Castle—recognises Nate from their school years. The younger brother of the missing girl is still pursuing his sister's cold case.

Adam and Nate are invited to take a ride.

Poster Girl (stand-alone title)

Backpacker Soleil 'Sunny' Reyer is gone. Tanned, glowing and star of the *Missing* poster; no one thought fruit-picking could be deadly.

Journalist Jessica Steyn was the last person to give Sunny a lift. Assigned the biggest story in her career, Jessica is on the job. Dig, dig, dig ... until she buries herself.

The cold case file never leaves his desk in the same way that Detective Nick Clarkson is stuck in Strand Harbour fifteen years after Sunny disappeared. Less hair, marriage over, no sign of Sunny.

Author Coen Watson's people are water people; his trust in it is marrow-deep – he's counting on Strand Harbour to cure his writer's block. Unpacking, he forces open a drawer corroded by salt air to find a faded *Missing* poster for Soleil Reyer. The author begins picking at old wounds.

Contact Jack

I don't hang around much on social media, but here's where you will find me:

Website: https://jackadamswrites.com/

Facebook: https://www.facebook.com/jackadamswrites

Email: jackadamswrites@gmail.com

www.ingramcontent.com/pod-product-compliance
Lightning Source LLC
Chambersburg PA
CBHW020334120726
47904CB00002B/406